PRAISE FOR
BRENT HAYWARD

"[*The Fecund's Melancholy Daughter*'s] uncompromising originality leaves the reader with few familiar signposts. Reading it is like waking up in the wrong bed, in the wrong apartment, under the wrong sun.... By turns surreal, macabre and stunningly violent, *The Fecund's Melancholy Daughter* is dreamlike in its strangeness and complexity. Like a dream, it is difficult to define and difficult to shake. The imagery lingers like archetypes dredged up from the sleeping mind."
—Mark Dunn, *The Globe and Mail*

"[*The Fecund's Melancholy Daughter* is] beautifully written and morally ambivalent, this complex tale will appeal to readers of Gene Wolfe and China Miéville."
—*Publishers Weekly* (starred review)

"Toronto's Brent Hayward has a knack for creating incredibly lush alternative worlds and mythologies, and *Head Full of Mountains* may be his most complex and demanding work yet.... [The protagonist's] journey suggests an allegory of human development progressing through different stages of life, but readers will probably come up with many other interpretations as well, perhaps seeing in it a nightmare of isolated and introverted consciousness, or the endgame of technologies that have left humanity behind. The result is one of the more different and difficult SF novels of the year, but also one of the most rewarding."
—Alex Good, *The Toronto Star*

"Hayward's debut [*Filaria*] is a powerful, beautifully written dystopian tale...."
—*Publishers Weekly* (starred review)

"...*Filaria* is simply one of the best books written in the last decade and is the best science fiction/fantasy book that I have read in a long time."
—Examiner.com

"A disquieting, claustrophobic, compelling hybrid of China Miéville and J. G. Ballard. I first read *Filaria* almost two years ago: its subterranean imagery has been stuck in my midbrain ever since."
—Peter Watts, author of *Starfish* and *Blindsight*

OTHER BOOKS BY BRENT HAYWARD

Filaria
The Fecund's Melancholy Daughter
Head Full of Mountains

BROKEN SUN, BROKEN MOON

FIRST EDITION

Broken Sun, Broken Moon © 2019 by Brent Hayward
Cover art © 2019 by Erik Mohr (Made By Emblem)
Interior art, interior & cover design © 2019 by Jared Shapiro

Distributed in Canada by
Fitzhenry & Whiteside Limited
195 Allstate Parkway
Markham, Ontario L3R 4T8
Phone: (905) 477-9700
e-mail: bookinfo@fitzhenry.ca

Distributed in the U.S. by
Consortium Book Sales & Distribution
34 Thirteenth Avenue, NE, Suite 101
Minneapolis, MN 55413
Phone: (612) 746-2600
e-mail: sales.orders@cbsd.com

Library and Archives Canada Cataloguing in Publication

Title: Broken sun, broken moon / Brent Hayward.
Other titles: Works. Selections
Names: Hayward, Brent, author.
Description: Short stories and a novella.
Identifiers: Canadiana (print) GBB8M0113 | Canadiana (print) 20190045035 |
Canadiana (ebook)
  20190047720 | ISBN 9781771484763 (softcover) | ISBN 9781771484770 (PDF)
Classification: LCC PS8615.A883 A6 2019 | DDC C813/.6—dc23

CHIZINE PUBLICATIONS
Peterborough, Canada
www.chizinepub.com
info@chizinepub.com

Edited and proofread by Brett Savory

Canada Council   Conseil des arts
for the Arts   du Canada

We acknowledge the support of the Canada Council for the Arts which last year invested $20.1 million in writing and publishing throughout Canada.

ONTARIO ARTS COUNCIL
CONSEIL DES ARTS DE L'ONTARIO
an Ontario government agency
un organisme du gouvernement de l'Ontario

Published with the generous assistance of the Ontario Arts Council.

Printed in Canada

BROKEN SUN, BROKEN MOON

BRENT HAYWARD

For Frances and Oliver, perfects

Contents

CLEANER

🐓 THROUGH THE THIN MAIL OF HIS gloves, Bristly felt it again, that rhythmic *thrum* in the superstructure's steel: vibrations not from strong gusts of wind nor a distant storm's buffet; not from an oceanic tremor, either, come rumbling up the supports. Not from any force Bristle had encountered before in his life spent hanging under the bridge. He lay on his back in the webbing and pressed his hand gently upwards against the girder. Beyond it, the sky was clear and pale blue. Bristle spread his fingers slowly, entranced, and licked his dry lips.

Somewhere near his feet, Scrub grunted a warning: *Back to work!*

The harness supporting Bristle squeaked as he withdrew his hand. Clips of his tethers jangled; Bristle rocked. Like other times, no one else in the crew had said anything about the strange vibrations. Bristle cleared his throat, decided he, too, would keep quiet. He had grown increasingly certain only he could feel the trembling, some sort of message only for him that he had not yet decoded, unpleasant news from far away. When it first happened, he had asked eagerly of the others, stopping in his work; they had stared back at him with frowns on their creased faces, eyes half-shut, as if gauging his sanity. He had even considered he might be the source of the vibrations, that they spread outwards from him, manifestations of his yearning and solitude.

He retrieved the scraper from his chest, where he had laid it moments before, and clenched it tight in the same gloved hand he had felt the vibrations with. When he tilted his head back, the world went upside-down. Great blisters of paint and flaked rust on the underside of the girder moved into his line of sight; buboes on the superstructure, waiting to be cleaned. The bridge narrowed, diminishing to a point on the horizon impossibly tiny and infinite, lifetimes away. The sky there met the gray sea. Bristle blinked away sweat and adjusted his goggles. Where his hand had been, the steel was already clean from his afternoon's work. It gleamed dully at him, fruit of his labour. Bristle scraped at the blistered part with his spatula, saw the flakes break off and fall past him, toward the ocean far below.

In the end, he thought bitterly, *everything falls into the ocean.*

FOUR DAYS AGO HE HAD FIRST felt the strange tremble in the superstructure, at shift's end, as the crew prepared to pull the nest westwards. The sky was clouded over; the air greenish, humid. Close and smelling of rain that did not come that night. One hand on the guy rope, the other braced against a strut, Bristle readied himself, moved forward in the netting—

And a reddish light burst in his peripheral vision, as if he had poked his head through a briefly glimmering barrier. The vibrations started then. He felt them in his arm, in his chest, but it was the red light that worried him the most. He could find no source for it; it was not repeated. He had told no one about this light.

Soon the vibrations persisted, diverting his attentions, and capturing them.

When storms raged out of sight, somewhere either far behind the nest— howling over and around stretches of the bridge cleaned last year, a generation ago, perhaps even by long-dead ancestors—or far ahead of it— blowing and raining on steel the crew might never reach in Bristle's life, or perhaps, if the storms struck closer, haul themselves under just next season—the vibrations were faint and random. Of course, when a storm hit much closer, or screamed through the segment of bridge from which Bristle and the others hung, making them miserable, the ensuing shakes and vibrations were no great mystery.

Sometimes wind made the girders sing.

Everybody in the nest knew the varieties. Everybody shared them. But not this pattern. Off and on over the past four days, these vibrations held a rhythm like Bristle's own heartbeat, a pace regular and steady, as if counting off his remaining time.

THROUGHOUT THE WANING SHIFT, BRISTLE CLEANED, and he scraped, and he tried to lose himself in work. But his thoughts were haunted.

Overall, the day had been still. Peaceful, it seemed, for the rest of the crew. He had heard few curses as they worked in the nest behind him.

Curious white birds wheeled on thermals overhead. And Scrub, supervising from his harness slung lowest in the webbing, also watched. Bristle could not see Scrub unless he twisted around, but he felt Scrub's stare boring into his back and he knew the boss suspected him of shirking.

Or of losing his mind.

Bristle worked steadily. He did not twist to see Scrub. His mind raced with memories he was helpless to stop, as if they had been triggered by the flash of red light and the recurring, throbbing pulse in the steel. Now he remembered a day when, as a child, he had asked the simple question: *Why?* Even then, endless water below and superstructure above, endless sky and storms and scrubbing this bridge inexorably westward, had seemed without reason.

The answer was a smart pinch on young Bristle's cheek and a terse lecture—

Bristle scraped with all his might, as if he could clean more than just the girder. His arms ached. Chips flew.

The lecturer, a gaunt man called Elbowgrease, had died long ago, tumbled from the nest down into the ocean. Bristle had since aged, and was moved to the front, and understood now what the dead man had meant.

We clean because our parents did, and because their parents before them did. We clean because there is nothing else in life except this bridge and the horizon that creeps away from us as slowly as we approach it.

When Scrub blew a shrill note with two fingers, Bristle sighed and rolled over in his harness to look down through the thongs of webbing at the ocean. Wind whipped whitecaps far below into frothing green. *If,* he thought, his mind racing, *a child were to ask me the same question today that I asked as a youth, I'd mutter the same platitudes.*

But that wasn't very likely.

There were no children.

CREAKING AND GRUNTING AND JANGLING, SCRUB climbed the mesh of the nest. The netting around Bristle tugged, pinching him, and now he did twist; sunlight played over Scrub's scarred face, glinted off his goggles and worn-leather helmet as Scrub hauled himself hand over hand upwards. Behind him, below him, as far as Bristle could see, the ocean churned.

"Free dangler," Scrub said. "What's with you? Keep your mind on your work. You're having a bad week."

"I'm no dangler," Bristle answered. He reached calmly into his hip pocket and drew out a flask, opened it, and gulped a swallow of warm egg yolk. Some cleaners had gone crazy in the past, leaving the nest to dangle and never return. It was something a supervisor was always on the watch for, but Bristle denied he was crazy. He said, "I was just thinking."

"I do the thinking on work time," Scrub grumbled, rubbing at his beard with the back of a glove and staring hard at Bristle. His dark eyes glittered. "You know your job, man. We need to reach the next support in five days, at most. If you lie there just stroking the steel we won't get anywhere."

"I'm not a dangler," Bristle repeated, and, after a moment, turned away. "I'm on my break."

Scrub came no closer. "I'll move you to the back, you know. Don't think I won't."

When Bristle did not respond, Scrub retreated, mumbling, to his low-slung spot.

In the rear of the nest, oblivious to the tension up front, one of the twins sang a plaintive song. For the rest of his break, Bristle listened to the lilting sound, eyes closed, lost in a haze of memories.

HE WORKED AND WATCHED EVENING CLOUDS blow in across the darkening sky. They mingled in the slow turmoil above him. He thought, *I have not touched another person in many spans of the bridge, maybe even a dozen.* He nearly stopped scraping again, wondering if it were his own body's loneliness that sent out the signals, who would ever receive them?

"Ready to heave," Scrub shouted, startling Bristle from his reverie. He grabbed the guy rope he had fastened that morning, braced his body against a girder and, on the count of three, pulled until his arms shook. Sweat coursed his face. Behind him, others in the crew also pulled and groaned as one. The entire nest lurched loudly on its pulleys, grinding several inches westward before settling. Swaying forward and back—while everything around him rattled and clacked and flakes of old paint fell into the ocean—Bristle watched the steel wheels roll to a grinding stop on the lip of the girder he had just scraped clean. Above his face now, more of the bridge had moved into range: a day's more blisters to remove from the steel, a day's more rust to pry free.

It'll be a week, he thought, *before the twins look up from their spot in the back and see this, cleaned and ready for their brushes. Slowly but surely, pull to the west, until water claims us and puts us to rest.*

So the cleaner's motto went.

NIGHT CLOSED IN ON THE NEST abruptly, like it always did. The crew gathered together, giant spiders moving toward the hub, spinnerets trailing cord. They did not speak much, but hung cloistered in the webbing as the winds picked up. Crouching upright, but remaining apart, at the front of the nest, Bristle turned to look toward the setting sun. His chin rested on one knee. The girders glowed like lightning. The ocean was momentarily becalmed with a vermilion sheen. Ahead, the support Scrub aimed for was not far off, rising solemnly from the sea. They would arrive there in three or four days; Scrub was always melodramatic.

The perspective of other bridge supports made them appear shorter and shorter into the distance until Bristle could no longer see them. But he knew they were there. Each one a resting spot, a week-end, a place to collect egg yolk and scrawny mice nesting under the bridge, and real spiders much smaller than the ones he imagined the rest of the crew looking like. Each support a passage of time. Each support an increment on the span.

Maybe at the next one, Bristle thought, *I'll touch someone again.*

Glancing back to see the faces of his crew, awash with blood-coloured highlights, he tried to imagine who might let him come close but, doing so, felt suddenly tired. More tired than he had felt a long time. Closing his eyes, he was asleep in a second, and promptly dreamt:

He lay in his harness under the bridge. But he had shucked his leathers, taken off his boots and gloves and his goggles, disconnected his tethers. Nightwind blew across his naked body.

On top of the bridge, where the white birds landed and fought and then flew from the nest's advance, where rain hit first when it rained and the sun beat hot on other days, stood a woman. At first Bristle did not recognize her as such: her body was unencumbered by cords and gadgets, by grime and calluses, but to see her there, upright, without anything to assist her posture, was astounding. And when she moved—the woman came closer to where he lay, looking up, paused almost directly over him—she lifted one strong, tawny leg and placed it down, then lifted the other, staying erect the whole time, with no webbing.

There was a maneuver that a cleaner used to get from one part of the nest to another, in an emergency, for it consumed much energy. Unclip all tethers, haul head-upward on the net, most weight on the hooked fingers but some on the legs. This was *standing*. Then, combining arm strength and pushing off alternating feet, short distances could be covered quickly before exhausted limbs tangled together or gravity took its toll. This part was called *walking*. Bristle thought of it now; these motions were the closest he could come to understanding the dream woman's quiet, astonishing movements.

Then again, they did not even approach a description of her grace.

In his dream, Bristle sighed. Although dwarfed by the rising scaffolds, the apparition seemed so tall to him; a vertical woman, beautiful, unfettered, a miracle.

He wanted her to come and lie with him in the harness, wanted her to whisper to him, to sleep in his arms.

Or better still, he wanted to be up there with her.

When he called out she did not look down. Instead—in her floating, upright fashion—she moved over to the edge of the platform and leaned against a rail there. She looked out to sea. Then east, where the nest had come from.

"You're around here somewhere," she said, softly, her voice alluring, like the sound the ocean sometimes made, when Bristle wished he could just fall into it and never work or wake up again. The voice seemed to come from somewhere inside his own head, between his eyes, maybe, or from the air all around.

"I can't pinpoint you, though. Nothing is working here." She paused, and smiled sadly. "In four days you've travelled three metres. So slow. The whole process should've taken seconds." The woman tossed her head now; the image of her body seemed to waver, then solidify again. "But you should be right around here, whatever you are. If you can hear me, I'll repeat what I've been trying to tell you for four days now. You've breached the two-hundred kilometre exclusion zone and are presently considered a threat to security. Any further advance west will be considered an act of aggression. Measures will be taken. I can't stop them. Turn around. Go home."

Though she made little sense to Bristle, the woman's speech caused him to long for her all the more. If only she could turn that sad smile upon him. He watched the wind blow hair from her shoulders as she lifted her face to the night and closed her eyes. What would it be like to be free of leathers forever, to move independently of this netting?

To be with a woman like that?

She turned away from him.

And vanished.

Bristle awoke.

Clustered in the centre of the nest, the others still slept. It was night now, but Bristle was no longer tired. Everything seemed clear to him. Outlines of shadows were sharp, precise. Moonlight on the girders. A light mist chilled his cheeks. The woman was a piece missing from Bristle, something he had wanted his whole life without knowing. He pulled at his woven corset, squirmed and tugged hard at his binding. With one hand, he snapped the cord of his scraper and then let the tool fall. It was swallowed quickly by the night. Below was the noise of water, shapes of glimmers on the waves, darkness.

Scrub would never forgive him now. He would certainly be moved back, relegated to fermenting bird shit for cocktails or painting the bridge with paintless brushes that had lost their hairs long ago.

Bristle untethered his limbs from the net and climbed carefully forward. Where the nest rose to meet the bridge in a bundle of thick cord, and a well-greased old pulley, he hooked one arm around a girder, then the other, and pulled himself up. The topside of the strut was just wide enough for his body. He kicked his legs, and lay there, balancing, feeling the steel against his chest, his chin. Exertion had made his head spin.

And there were the vibrations again, matching his heartbeat.

Looking up through the lattice of the superstructure, he caught a glimpse of the crescent moon watching, darker shapes of clouds blowing in.

Dangler, he thought. *You are a free dangler.*

After catching his breath, he pushed on, wriggling forward until he came to an angled girder that led from the distant support past his face, up past another horizontal strut, to the platform where he had seen the dream-woman standing. Another girder crossed in a giant X. In case his waning energy gave out altogether, Bristle reached out to wrap one of his wrist tethers around the steel, securing it tightly just above the head of a large rivet. Uncleaned, the superstructure here was crusted with the rust of ages, which broke off in great flakes. Bristle pulled his upper body along the angled girder, getting higher with each grunt, each tug, so he was soon lying at forty-five degrees. The toes of his boots just touched the beam from which the nest was suspended. He was higher in the world than he had ever been before.

Far below, wind slapped through the ocean swells.

He wound his free wrist tether farther up the angled girder, leaving enough slack for him to loosen the first. Soon he could grip the next horizontal strut, and he heaved himself onto it, managing to get his chest and hips and boots up. Breathing in the air was like breathing fire. Trembling, he looked back.

The nest was a mass of shadow, the sleeping crew a clump of darker, unstirring shapes, farther away and smaller than Bristle had thought was possible. He was already halfway to the next bridge support. Disconnecting his wrist tethers altogether, Bristle left them behind and scaled the last stretch of the angled girder, clenching it tight with both arms. Finally he hooked his left forearm over the lattice platform. For an instant, as he tried to get up this last stretch, his legs swung out over nothing. His fingers clenched the bridge so tightly, it felt as if the mail of his gloves pushed down to his bones. Gasping, he heaved, and rolled.

He lay on his back on the platform, breathing hard and staring up at the purpled sky. For the first time in his life, there was nothing between it and him: no beams, no girders. No superstructure. He tore his helmet off and closed his eyes until the dizziness faded.

There was no going back to the nest now. Without his tethers, the logistics of going down were unthinkable.

And, without his spatula, he was useless.

He was truly a dangler. A bad egg.

Bristle struggled to his hands and knees. Through the grid of the platform he could see glimmers of moonlight on water. He swayed with vertigo. Ahead of him, to the west, the bridge went on forever, darker than the sky. He looked over his shoulder; behind him was the same view, but without the crescent moon. The eternal bridge. Bristle wondered if it really did go on forever, as some said, doubling back on itself in a massive, never-ending loop.

Well, he was free of cleaning it now. *Free*, he thought, with only a trace of self-recrimination, *to chase some phantom*.

Bristle tried to get to his feet. He managed to squat for some time, hands held out to either side, but he soon tumbled over. His legs would not respond to his wishes or hold his weight. And the bridge was too sturdy. The lack of motion made him feel ill. Slowly, woozy, he crawled westward.

Before too long (but easily several days' journey for the nest: he was almost over the support, where the scaffolding either side rose to incredible peaks), he heard a commotion beneath the bridge: Scrub's shout, the nest rustling. The crew was awake, looking for him. Bristle froze. But could the others see him here, so far above, just a dark shape on the mysterious upper surface? They probably would not even think to look up. Scrub would decide that the ocean had claimed Bristle's body, that Bristle had fallen while trying to dangle free, or maybe had finally jumped. There would be a crew meeting first thing in the morning, a talk on the dangers of spending too much time thinking or staying apart from the rest of the cleaners. Bristle could almost hear it now.

He resumed his painful crawl.

The platform of the bridge was not as different from the underside as Bristle had imagined it to be: it was steel, in filthy condition, pale with mottled bird shit. Welded and riveted, all sharp angles and interlocking framework. But gravity pushed down on him here. The world was reversed. He no longer swung from a soft web; his bones and muscles ached. His knees would burst apart if he kept this up for too long. His bones would shatter. Could he wriggle forward on his back?

The misty wind carried Scrub's voice to him: "Bristle? Briiiistle . . . ?"

Where, he thought, looking into the distance, *am I going to go?*

"Briiiistle?"

He saw the sheet of red light too late to pull back; one instant it was not there, then, when he moved his head slightly, it erupted, a blazing curtain. Bristle collapsed, moaning, onto the platform. When he blinked away afterimages, the woman was back, *standing*, two metres away, looking down at him.

"Who are you?" Her eyes widened; one foot moved backward. "You're a . . . man?"

Bristle uncurled himself, teeth clenched. "Yes," he managed to say. Pushing his torso off the bridge with trembling arms, he could look up at the woman's face, return her gaze. He saw the shape of the moon shining through her body. "My name's Bristle."

A beam of hazy white light stretched from far out to sea, from one side of the bridge, many lifetimes west, onto the woman's back. Her robe blew in the wind, though right now there was no wind.

When she did not answer, he said, "I'm a cleaner."

The woman had made a small, gasping sound; she put one hand to her mouth. "You talk so strangely. But I can understand you. You said . . . you're a *cleaner*?"

Bristle nodded.

"That's funny. I'm a cleaner, too."

She looked beyond Bristle, to the east. Her eyes seemed sadder and more desirable than anything he could ever have imagined.

"You? A cleaner? But you're *beautiful*."

"I just don't see how any of this can be happening," the woman whispered. "I was woken up to investigate, but nobody else seems to be around to answer my questions or to hear my report. I don't know what to do." She returned her gaze to Bristle. "Surely," she said, "you haven't crawled all this way?"

"No," Bristle answered.

"You weren't here last night. I looked."

"I was . . . underneath the bridge." But he thought: *That was in a dream. I'm not dreaming now.* "What's your name?" Bristle lowered his torso again and rolled onto his back. Though the steel was much harder than the netting had been, he felt more comfortable like this. He looked at the woman upside-down, at her pale, sad face, at the sickle moon showing through her chest.

The woman watched him. "I don't remember my real name," she said. "But I'm part of a system called IDEBCATS. At least I was. It's an acronym. You can call me Deb."

Though Bristle still did not know what the woman was talking about, just hearing her voice was enough to make his heart thud. So poised and smooth-skinned, it was as if Deb was not even the same animal that he and the others in the nest were. Women and men he knew were seldom a comfort. They were tough and, in the rare times that they touched him, they creaked in their layers of leather and hide and woven debris, their skin dry and cracked and scabby. "I came up here," he said, "to be with you."

She smiled wistfully. "I've tried to contact you several ways: beating out Morse, hypnopaedic mist—"

Under the bridge, Scrub yelled again. Maybe they had seen him up here, or followed the beam of light that shone from far away onto Deb and him. Bristle opened his mouth to explain about the nest, but the woman had moved quickly to the railing and stood there, looking down. "Are there more of you?" She was angry now, and when she turned back to Bristle, her face was creased. The beam behind her danced, flickered, following her motions. "Is that it? While you distract me? They sneak past?" Her voice became louder and louder, almost shrill. "We've got a fix now, Bristle. A lock on them. You are a treacherous man!"

"Just cleaners," Bristle said, alarmed at the change in the woman's demeanour. "They're just other cleaners."

"I couldn't figure it out. But you were tricking me."

"No," said Bristle, desperate. He wanted her the way she had been, not like this. He wanted her to like him.

She stared for a long time into the distance, as if listening to a sound Bristle could not hear. Her lower lip—that impossibly red, soft, full lip—shook. "Oh, I don't know, Bristle. They left me all alone. I don't know what to do. I don't know what to do in this case. I don't want to kill anyone."

"Kill?" Bristle was shocked. Was this woman a dangler? This woman of light and wind who came to visit him in and out of his dreams: was she crazy? "Why would you kill us?"

"It's my job," Deb said. "That's what I do." There was a certain pride her in voice. "Interactive distant early bridge cleansing and termination. That's my duty."

"Maybe—"

Scrub shouted once more.

Bristle licked his lips; it occurred to him now that the beam was like a tether on Deb, that she was not as free, or perhaps even as beautiful, as he had at first imagined. "Maybe," he said quietly, "you don't have to do your job anymore."

It seemed as though Deb had not heard him. She returned from the railing to stand by his head. "I'm isolated, Bristle. Cut off from everything."

"Me, too," Bristle said, and he reached up to touch the woman but his fingers passed through her.

She said suddenly, "Will you come back with me? Stay with me, Bristle?" Pointing westward. "Just a few metres away, the moving walkway starts. You'll be at the terminal before you know it."

Thinking that nothing was ever what is seemed, Bristle said, "Don't kill my crew." Inside his chest, there was a chasm of disappointment opening, a hollowness. The wind blew tears from his eyes.

Deb stared at him. "If you don't come with me, I'm afraid another part of the system will kill you. The laser has become active. It's got a lock on your position. I don't think I can stop it."

"I don't want anyone—"

The beam of light winked out and the woman was gone again, suddenly, leaving only Bristle and the moon and the shouts of his name coming up from the dark nest below.

HE CALLED THROUGH THE GRILLE OF the platform for a long time, trying to explain to Scrub that he felt the crew was in grave danger. Scrub yelled back that it was he, Bristle, who was in trouble, and that he had better get his ass back down into the nest. He called Bristle all sorts of names, made threats, screamed until his voice went hoarse.

"We saw you up there, talking to no one," Scrub shouted. "Man, you've lost your mind. And your position."

As Bristle wearily crawled westward, away, Scrub's shouts faded.

When his energy was spent, he lay on his back near the railing, surprised to find the platform moving slowly under him, bearing him along. He was too tired to be alarmed. He watched the night sky above him and thought about the people he had left behind, people he would likely never see again, and he wondered if the whole thing had been a mistake. Maybe Scrub was right. Maybe he was crazy.

Eventually, he fell asleep.

THE DISTANT CRUMP OF AN EXPLOSION woke him. It was raining, a misty dawn. The sky was gray and uniform. He was still being delivered westward by the moving platform. He propped himself up on his elbows and saw darker smoke rising from the bridge far to the east, a smudge that struggled to get into the air. Was the crew dead? Had he been responsible for the nest's destruction? Feeling a surge of horrendous guilt, Bristle opened his mouth and let drops of rain wet his tongue, his throat. He took a swig of egg yolk from his flask. His hands shook.

A white bird cried out nearby as he unfastened his leathers, complaining about Bristle exposing his flesh. Tossing his woven corset aside, and his leggings, so that they were quickly left behind on the stationary part of the platform, he wondered if he would ever see another person, or if he had already passed from the world of the living. But the rain felt good on his skin. He rubbed his hands idly over his chest and belly and face, felt the grime there softening, and knew he was alive.

The vibrations in the bridge began once more, up through his spine; he felt another shiver of remorse. *Free dangler*, he thought. *This is what happens to those who go bad.* His heart pounded strongly.

When there was a brief clearing in the cloud cover, and a glimmer of the sun showed through, he was sure he saw Deb again, running on the bridge next to him. This time her tether of light came from the sky. She was faint, though, hardly more than a phantom in the golden mist. Her mouth worked silently. He got the impression she was trying to apologize for something. Her faint hands waved at him, and her expression seemed charged with elements of hope and excitement.

She could not exist. Bristle had imagined her into being. The rain clouds closed in and Deb was gone.

Some time later, though, when Bristle rolled onto his side, curling in on himself and tilting his head so he could look west into the rapidly approaching future, he saw a thick, dark mass along the horizon that took his breath away: a smear of something solid slowly widening as he stared. Not sky, not bridge, not the restless swell of ocean.

Broken Sun, Broken Moon

1.

THEY WOKE ME, FROM ONE NIGHTMARE to another, with news of a perfect child. Out the tiny shed window, dark sky, no sound of wind or ticking of the moon. I lay still for a moment, more than a little disoriented.

A young perfect?

Mists had coiled my ankles—

Sitting up, I could see the mayor's absurd headdress, limned white as he leaned in, squinting, and glimmers of lantern light on ugly, stoic faces either side: two municipal ogres, jaws underlit, brows harsh. *Entranced.*

Every night since the storm passed there had been some unpleasant reason for council men to come knocking. Mumbling, *I'm coming*, I got dressed quietly, pulling a shawl over my shoulders and cinching it at my waist, though where I'd been staying was a structure set apart from my mother's house.

When I opened the door, I surprised four grunts, cowed at Mayor Richer's feet (who surprised me too): the little men blinked up from behind the legs of the larger men. I hadn't seen them through the window. Mayor Richer, apparently, was now using low-cog types as bearers: grunts were only able to carry the lanterns and a few tiny bags because the items were strapped directly to their backs. Recoiling in the bobbing glow cast over them by the lights, they betrayed an incomprehension of proceedings I could maybe approach but never fathom.

Our town council was reduced to morons, muscle, and me.

Patting my shawl's pocket to locate my key, I stepped outside.

Mayor Richer, a piebald, at thrice the grunts' height (yet, without the headdress, half a metre shorter than either of his ogres), appeared diffident, possibly even terrified. His blotchy skin was peeling—I could tell, even in this unreliable light. He set his mouth tight. "Hurry, scribe."

"Where are we going?" As I locked the shed door, a turgid gust, risen from the ocean, rolled over us; I hugged myself. "A new child, mayor? Really? A perfect?"

He turned away without replying, grunts scurrying from his feet, lanterns wild and clanking at the end of their poles.

The ogres, blinking semi-alert, spun on their heels.

We left my mother's garden, shutting the gate there, too.

UNLESS ENGAGED—PILOTING SLEDS, LIFTING ROCKS AND moving them, or ambulatory—ogres, the largest type, spent their waking time staring inland, over the roofs, toward the hinterlands and the paring of set sun there. Doctor Face would say they counted cosmic rays, bouncing over the obsidian between the crippled orbs but, unable to see any such phenomena myself, I was not wholly convinced. Walking, they moaned, and their moans echoed forlornly.

Descending the deserted street, sleepy homes either side, we headed toward the beach. The night was clear and quiet. Either a body had washed up on shore or we were going to the sarsen stone. I treaded lightly. Grunts dropped back and ran forward in short bursts, as if they were trying to escape their loads, bags thumping against their flanks, lanterns making the bobbing light crazy. I never liked men walking behind me, whatever type.

I had not put shoes on. The hard, smooth surface of the stone road was warm as the breeze, which continued to pick up—

One of the few trees in town had fallen. Flat rootmass vertical, unable to cling any longer to the glossy bedrock. Gravity must have shifted. Mayor Richer slowed the procession as we passed. Trees were under his jurisdiction. He had not replaced the garden appointee, a prentiss whose name I could not recall, and who had vanished, several weeks ago, as citizens of palmetto sometimes do. Our meager soils were almost entirely dispersed. One or two more storms and there would be none left.

You could fool yourself into thinking that inside each home were modicums of tranquility, snoozing citizens—at least until fragments of the wounded structures broke free and drifted up into the night.

"Hold onto your stuff, scribe."

"Tell that to your grunts." Who were certainly having some form of trouble keeping it together; I wondered if the mayor had slipped weights into their bags to keep them anchored.

We crested the bunkers, revealing silvered waters of the ocean, beginning to encrust. I had suspected as much from the smell on the breeze. In another night or so, the hardening layer would be thick enough to walk on. Exoskeletons of a million dead crabs, fused together. Difficult to imagine—almost—these now-subdued waves raging, waters rising, killing—

Stone embankments rimmed our town and could easily be seen from here, standing atop the spine of the bunker, awash in muted sheens of paler glare from the moon, oddly low on the horizon. I still had not heard any movement from the orb, not since they'd woken me, and wondered if it had finally broken down altogether.

On the beach, debris and wrack—amid larger fragments of houses, too big to drift away during the losses, or having come down, inert and drenched, when gravity suddenly increased—were dragged clear of the torrential streets to gain access during rescue attempts.

I attempted to blink away a rush of sudden, breathtaking memories, dreams and corpses and the broken moon—

Nightsleds.

Not palmetto junks, but two sleek frigates, from the capitals.

Government craft, parked on the eastern flank of the embankment, running lights dimmed and sleeping sails. I had seen a quick movement, almost invisible against the dark background. A peeper's eyes were sharp. The dull sheen of a bodysuit as a crew member stepped, lanky in his uniform, onto the frigate's deck.

Government men watched us.

I scowled in my own fashion at the mayor; his studied indifference and hardly concealed fear meant he knew full well about our nocturnal visitors. Government men had been waiting here for our approach and were coming out now that we had arrived, to get a better view.

I had many questions.

I asked none.

The grunts trembled and held back. Maybe—despite their low cog and poor eyes—they, too, had seen the sleds, and could smell something awful besides the hardening sea?

Mayor Richer saw fit to threaten the little men with his staff; this ceremony was vital to him.

Ogres stared blankly inland again, over my head.

At least the row of dead citizens—some having lain on the beach, wrapped in shrouds for the past three days, until I could get to them—were gone.

THE OGRE TO THE MAYOR'S LEFT—THE one with a lightning scar over his left eye, a sigil etched there by some mishap—carried the perfect infant in a pouch, under his pareu, and I hadn't noticed. Not until the giant withdrew and gingerly placed the silent bundle onto the sarsen stone with ridiculously huge hands.

I covered my mouth.

Flicking open the binding (fingers the size of the child's forearm), the giant looked at me directly, eyes tiny and black, then at Mayor Richer, seeking criticism or perhaps praise but getting neither.

Ten fingers on the child; ten toes; soft skin a consistent hue. *The perfect male.* Not too distinctive from most other types of men, including my own, though who knew the endocrinology, pattern of viscera, or genetic time bombs within. Maybe Doctor Face. Not me, that's for sure.

Awake, eyes open, a calm, symmetrical baby, looking up with benign curiosity at the night sky over palmetto's gusty beach.

Mayor Richer took a step closer to the stone but the grunts continued to hold back, lanterns trembling atop their poles, as if the infant could transform into some primal creature, leap at them somehow and tear their little hearts out—

I exhaled slowly. I had to stay calm. Time was fucked up. My thoughts could bolt unpredictably when I worked, making things worse.

Once, long ago, there had been a perfect in my class. A male, he was tiny and painfully clean and he sat in the front row paying rapt attention to Miss Bridge's lessons. His face was delicate. Cold blue eyes, full lips, white, white teeth.

Not this young, of course.

After he died, of cancer, there were no perfects left.

Until now.

Two nightsleds watched, and waited.

Something finally whirred far out at sea, and the moon clicked up one notch. In that brightened moment I remembered a flash of my dream, as if it had been jolted free: in the cavern, belly up to the steel ladder, coming up anxiously from mists—

Government men had brought this baby with them. Delivered it to our esteemed town council, commanding—while I slept—this ceremony.

With a full head of blond hair, the perfect was alone now, out here on the exposed stone. Blinking, twisting, hands grasping at nothing. In a very different place than where he should be.

I looked directly at the frigates, saw the small flash of a government device from the cabin on the right. They were taping us? Recording, or aiming their weapons in our direction.

What was the crime, the intent? What was the point of this?

"Can you see everything, scribe?" Mayor Richer's sudden words, clipped and parched. "Can we proceed? Are you in your, uh, trance?"

He was sad and old and ill.

I nodded, not for the trance, which was a stupid thing for him to say, but to tell him I was ready. Moments streaked after images, permutations, possibilities. All dark. Nodding, stern as I could, was easy with my peeper's face.

The tiny lanterns, at last held aloft and steady. A pristine clarity in this tableau. *Alive*, midway between the broken sun and the broken moon, on the coast of a stone continent, this moment teetering but about to slip irretrievably, taking a life with it—

Mayor Richer cleared his throat. "*Scribe*?"

I would recall every detail, every track of white vernix like a map on the perfect child's skin, trying to discern milky patterns there, mnemonic tricks—

"*Scribe!*"

The ogres had already lifted the blanket.

My polluted blood sent wires into my bones. I had to remember every detail, every movement, every sound. That was my job.

An ogre's stink, when they exert, is horrible.

Mayor Richer began an uncertain passage—I saw him look over, too, toward the frigates—but I didn't pay attention to his words or to the government men; everything except the perfect child detached from the vanishing moment and drifted out over the calm sea.

We would all be dead one day. Me, Mayor Richer, the grunts, the ogres. All types of men. I wanted to tell them this. I wanted to shout: *You fucking idiots!*

Who would memorize my last breath?

Deaths filled me, yet drained me.

Mayor Richer stepped onto the lip of the sarsen stone. He was jittery but still pretty nimble. Even the grunts came forward. We were all ready now. The municipal ogres raised high the almighty blanket, arms straining under the stone's weight, tendons like blades.

I'd almost finished my part.

Beyond the ticking moon and the widening wedge of light yawned a black rift. No man could know a thing about that blackness, not even if they were of the highest cog and lived through a thousand storms.

The blanket's clap—stone slamming against stone—sprayed a wave of the perfect's blood and guts across my bony shins.

AFTERWARD, WE DISPERSED. I DIDN'T CARE anymore where the government men went or what they had wanted. A lesson? The final condemnation of another type? I was left gutted after each death and could think only about my bed. Well, not my bed, exactly, but the bunk, in my mother's shed, behind her house.

I never looked back when I left the beach and headed home. Government men and their motivations were the mayor's problem. My job was to remember the deaths, and write a ludicrous epitaph about each in the ledger.

Wiping blood off my skin, best I could, my head pounded.

I returned to the shed, but by the time I had finished recording the last moments of the perfect child's life, dawn was breaking—I heard the sun clank, coming up, and the moon drop once. Before the vibrations hit, a sudden, mild gravity surge caused tiny bits of our wrecked houses to patter down on the shed roof like slow rain.

Perfect infant,

I had written in my painstaking lettering, tongue between my teeth:

Male (brought to palmetto by two nightsleds?)
Summarily crushed by municipal ogres
Between blanket and sarsen
A quiet end

I regretted the question mark, and the entire parenthetical line about the frigates, as soon as I'd finished it. I could not erase words, nor scratch them out: paper was rare, and ledgers were audited to ensure entries were acceptable.

I placed the pen down gently.

Above the new entry, in ink barely dry, a list of recent dead: victims of the storm and gravity's fluctuations; another sacrifice; cancers; malignancies.

My breathing got funny and my eyes stung. Releasing tears is an excruciating process for a peeper. I did not actually cry, but I was so tired, so fucking wiped out. No one would ever let me rest.

I lay across the bunk with my shawl still on. I did not sleep. Staring at the old rattan wall, shapes of black mould creeping slowly up, seeking to escape.

I could see faces of the dead, hundreds of them, whenever I closed my eyes.

An alarm clanged from the town hall. An assembly to start the new day: government men had not yet left town.

Putting the ledger back on its shelf, I kissed my fingers, touching them to the cover twice before dragging myself outside again. The day was already sparkling. Inland, the sun had cranked into view and the moon dropped lower over the sea. Glimmers of light ambushed me, cosmic rays I could not discern, stabbing eagerly at my eyes.

To THE LEFT OF PALMETTO—IF YOU face the sea (and the broken moon, of course)—a day's journey by sled, tacking the way frigates do, once they're out on the open hinterlands, are the twin capitals of rios and popu. Only the mayor ever went beyond palmetto's embankments, mostly to rios, the nearer of the capitals, when government men in the palace there beckoned. I had visited neither city in my sixteen years and had no reason to believe I ever would. Individuals were brought to palmetto from the capitals, and left behind, not the other way around—you could go to the immigrants' camp, where palmetto's citizens were first placed, out by the crater, and ask any recent arrival there about the capitals, or details about their past, but immigrants had no such recollections.

Some, like the young perfect, came to town for much shorter, and more dramatic, sentences.

In his ridiculous seminars, Mayor Richer told us civil servants stories about rios and popu, and about his stays there, and of the strange men who gave him his orders—and occasionally paid us these unpleasant visits.

Standing upright, government men were tall as an ogre. Thinner, though, with a straight back, and limbs that didn't bend quite right. They wore full masks, almost like the one Doctor Face put on whenever he tried to see why citizens were getting sicker and dying younger. (Doctor Face told me these masks protect from *spores*, which cloud up from a citizen's insides, when they're cut open. I can't speak to that, either. The one time I gashed my foot on a shell, splitting the meat of my heel wide open, I saw only my watery blood.)

"Unable to compete," this government man shouted from the stage of the town hall, where he stalked on those long, thin legs, "dwindle and kill! All of them!"

The uniform was dark and lustrous, a bodysuit. Piping on the seams carry essences that make hissing sounds whenever the government men move. They wear black gloves to their elbows, and tall black boots. Through the masks, their voices boom and screech and the words distort and you can never see much detail in their faces anyhow, with the collars up over their cheeks and the dark shades.

I did not understand what government men said. I understood less and less at each assembly. Those around me seemed to pay attention, and possibly understand, but perhaps they, too, did not want to admit their incomprehension.

Mayor Richer sat near the stage, facing the chairs on the floor. His peeling face looked terrible in the town hall's tungsten lighting. He appeared so close to dead that I had to grind my teeth to stop from memorizing everything about him. The government man addressing the hall could have kicked the mayor's headdress off, had he wanted, and seemed about to do so, several times. The mayor was dejected, folding in on himself. At the best of times, he never liked any meeting where he was not the highest ranked. Maybe the death of the perfect child brought him to an endpoint. I often wondered why government men had selected him in the first place, of all citizens, to run palmetto.

I sat in the front row, on one of the folding chairs, with Tang, the counter, on my left, and Seminural, a prole in charge of palmetto's zoning— wheezing with each breath—on my right. We had gone to school together. Prior to coming into the assembly, I had met them on the steps of the town hall, as we were wont to do, and had told them about the perfect child, and the watching frigates, and how the baby's guts had spurted out from under the stone blanket. Maybe another type had come to an end, I told them, but my associates had problems of their own, and only half-listened.

In the back of the hall, the municipal ogres stood at attention, staring straight ahead. There were perhaps thirty citizens in attendance, maybe thirty five. A poor turnout. Mayor Richer would lecture us later, in the debriefing—

Two hunters lingered by the back door, sniffing, leaving when they saw me looking. Grunts didn't come inside; their pinched faces crowded the big window.

Mostly, when my mind wandered, I stared at the government mens' weapons. Blades, with an unnatural sheen, like that of their bodysuits, and those long, sinuous guns, whose power and malicious intelligence were evident. My palms grew wet. I always daydreamed, oddly, about being touched by these weapons, lying naked, letting them latch onto my flesh. I hated both contact and nudity. Sometimes I became convinced the weapons whispered to me, secrets I should know but had forgotten.

Once, I imagined I'd seen the palace at rios from the deck of a frigate, as the craft coasted through a massive gate made of curved bones—

The government man shrieking on stage, I could tell, was female. Like me, and my mother, and Miss Bridges, the teacher. I could not really see her eyes, behind the shades. The eyes of other men, viable types anyhow, higher cogs, were always on me, wherever I went. I never liked the way men looked at me—male or female. My mother said I would suffer if citizens stopped looking at me but I was not like her, despite her claims. *Men feed us with their stares*, she said. But I hated the attention. Without it, I would not retain details about death. I would not be the scribe. Attention fueled a peeper: a cycle I'd like to smash.

Underneath their uniforms, government men must not be flesh, or blood, like the varied types of citizens, but maybe gears and spiny rods.

"Cut, cut, cut," screeched the man on stage.

When I shuddered, and took my eyes off the gun, deigned to pay more attention, she was, without a doubt, looking right at me.

Slicing silently one behind the other, the frigates raced across the obsidian plain, leaving twin tails of sprayed dust, heading back to rios, or maybe popu. The monstrous sails had awoken, unfurled and, braced around the masts, did not look back at us, watching the nightsleds leave from the steps of our town hall, high on the embankment.

Up here, one could see out over most of the town, set in the depression before us. There was a grey smear to the sky now; the murderous glitter that had greeted me in the morning was gone. The sea, equally grey, and still, was as much a slab of stone as the land. Our own miserable sleds, palmetto's junks, parked haphazard in the corral, having been tossed by storm winds. Only able to travel the ridge of stone behind the town, with an ogre impassive at the helm, they were bad jokes compared to those swift crafts now vanishing into the distance.

The few sails we owned huddled together, dozing around their nesting pole, smaller creatures, a washed-out green, sickly and inert.

Stepping down, I noticed tendrils, rising from the crater, around which rimmed the immigrants' camp. In my dream, I'd clung to a ladder anchored to the side, afraid of moving either up or down. Below, in the dream, were mists. Above me?

This.

No breeze today. The tendrils rose straight up. Gravity seemed less than normal again—certainly over there. Maybe when the obsidian crust collapsed, massive obelisks tumbling, smashing into the cavern below, the sun and the moon had been broken. Artefacts were destroyed. Any structures that had fallen in the collapse broke apart slowly as they decomposed and floated up piecemeal from the crater. Even when gravity was constant, our houses shed components. A battle to retain them. On days like today, traces could be seen, rising, fine as smoke.

Mists had curled around my ankles like fingers.

"Scribe? Three, two, one. What you looking at?"

Tang, grinning, all teeth, withdrew an egg from his shroud.

Grunts who had been gathered outside the town hall scurried past us in small groups.

Tang put his thumb through the eggshell; I saw the zygote within trying to get away.

The grunts were going back to barrios now that the crowds were mostly gone, to hide there unsuccessfully from whatever might come next.

Tang was shorter than ever. Up to my crotch now. I had to stoop to pass him back the egg. Seminural joined us. Tang swallowed the zygote because he was the one who found the egg, scooping it out of the yolk with his fingers and dropping it whole down his gullet. Me and Seminural broke off pieces of yolk and sucked at them; the egg was not very strong.

Not so long ago, Tang and I had walked together along the line of the coast. He was taller then. We looked for flotsam or just sat there, in the pre-storm breezes, getting high and talking. We even shared an office briefly, when the mayor had wanted his team on site, but that didn't last long and Tang wasn't feeling well lately and we didn't speak much anymore anyhow. His grouper features, too small for his head, puckered even more around his broad mouth, as if they were getting sucked in. He was pretty high cog, viable but prone to a grouper's degenerative biology.

Seminural seemed sick too now, bags under his eyes.

We stood there, the three of us, a fine trio, looking out over palmetto as the egg took over, each with our own warping perceptions, trapped inside our heads. I hoped at least for a decent vision or two.

2.

My mother stood at the stove, preparing second breakfast. A kettle steamed on the counter. Against a frying pan, she ground sluggish crustaceans to a pulp with a fork, her meal hissing and flailing as she pestled them out of existence.

The side door of her house had been open; I hadn't had to knock. My mother seemed sluggish, too, not recovered from her own evening. Diffused light came through the kitchen window in a broad column, motes of dust struggling within. Light always looked a bit off inside my mother's house.

"You've been crying," she said.

Rays of light gave her an amber aura. Her face, turning quarter profile as I stepped fully into the kitchen, remained an image of beauty so poignant any words I had planned to say were caught in my throat.

"So have you."

My mother snorted. "What did those fuckers want?"

"Who? You saw them? The mayor and his ogres?"

"No, you idiot. Those freaks from the palace."

"Oh." Sitting down at her kitchen table, I inspected, and sniffed, a plate of heavy bread. There were several slices; she was making a lot of food. I shrugged. "I don't know."

Selecting a slice, I took a bite.

With a practiced movement, my mother flipped an errant crustacean back into the pan. "You're full of shit."

"They left," I said. "Right after the assembly. They came last night. They were angry about something."

Behind my mother's head, on the kitchen wall, a new crack ran from stove top to ceiling. Trickles of particles made their way upward. Some houses seemed to attract and even contain gravity fluctuations: my mother's was one of them.

I watched her face to see if any traces of emotion were evident but none betrayed her features. Like me, she was a peeper, and peepers don't emote much, unless it comes out when we are in the process of comforting a citizen, like she did, or maybe trying to remember every detail of a citizen's horrific death. Just like her house, new cracks had recently appeared on her once-flawless skin. Peepers are beautiful, but deadpan, with faces of stone.

"Did you talk to them?"

"No."

She turned. "Did they ask about me?"

"No." My voice quiet. *Dressed in a summer shawl, thin limbs bare, expressionless face exposed, my blue eyes always wide, my skin shining. Men watched me as I accompanied my mother in the market, or shopped on the street of crocodiles, in barrios. Men watched me as I ran, by myself, to school—*

The eaves of my mother's roof were damaged. Tiles needed repair. Few houses ever grew back correctly.

Heat and the grinding fork had silenced the last of the crustaceans. They simmered. My memories were acting up. Maybe the egg I'd eaten earlier was stronger than I thought. I sniffed at the bread, wondering what might be in it. I kept thinking about the grunt toddlers, trapped in their daycare during a surge, on the first day of the storm. Bodies of children lay arranged before me. I saw smashed faces in the lantern's struggling light or, worse, untouched faces, as if pulled from the rubble asleep. I studied swollen tongues, eyeballs pulped to jelly, the dust-covered shapes of thin blood like birthmarks appearing too late to mean anything to anyone. All told this year, excluding last night's sacrifice of the perfect child, twenty-three citizens had died in the storm and its aftermath. I was called to each one, either during the throes or as soon after as possible. Twenty-three dead, memorized and recorded, all lodged within me, joining others from previous storms and from the slower seasons of relative respite that lay between. Palmetto's dead, trapped inside me—

"Wake up," my mother said. "What the fuck's the matter with you?"

"Huh?" I wiped moisture off my chin with the back of my hand; something squirmed in the fluid.

She sat across from me, pushing pulped crustaceans into her mouth with her fingers. Even gorging, in her slow decline, my mother looked remarkably beautiful. Her blue eyes were still wide and her teeth still strong and white. No man could pass her on the street without stopping, even now, unless they were of the lowest cog.

"I want to come home," I said, abruptly. "Council won't fetch me in the middle of the night anymore. Not for a while. The season's over, mom."

Chewing, she said nothing.

I looked down at my hands and tried to keep my voice steady. "I can't stay in the shed anymore. I can't sleep with the ledger at my feet. I want to come home. I want to—" I met her gaze. "I want to resign. I can't be scribe anymore."

She chuckled. At least, I believe the noise my mother made was a chuckle. She was hardened and mean—

Beyond the short hall off the kitchen, through the open door to her bedroom, a recumbent body shifted. On her unmade bed, in shadows, under a sheet in the gloom, a citizen waited for her.

My mother saw me looking. "You can't stay here. Vanishing like you do and then showing up. Eating eggs all the time. With your friends. And I don't want those bureaucratic fuckers coming over."

"They won't, mom. I just told you. The season's over."

"I don't like to see you stumbling around palmetto. Didn't you learn anything with that fucking fish teacher, Miss Bridges? Aren't you supposed to be the smartest person in this town?"

I looked at my hands again. Unlike my face, they were not pretty. I never wanted to be high cog. I never wanted to be pretty.

"Go outside and play."

My mother wanted to rejoin the man in her bed. She had not finished with him yet; the breakfast was for him.

"You need fresh air," she said. "The sun's up."

"The sun," I replied, "is fucking broken."

She had risen from the table before I'd even slammed the side door. I heard her chair move, heard her walk back to her room, heard the citizen there say something to her, sort of a moan, his voice deep inside the ebullient mood she had put him in.

MISS BRIDGES WAS MY TEACHER; SHE was the one who first nominated me for my current position, as palmetto's scribe, though even before the naming ceremony town council had begun tracking me. I was an uncommon, viable type, only daughter of palmetto's comforter—attractive, of course, stoic, and getting exceptional grades.

Eyes were upon me.

On the beach, dressed in kelp garlands and an embroidered shawl, with the moon cranking up over the sea and the broken sun barely visible behind the silhouetted town, warm winds blowing in—

Miss Bridges was nice to me. True, she was nice to the other children, too, regardless of their type, or cognition—patient with our lassitude and blank looks—but she was my *friend*, my mentor. She was also what used to be called a *fish*. A fish is a type of man whose blood runs cold. She had scales around her ears, vestigial gill slits, no hair at all. A shrill laugh. Excess saliva, too: no one wanted to sit in the front row of her class, except myopic students, like stains, who are virtually blind and have little choice.

Fish also die young, mostly from lung infections. Their deaths are as terrible as any other to behold. Doctor Face long ago deemed the type recessive, a biological failure. Miss Bridges was the last fish. Death comes for the mean and the nice alike.

"CELESTIAL ORBS COLLABORATE."

Unlike my mother's harsh admonitions, Miss Bridges' voice was soft, soothing. Memories of her tone—barring that of her final words—made me feel a warm sort of sadness that was almost pleasant. She had a salty smell, one I associate with my youth. Sometimes she would pant. Her smell, I know now, was related to crystallization of urine in her kidneys, a shortcoming, but at the time I liked it.

Intricate cradles of string wound the webbed fingers of her cold fish hands.

"Though less and less," she said. "They're linked, a couple. Threads of light saw back and forth between the moon and the sun. These are known as energetic particles. Some say the adenomas can see them."

She smiled.

Ogres, she meant. *Adenomas. Cosmic rays.* Miss Bridges had a different name for all types of citizens and used only them. (Was she hurt by the term *fish*? I don't remember what she called herself—or me, for that matter. Amara something? An amaran? I was possibly an adara. Or maybe the other way around.)

String sloping to the left, then, with a deft movement of her fingers, to the right. Miss Bridges told my class how the continent had once worked and would never work again. She showed us on a piece of damp string:

"Stripped of shells, beta particles race back and forth. These erode us. They jostle us. For the same reason the beach flickers, or why sleds go, or why we feel heavier some days."

Storms would continue getting worse and worse until they wiped everything out, except probably government men, who would no doubt evade the effects of entropy inside their capital cities.

"We can employ a formula together, here, right now, on the board, to calculate the number of degrees each celestial body fails to rise above the horizon. We calculate how much less they rise each year."

Was I the only one in my class paying attention? *Everything is falling apart*, she said. A simple lesson. The sun can't rise fully into the sky, nor can the moon. We are victims to their failing light. Just look into the face of a dying grunt. Look into the face of a piebald as he draws his last breath.

Types come and go. Men slip further from an ideal no one can remember.

Cancer killed Miss Bridges, not lung infection. I watched her die, of course. I sat by her side, in the infirmary. I remember every detail. When her heart stopped, I went back to my room and wrote about her death in the ledger, using the words *placid* and *peaceful*, as a good scribe should, though I saw, in her eyes, as her life departed, something very different.

INLAND, INSIPID STREAKS OF CLOUDS WERE faint bloodmarks against the washed out flesh of the sky. These were remnants of this year's storm, several days away now, about to vanish off the inner rift. Beneath the clouds, a broad paring of the celestial orb had frozen in place, almost as high as it could go, extending across most of the horizon. As the sun struggled to ascend, a distant *boom* from its efforts shook the bedrock.

I felt a tremor pass beneath me.

Citizens on the streets all had the same sort of look, no matter what type: thankful to be ambulatory, but somewhat guilty to find they had survived another storm while others had not. Most looked at me, or smiled briefly, but uncertainly, in their varied forms of smiles. A few doffed their hats. Did they feel resentful of their attraction toward me? They knew I would never help them feel better. Were it not for minor tweaks in luck, I could easily be studying their corpses, and one day probably would, instead of lying with them in a comforter's bed.

On the beach, day crews were assembled, grunts mostly, throwing collecting nets into the water. I heard the *slap* of the woven mesh. The nets sank slowly, pulled down by rocks. Grunts had cleaned the surface of crab exoskeletons for some way out from the shore but the viscosity of the exposed ocean was nonetheless thick: lots more protein than usual in the water. Krill, churned from the sea bottom by waves, remained in abundance for weeks, small compensation for the damage and deaths.

When I passed the rope bridge at the end of orion blvd., where stairs were carved into the embankment, leading up to the storm lookout— heading to the office, to see if Tang had another egg he'd be willing to share—Doctor Face startled me, hailing from one of the chairs on Lucky Jym's patio; he sat in the shade there, drinking a cup of spiked brine.

I approached, wondering what, if anything, Doctor Face knew about last night's sacrifice. I hadn't seen him at the assembly, but I'd not searched the crowd very closely.

"Funny," he called, when I got closer. "I was just this second thinking about you, scribe. Looking at the sea and wondering about you."

"Oh?"

"Can you come by my home? I'd like to show you something."

"I'm going to work now. Maybe later."

He was wearing his gown, a dark stain over the left breast. Big gloves and filter mask rested on the table before him, several empty glasses arrayed by his folded hands.

"Later in the day," he acquiesced. "Sure, if you can. Nothing to get worked up about. Plus I have some questions about the, well, the position of limbs, relative to each other, things of that nature. Especially in older specimens."

"When citizens die, you mean?"

Nodding, he took a healthy sip. "Startling theories occurred to me last night, scribe. Obstacles shifted out of the way, did they not? While the town slept? Did you feel it?"

"No."

"Things became clearer. To me, anyhow. Soon we'll have a breakthrough, you'll see."

Doctor Face had large yellow teeth, which he exposed often under his moustaches. He was a prole, very high cog, of course, and though I could not see his eyes behind his glasses—lenses were stitched to the perimeter of his orbital bones—I'm sure he winked at me.

"Can you sit for a moment?" Indicating the chair across from him. No one else was on the patio. "I've tried to explain my theories to Jym here, but he's a fool. A good fool, mind you, healthy as a hunter, but he doesn't get it."

The proprietor listened from the kitchen. Lucky Jym was also a prole. Smart, functional, viable. A regular at my mother's house.

"But he does prepare a good cup of brine." Doctor Face made a show of draining his fourth drink. Pale foam coloured his moustaches. He grimaced. "Are you sure you're all right, scribe?"

"I'm fine. Why?"

"You're one of the few in this town who understands me."

"I can't stay." I did not appreciate his concern or circumlocution. Another egg is all I wanted—a stronger one, this time. And I still needed to sleep. "You're wrong, doc, I don't understand you."

He grinned as sudden flickers of light, released off the beach, made me wheel: there had been a loud click, from across the sea, but it did not sound like the moon. I put my hand to my brow, to look out as far as I could. The moon had not moved. At the horizon, between water and sky, a grey line was scratched.

"Scribe?"

Grunts struggled with a net. Several, I realized, were standing on the exoskeletons of the crabs, fishing through a hole. I had never seen this behaviour before and—

"There!"

Startled again, I wheeled to see the doctor, clearly excited, pointing across the street, toward a brightly tiled house that belonged to an ancient prentiss no one had seen in ages. The house had partially collapsed during a surge and had never repaired itself. Near some weeds at the cracked foundation, I saw furtive movements, fronds bending. "What is it?"

"*A creature.*"

"*What*?" Was the doctor messing with me? "What sort of creature?"

"Mangy and scrawny. A cat? Isn't that what you learned about in school? A cat? It was watching us." Doctor Face laughed. "Or maybe just watching you, eh? Taking notes. Now please, scribe, sit for a moment. You're worrying me. There seems to be a form of— Something is going on."

Out the corner of my eye, I could see Doctor Face craning, trying to see what I'd seen out at sea, but there was nothing there of any interest, not to him anyway, so he just scowled.

I said, "Can you smell it?"

"Smell what?" His moustaches lifted.

"Usually, when the storms pass—when they're inland, like they are now—there's a smell coming off the ocean. You know, with the new year. And the crabs. The smell of their bodies. And the moon is—"

I was unable to continue.

Nets plopped again into the water.

He fixed his lenses upon me. "Have you ingested a zygote?" Taking another draught, and wiping his mouth. "Do we need another intervention?"

"No. We didn't need the first one."

"All good citizens need them periodically. Have you had any, well, disturbing dreams lately?"

"Are there any other sort?"

He grinned again, gesturing toward me with his cup, as if I'd won this exchange.

Doctor Face had gone down into the crater, when it first opened. A team of a dozen citizens went down. Young, keen Doctor Face. Miss Bridges told us about that day over and over but maybe those stories had been in my dream, too? Arcane devices, retrieved and studied, poked at, prodded, eventually destroyed: items that would never surrender their purpose and could only, council deemed, hasten the breakdown of palmetto—

Doctor Face stared, somewhat alarmed. My mouth had gone dry and I struggled to remember what I had been saying. Machines dropped into the ocean? A creature watching me?

Doctor Face himself, in a second, smaller expedition, brought up the school books.

"I remember the feel of the ladder," I said. "The rungs on my feet. Cold metal against my palms. What was down there, doc? Under the mist?"

He grabbed at his gloves. "Let's go to my home. We can't talk about this here."

As I was about to protest, my shawl was tugged hard, suddenly, from behind:

"Scribe, scribe! Come quick!"

I turned to see Hartwell, the council's message runner, a priori, standing before me. Hartwell's scoliosis was so acute they called him a *spring grunt*, though he clearly wasn't low cog or a grunt. Still, he had to look up at me. He coiled in on himself and got lower and lower every day. Like Tang. Hartwell's neck was a hard bulge over his left shoulder, yet he could lope faster than anyone I knew. His hair was a mess. He looked utterly frantic.

"What is it?"

But I knew. I could see, in his eyes, there had been another death, or a citizen lay dying, and I needed to watch.

"Better come, scribe. You, too, Doctor F. *Come*."

The doctor fixed his lenses upon Hartwell. "Slow down, son. Nothing is achieved by panic."

"*Come!*"

"Who is it?" I reached down to grab Hartwell's hunched shoulder. "Is Mayor Richer there?"

Hartwell shook his head best he could. "Not yet, scribe. At barrios—" he indicated with a lurching twist of his body "—you'd better come."

Doctor Face, empty cup still held frozen in mid-air, stared at the square behind us, where a small crowd of assorted types—predominately grunts—had already gathered.

THIS YEAR, THE POWERFUL GRAVITY SURGE that the storm had initially brought nearly reduced what was left of barrios to complete rubble, most of which had, in the days following, crumbled and drifted off. The street of crocodiles, where citizens of all types used to shop, my mother included, for everything from sweet treats to companions, was now altogether gone. Building materials for barrios were shoddy, and the small houses— shacks, really—took longer to rebuild than residences in any other part of town. With each recent storm the area weakened further, and had grown slower, more delicate, twisted. Mostly grunts lived in barrios; probably half the entire population of palmetto was grunts.

As we neared the crowd milling on the border of the cluttered slum, I could see no other council members, like Hartwell had intimated: scores of little men; three prentiss—and the hunters I'd seen at the town hall, awkwardly hunched, their backs to me, muzzles down. Hunters did not often leave the vicinity of their pen and their presence here was further off-putting: twice today I'd seen them. There were only three left in palmetto and one was ancient, feral, in the infirmary full time, tied to a stake in a back room.

I could not see what anyone was looking at. I could not see the body. But I knew it was there. Colours took on saturated hues, sparkled; my sinuses were swelling; time fucked up—

Huffing, Doctor Face arrived. "I say, scribe," he wheezed, "you sure move pretty fast."

The hunters' long faces turned my way. Had I not suspected some truly awful event all day? Sniffing at me, black lips curled over sharp incisors, gums a bright red, eyes wild. I had never seen a hunter die. This thought occurred to me, smelling their adrenaline, their foul breath. I had never written a hunter's epitaph.

"Scrrribe," one growled.

"*Look*," said the other, pointing between the legs of those before us with a foreshortened paw, black fingernails like claws, but I could see for myself now, as a citizen stepped aside: the oily uniform, the long-limbed body, broken-backed, the smashed mask and last twitches of a dying government man.

ALONG THE COAST OF A GREY, sluggish sea, standing on the edge of a town square, I was a mote, passing through faltering light. We all were. The continent lay silent. A tremor passed through me, and the bedrock trembled, from one rift to the other.

Then I was kneeling, holding the gloved hand of the government man. With the two fingers I kissed to the ledger, I gently touched the bridge of the man's mask, feeling the warm, strangely pliant material *move*: it had split in two. Dark red fluids leaked out of his face.

This was the female, from the stage. Hadn't they all left town? I'd watched the frigates leave. Why had she stayed behind? Struggling weakly to breathe, the government man was bleeding from a chest wound, from her face, from a rent in her uniform by her stomach, yet the consistency of her blood was thicker than any blood I had ever seen, a brilliant crimson, turning darker as it spilled, and gelling. Hotter than any blood I had touched. Nor did it smell familiar. Trembling, I brought traces very close to my nose, on the tips of my fingers, in order to fix the unusual scent, and I even thought, for a moment—madly—about licking my fingers, tasting them, but I shuddered off this primitive and startling urge.

How many times would this government man be able to fill her lungs again—if she even had lungs? Ten? Twenty? I let my eyes move over her body, remembering. Bodysuits were not black, nor as smooth as I had imagined they would be; the fabric was covered with tiny pores that opened and closed like mouths. I brushed my knuckle over the smooth breast and the uniform sucked at my skin. The shattered mask was a broken shell, like that of a mussel, stepped on. A trickle of red blood ran from the government man's ears now. Under the mask, and fractures shades, I could see her eyes—one of them, anyhow, blue, just like mine. The second eye was gore. But that one blue eye was a window to another, stranger continent—

"*Scribe!*" The mayor, frantic, half-dressed, came running across the square as best he could, one hand holding his headdress in place. "Get away from there!"

A few council men came with him, hastily—two bean counters, Ron and Simon, both proles, and Havershad, a stain stenographer. I turned away from them to look once more into that dying eye, to memorize what I saw there. I understood, with certainty, they were not like us.

"*Scribe!*"

I think the government man tried to speak then, but only pink bubbles came to her lips; her eye dulled.

"Get up," Mayor Richer shrieked, wheezing and breathless himself, right next to me now. "What are you doing, you idiot? Don't touch that—*Get up!*"

"Memorizing," I said flatly. "I'm doing my job."

Turning to the pair of hunters, screaming at them: "How did this happen? Low cog idiots! Doctor Face, didn't I tell you? *Doctor Face!*"

The hunters kept their eyes on the ground and did not whelp, or cringe, even when Mayor Richer beat them with his staff. "You're the last of your fucking type," he shrieked. "I promise you that! The last!"

Doctor Face put one hand on the mayor's arm, to hold him back, but the mayor wrenched free.

"That's not up to you, mayor," he said.

The hunters, baring their fangs, slunk away.

"And don't go into your trance, scribe. You're not putting any of this in the ledger." Mayor Richer raked at his cheeks with curled fingers; there were runnels in his loose flesh and bloody strips dangled from his chin. "These fucking hunters, Doctor Face. I listened to you and now look what they've done. Get up, scribe! That's an order! Get up *now!*"

More grunts were filling the square behind Mayor Richer, drawn by his shouts. He tried to grab me but the doctor held him back.

"I've seen their rage," Mayor Richer hissed. "Trust me, I've seen it. How did this happen? Scribe? Was it those fucking hunters? They'll be put down," he promised. "Doctor Face, you hear me?"

"We don't know what happened here, Richer," said the doctor. "And, like I said, it's not your call who lives and who dies."

"Don't tell me what my call is. There'll be consequences for this. Every storm or gravity surge, or even the sacrifices, are forced on us from outside. *But we did this*. We did. One of *us*." Mayor Richer turned to the left, toward rios and popu, as if sleek frigates would appear on the horizon any second now. "We've hit rock bottom. We've failed."

"I memorized her last breath," I said, insistent. "I watched this man die and I'm going to write her epitaph in the ledger."

"*You cannot!*" Mayor Richer spun, spittle exploding from his lips.

For the first time I wondered if his fear came from some concept larger than personal demise; I was surprised by the possibility of his selflessness. Mayor Richer's thin blood dripped onto his gown like water; he was literally coming apart.

"*Her* last breath? What's gotten into you, scribe?"

I shrugged, and might even have smiled, though no one would have known.

Doctor Face meanwhile held his gloved hands up, palms out. "We'll weigh evidence. Let's not jump to conclusions, Richer. Hard to imagine that the hunters killed this, uh, this man, or that anyone here in palmetto can kill of their own volition. Let me have this body and I'll soon tell you the truth. The answer to every question is within. I can finally crack it, Richer. I can. I'll turn things around. No one will ever see this government man again, I assure you."

"You're both mad," the mayor said. "And I should have *you* killed for addressing me like that, *Face*."

"Apologies, mayor. You know I forget my Ps and Qs when I'm excited. No disrespect meant."

"We need to wrap the body in a shroud. Decompose it. Carry it to the beach—"

I could see a series of reflections in Doctor Face's lenses, my own central and foremost.

"Mayor," he said, pointing one finger, "this, er, this event, could be most, well, most fortuitous for the future of all citizens."

"*Fort—?*" Mayor Richer's face got even redder. "I'm not listening to this shit anymore." He had to hold his headdress in place with one hand. "You both insist on disobeying me. Scribe, you cannot capture this death in the ledger. That is what *I'm* trying to say here. You have no idea! The ledger is for palmetto and, and Doctor Face—" He wheeled, scattering grunts with his feet. "You may not have the fucking body! You need to find the hunters, that's what you need to do. Scribe, go with him. Find those fucking hunters." He looked about, as if realizing, for the first time, the number of men watching. "Disperse! Go back to your homes. Your council will deal with this! Go home!"

Slowly, the crowd did disperse, except for a few of the grunts, who had not comprehended the situation.

"Why was she here?" My words fell like pieces of a broken home into the town square.

Mayor Richer turned slowly to me. He pushed his headdress straight.

"The frigates left," I said. "After the assembly. They left town. We all saw them go. But she stayed behind."

"What is your point?" But there was a flicker behind his eyes, a doubt there, among others.

"Why was she here, in barrios?"

"Stop saying *she*. You've truly gone mad. And I don't have to tell you anything." Watery blood ran down the mayor's neck; his gown was ruined. "You must erase all details from that peeper memory of yours." Mayor Richer wiped more blood off his face, and began, surprisingly, to weep. Tears dripped freely from his cheeks, making everything pink and messy. "We're fucked," he said. "We're just fucked."

A FOG LAY ACROSS MOST OF the sea. The doctor was limping as we walked the residential area. I could see the fog periodically between the houses. Doctor Face looked significantly older all of a sudden and I was not sure how. After Mayor Richer had the slim corpse of the government man wrapped in a shroud, his bean counters and Havershad had carried the body to the beach, where it lay now like another victim of this year's winds—one last recovery, a loved one found under a collapsed building, or drowned in the sea.

Miffed he had not been given the body, the doctor called Mayor Richer a fool. *Incredible secrets in that blood*, he said. *Did you see the red blood?*

Clear-headed—maybe more clear-headed than I had ever felt—I told him I had. I was looking for the hunters. Had they returned to their pen?

Palmetto was oddly still.

The sun ratcheted down another loud notch and tinged the approaching evening mellow amber. Our shadows stretched before us. The continent trembled and I imagined rays of waning light hitting my back and crawling over my skin, breaking me down.

What I could discern of the sea was so flat and calmed by the fog I could walk across it, to the outer rift, stepping on dead crabs all the way. I stopped for a second, to consider this.

One edge of the sarsen stone peeked out from behind my mother's house, which I could see below us now, tiny, and to the right. Doctor Face muttered about missed opportunities. *Wasted time,* he said. *All those damned days.*

Was my mother alone? I remembered the man waiting for her in her bedroom, the plate of heavy bread on her kitchen table, and my surge of anger.

Doctor Face wanted me to forget the mayor's directive, forget the hunters, and said more than once that I should come with him, to his home; he talked about this prospect again, said I seemed distant. He still had concerns about me but I could not focus on what he was saying. At one point, he startled me by shouting, "We are asleep, scribe, and forgetting!"

Even though the doctor was a prole, and very high cog, he would never understand the workings of a citizen, no matter how much he broke us apart and studied the bits.

"A sled is missing." I pointed. We were passing the corral, where palmetto's junks parked; I had grabbed the doctor by the arm and stopped him cold. Stumbling, he spun on his bad leg, nearly losing his footing—

"A sled? I don't—I say, scribe, how can you be sure?"

"This morning, after the assembly, there were seven. Now there's only six."

His brows constricted around his lenses in a squint, counting already, lips moving against the barbs of his moustaches.

Two of the old craft, damaged by the most recent storm, leaned against each other, as if in commiseration. Smaller components had since drifted away into the sky. On the nesting pole, one of the sails appeared to be wounded, more off-colour than the others, sagging weakly, while the rest huddled as high on the pole as possible.

Doctor Face frowned. "Perhaps the hunters—"

"Hunters couldn't pilot a sled."

"True . . ."

"Doctor Face, I hereby deputize you."

"What?" He was shocked. "What are you up to, scribe?"

"Go get a municipal ogre. Find the one with the scar over his eye. Tell him we need a navigator."

"A *navigator*? What? You can't *leave* palmetto. You can't— Only the mayor— You heard what he said, scribe. And I certainly can't *go* with you, running about and such. My knees are inflamed and my heart— I have important research *to do*."

"*This* is important. The hunters didn't kill the government man." I released his arm. "Whoever took the sled did. Meet me back here as soon as you can. Hurry."

"There's no killer, scribe." He looked toward the sun, putting his hand to his brow, as I had done earlier in the day. "Trust me. There's no killer out there."

"Just go, doc. Get the ogre. I'm pulling rank, as council."

"What you're proposing is madness. These sleds aren't made for distances."

"Go."

"Scribe, listen, listen to me, I should tell you I've been asked to keep an eye on you, on your behaviour."

"By who?"

He grimaced. "And now you've hurt me. Your grip is like *iron*." He rubbed his upper arm with a gloved hand.

I thought he was going to defy me, continue arguing. His stained moustaches covered his mouth like yellowed baleen. I could smell his stale sweat and the tang of concoctions he used in his work. But he said nothing more, and limped off, to get the ogre—or so I hoped.

I turned away. Clues, I should have told the doctor, are elsewhere.

THE HUNTERS WERE JUST EAST OF the town hall. One was peeing against the storehouse wall while the other stood guard, sniffing at the breeze. The red on their gums was the government man's blood. Like me, they had been drawn to it, but were unable to resist a taste. I knew this now. They had lapped up the government man's blood.

I stopped.

The hunter was not standing, but peed on all fours, squatting, like a creature.

They saw me watching, and they snarled.

AS THE SLED WAS PREPPED AND checked, which involved the ogre moaning and clambering about the deck in an apparently aimless fashion, standing on each runner, staring at the inner horizon, no government men came over the embankment. In fact, palmetto remained preternaturally quiet. Evening closed in and the sun went down in increments, just like other evenings, dropping with distant *clanks*, which manifested as tremors, shaking the bedrock.

Before long, the ogre pushed the sled from the corral. The sail—he'd chosen the ill one—clung to the mast overhead, rippling in its restraining cords. Doctor Face had not returned, but the ogre with the lightening scar over his eye, arms thicker than my legs, had, to my surprise, shown up, bringing several municipal grunts in tow, who had been carrying a sign between them that read:

YOU CANNOT LEAVE!
SEEK HELP SCRIBE

The doctor's handwriting was awful.

I chuckled, for the first time ever, I think, an awkward, barking sound, just like my mother's.

Looping kelp ropes around each hunter's neck, I had led them back; they could not resist.

Doctor Face likely ran to tell the mayor, or maybe my mother, what I was planning.

No one came to stop us.

When the ogre stood on the deck, feet wide apart, encouraging the sail to unfold, I took a seat behind the mast. The grunts crouched around me. Hunters were tied, one to each runner. They might be a furtive type, low cog and maybe recessive, yet they possessed an inability to disobey anyone in council. Tethered now, they glanced sidelong at me, resentful, fearful, compelled. Did they know I was trying to save them? How did they perceive me? Hunters were close to a genetic precipice off which there was no recovery, but they were not killers, and need not be condemned. There had been enough death.

As we headed up the embankment, into the hinterlands, we picked up speed. By the time we were clear of the ridge curving behind the immigrant's camp, leaving the last few municipal buildings behind, it was almost night.

AT THE HELM, THE OGRE HELD the lower half of the sail in one hand and kept pushing the beast skyward with smooth, pumping motions; the sail fanned out more and more each time and the runners of the sled engaged fully, hissing against the black stone. I strained to see the sail's extensions drifting out from the beast's core, which nestled tight against the mast.

Sails are bigger than you can imagine, Miss Bridges used to say. *Sails exist in a different plane.*

Ogres use them to catch light.

I had never been this close to an *adenoma* as they piloted: I did not recognize the level of attention in the giant, this degree of cognition and *connection*.

Several times I caught a glimpse of the sail's dark eyes and row of soft, sad mouths.

Ahead of us, the low arc of dim sun shimmered.

As the hunters loped awkwardly alongside, I wondered if I was truly trying to save their lives or kill us all. The men snarled at scents I could not detect. Did they want to drop to all fours?

Viability was a veneer of varying thickness, but a veneer nonetheless.

The sun went down another notch. One last time, I thought. The ogre watched the falling orb intently, and the tremor, when it hit, shook us with vigor.

I had never left sight of palmetto before; now I could not leave fast enough. My experiences in a sled were very limited, so I was unable to assist; the ogre, however, seemed practiced, and confident, and we progressed apace.

There was really only one route, straight along the light which stretched like the string between Miss Bridge's sweaty fingers, directly into the sliver of broken sun. The sled was not made for distances, as the doctor had pointed out, yet we aimed toward the inner rift and we moved swiftly away from the town.

Behind us, watching, the moon raised high over the sea.

HINTERLANDS DID NOT GET COLDER AT night; I imagined they would. We travelled in a strange quietude. At times, the hunters ran close enough to touch. I spoke to them at several points, but they did not reply. I tried to assure them nonetheless they would never again face Mayor Richer's wrath.

Before long, they began to yip and growl, eerie sounds, and I realized they were trying to communicate with the ogre, who paid them no notice at first, but soon shifted, heaving down against the sail. Baffled by the exchange, I was about to ask what was going on when the hunter on my left, the one I'd watched pissing, ran close, turned his muzzle toward me, and said: "Ssscribe: there are nighteggsss nearby. . . Ssstrange eggsss. Ssshould we sssstoppp . . . ? You like egggsssss . . ."

Saliva sprang into my mouth, unbidden, colder than ever. I could see the shallow depression of the nest just ahead, and the clutch within.

"Stop," I said.

The hunters braced themselves and the ogre had to physically restrain the sail, tugging the creature and rolling it toward him to hold it still.

When the sled ceased moving, the silence of the night roared.

There were a dozen moderate-sized eggs in the cluster. All white, all aglow. I was mesmerized. Larger eggs than any I'd seen before.

Was this sort of treasure standard outside of town?

I looked at the hunters, and the ogre, but it was too dark to see their expressions.

The grunts went into the dip without hesitation. I shouted out to them, a blessing, a warning, as they picked up one egg each—almost as big as their heads—and turned toward me, waiting for further instruction.

Nearly delirious, I beckoned them closer.

The ogre had returned his resolute stare to the inner horizon. Perhaps cosmic rays played out a vision for him as beautiful as these eggs were to me. He held the sail with straining forearms but the sail struggled. The interaction between them was almost lustful. Unseen tendrils writhed into the dark sky, seeking purchase on some plane or other.

When I disembarked, the hunters growled; I paid them no heed. After gathering up the proffered eggs in my shawl, I returned to my seat. The grunts climbed back on, and the ogre, on my command, tossed the sail up into the night.

Rubbing the eggs together in my lap, I took the largest, licked it, caressed it, and bit through the thin shell; within, the zygote turned away.

Zygotes live inside us, Doctor Face said. *Zygotes live forever.*

I looked up, as if he were addressing me; he was not, of course. Instead, we were hissing into darker hinterlands. I saw our path stretch out, a track of glass dust and faint beams of light, populated by faded memories of types come and long gone.

With two fingers, I retrieved the zygote and pushed it, squirming, down my throat.

DECREES WERE WRITTEN AND LEDGERS MAINTAINED to ensure the citizens of palmetto remain *civilized*. Wear shawls, they said. Get a haircut (if you were a type able to grow hair). Record the lives, record the deaths. And, of course, walk on two feet. *Head to the sky*. That was most important of all.

But when I knelt in the shallow dirt at the border of the town square, under the hunters' primal glare, when I felt everything inside me *shift*, I knew that palmetto, the ledgers and the decrees, no longer held any importance, nor likely had they ever.

I was no longer the scribe.

I was no longer a citizen.

We might have caught up to the other sled a few hours after dawn were it not for the zygotes I consumed, and the accident that soon befell us.

VISIONS BEGAN TO STRIKE ME, EACH more powerful and vivid than the last—certainly more powerful than any I'd experienced before. I imagined myself alert in the seat of the sled the whole while though I must have been slumped as the hunters and the municipal ogre maintained the craft. Among such company, under such circumstances, foolish of me to relinquish my wits, yet I had, readily, at first sight of the eggs.

I was unviable, the lowest cog, a cripple.

In one of these visions, I saw my mother, in her prime, when her face was gorgeous and without any hint of expression. She slept on her back, snoring lightly, in the shadowed interior of her bedroom. Next to her lay a man, an unfamiliar female, also asleep. Both were naked. A sheet covered my mother. The other's exposed skin—except for her face—was mostly scales, with a ridge of dark bristles down each shin and forearm and at her pubis. Her eyes, closed but aflutter, were so near to each other that there was barely a gap between them. When I was perhaps five years old, a group of such men lived in a cluster of shacks near the crater. They used to stare at me slack-jawed whenever I played or passed nearby. Some kids would throw rocks at them. The type no longer existed. I believe they had ceased to be citizens by the time I was six. Yet here was this man, inside my mother's house, at least in my vision, being comforted: I could see traces of spent endomorphs over them and on the sheets. Fragments of my mother's empathy still caught in the ridges of this stranger's scales and on the bristles of her long legs. I knew what my mother's exhaustion felt like, what a peeper expends when they work—

The man opened her narrow-set eyes and saw me standing in the doorway; I stepped back, into the darker hallway—

In another vision, Doctor Face wore a band around his head, a small lantern attached. He was reading one of the delicate books he had brought up from the crater. His home was a mess—devices and arcane apparatuses on every surface. Nothing I had ever seen before. Cables, tubes looped. On one bench, a dissembled government man's gun twitched, as if to warn the doctor I was there, but he frowned at the glowing pages, which were scrolling slowly on the dim screen—the book's energy was weak—and paid neither me nor the gun any attention. He was about to adjust his left lens with a knuckle when a noise made him look up. I heard it, too. From outside his home. A strange cry. With difficulty, the doctor rose, favouring his left knee, and went to the window, peering out; beyond was darkness. Something out on the beach? Tiny glimmers of light: lanterns? A municipal crew?

Two frigates, silent nightsleds from the capitals, were parked on the slopes of the dark embankment.

Suddenly I had the feeling that Doctor Face lived inside a small and cluttered sled, floating through the night sky between the sun and the moon.

We all did.

As I was about to ask for help, a grunt woke me, trying to get close, presumably; I swatted at him.

I could hear the runners hissing against the obsidian and it sounded like static; vibrations rattled me. Progress and velocity were impossible to ascertain. Had I been out cold? Or was I lying on a table, prodded by the guns of government men? It seemed as if a long time had passed. My head was full of strange lights. I, too, was hurtling through the void. Powerful eggs rampaged in my blood and zygotes fought in my belly.

I pushed another grunt from my lap, where it had been snuggling. My heart pounded. I think the grunt might have stumbled over the side.

I sat up straight and tried to steel myself. The hunters crouched on the runners of the sled now, either side, hunkered low, sniffing the wind with their eyes locked on the horizon as if they, too, were ogres. Above, the sail had spread fully; we were moving fast. Could they see anything up ahead, smell anything?

They would not look at me. I tried to address them, but had no voice.

All I could see of the municipal ogre was a silhouette, at the helm, moving ponderously with the sail.

Would he kill, I suddenly wondered, with his bare hands, if I told him to?

The first tremor shook the sled and caused us to become briefly airborne. We lost another grunt. When we came down, the sled jolted heavily and the runners threw up a thick mist of ground particles; the hunters, howling, sprawled headlong and the ogre was thrown against the mast. A rail detached from the rear of the sled, spinning behind us for a moment before lifting into the sky; gravity was altering. We had hit a pocket of fluctuations—

The continent brightened. Our wounded sled trembled on a track of light.

Ahead of us, the sun was a degree higher.

I remember realizing that increased proximity to the inner rift might be more dangerous than I had thought but we did not stop. We were closing the distance between us and the stolen sled. I looked back, expecting, absurdly, to see distant palmetto, or traces of the ocean, but I saw only an endless expanse of hinterland.

"Srrrribe," one hunter growled. "We will die out here."

"Chewed by the ssssun," hissed the other.

I did not reply, except a gesture, to continue, onwards.

When the sun rose another notch, sending a crashing ripple we could all see and feel coming, we were thrown into the air again. This time, when our sled came back down, the left runner broke off altogether, sending the craft spinning out of control; the ogre was thrown, relinquishing the sail, which seemed to slip immediately through a black hole opened in the sky.

Through some miracle, I was able to hang on until the craft came to a stop. I did not see what happened to the hunters and would never see them again. As I lay, dazed, still very high, the mast creaked, and snapped, and though I tried to roll out of its way, my legs were not responding. The heavy structure came down upon me. My vision went black.

THEY DRAGGED ME INSENSATE FROM THE wreckage and threw me into the nightsled's hold with my hands bound behind my back and a sack pulled down over my head. My legs had been broken. Nonetheless, I felt nothing. The eggs I'd ingested were like none other and those zygotes raged inside me.

Government men were rough: when they hauled me into their frigate I fell forward, smashing my face; I spat out several of my teeth and, as they grew back, lay bleeding throughout most of the journey.

They brought me onto the deck in time to see, through eyes swollen nearly shut—tearing the sack away—a massive bone archway sailing overhead, and, beyond that, the glittering palace of rios.

I swooned.

I remember very little of my transformation.

3.

BATHED IN LIGHT, WHICH FELL OVER him in a blurry-edged form, as if through a window, the buttons of his vest winking as he breathed, Doctor Face dozed in a chair by the side of a narrow bed in which I lay. I tried to blink the good doctor into focus, to rub at my eyes, but my hands were too heavy; a white sheet, pulled to my chin, had been tucked very tight over me.

I ached everywhere but was not in any real pain. Nor did I feel tired. There had been a dream? Movement, and darkness? But that was over now, whatever it had been. My thoughts were placid. *Peaceful.* And though I presumed my current state and situation should have been alarming, I could not generate appropriate concern.

I yawned.

I had been in this room before, seated in a chair similar to the one Doctor Face rested in now. I had watched patients die here, lives come to an end: I was in the infirmary. On a metal tray next to the bed, nestled with a thermometer, a small flashlight, and devices I had, however, never before seen, the large chamber of an outrageously large hypodermic needle held watery contents alive with green—

Struggling to sit up, to get free of the sheet again, I made the doctor snort, and start; he grinned suddenly from under his bristly moustaches, awake, holding out a gloved hand to restrain me by laying it on my shoulder. "Not so fast," he said. "You need to take her easy, scribe."

"Did you put those things inside me, Doctor Face?"

The doctor, glancing at the needle, nodded cautiously.

"You shouldn't have done that."

"I had no choice. Save the peeper, you know. All that. A viable type. One of the best. Some issues, but don't we all have a few of those?"

"They're going to die inside me."

"Relax," said the doctor. "They're not going to die."

"How did I get here?" Now alarm was trickling in.

"We found you outside of town. Comatose, barely breathing, toxic. Do you recall? Your, uh, limbic system." He tapped the bridge of his glasses with a forefinger. "Your amygdalae went septic."

I closed my eyes. Doctor Face was lying to me. I was not lucid enough to understand why, or what the truth might be, but I knew he was lying.

I could feel the unfortunate creatures moving inside me.

Beyond Doctor Face were nine other beds, in two rows, mostly made, and empty, though in one a very large man lay in traction, swathed head to upraised toe in dirty-white bandages. An ogre? Was that possible? His entire bed was in shadow—

I recalled the accident. I had been in a terrible accident. I was startled by the violence of the vision and could not speak of it had I wished.

Taken from the wreckage by government men, bloody, my legs smashed to ruins, I had been imprisoned in the palace.

And this large man, in traction, had been with me.

He was part of my crew, the pilot of the sled I had commandeered.

I could describe to the doctor the holding cell, in rios, down to the last rivet. I could describe the city itself, and the palace, as we coasted in, and they tore the sack from my head.

After my legs had healed, I paced the floor of my cell during waking hours, to keep blood flowing and my muscles from atrophying. Higher than I could reach, there was a single window, through which oily light fell at irregular intervals, sometimes for the duration of a day, other times only for an hour or so. The walls and floor of the cell were a form of soft, warm cement, painted pale green. I had a cot, and a bedpan.

Government men would come, on occasion, to feed me, or bring me—by means of an enclosed, floating sled—to other rooms in other buildings where they'd force me onto a mattress, interrogate me with questions I could not understand, and latch their guns onto my skin—

Now, I looked out the large window next to my bed. There were iron bars over the lower half and the glass was spotted with circular flaws that looked like tumours, distorting my view. Beyond the bars—which I could have touched, had I been able to move my arms—was an expanse of the placid ocean. A bright day in palmetto, but the sun itself was behind the infirmary, of course, where it always was, and this was the moon I saw, large and high over the horizon. Too high. I tried to frown. Not only did the height of the moon seem wrong, but there was a stillness out there, a tint to the sky, a translucency to the washed-out colours that made my heart skip a beat.

"You okay, scribe?"

Had I not talked to the doctor just this morning, on the patio of Lucky Jym's? Which would mean I was wrong about the ill-fated trip into the hinterlands. Wasn't I a prisoner in the palace for weeks, months?

Memories of being captured, and brought to the capital, memories of government men holding my arms and pulling off my shawl, could *not be false*. These could not be false. My tears were burning me.

"You okay? Scribe? Are you *crying*?"

"No," I said. "But this is messed up."

"What is?"

"All of this."

"You'll rest here for a few days," he said. "You're lucky to be alive."

"I don't need to—"

"Look, scribe, a volunteer will visit you tomorrow morning, take you outside, to the mess, if you feel like walking, or eating. If you're up for it." He looked around before leaning quickly closer. "And if you remember details from before," he whispered, "don't draw attention to yourself. You'll be under a lot of duress shortly. Best keep quiet. If anyone else comes in here, council people, to talk to you, feign sleep."

I searched his lenses for signs of a joke but could see none.

"It is good to see you again, scribe, I must say." He slapped one large thigh. "We'll take this slow. Because there are a few citizens anxious to see you: your mother, for one, and the, er, well, the new mayor." He paused, waiting for a reaction, I presume, but I gave him none. "I won't tell any of them you're awake. Not yet. So you can continue to rest and gather your wits. You peepers are a stronger type than any of us know, aren't you?"

I thought about the dead government man, and my absurd flight. Red blood, on the hunter's teeth. When I turned back, to look at Doctor Face, I caught him fiddling, both hands, with an item I could not see, hidden below the edge of the mattress; he stopped abruptly and raised his round lenses again to meet my gaze. His grin crept back.

"I'm thirsty," I told him. My arm, where I presume the doctor had stabbed me full of his creatures, was sore and getting worse. There was a void in my head, a cool, open void. I asked him what the hell he'd put inside me.

He gestured to the giant hypodermic. "Leucopenia."

"So I was close to the sun."

"You are a smart cookie, scribe. Normally, that would be true, but not in this case. You were no closer to the sun than you are now."

"Was it the eggs?"

"Eggs?" He frowned. "Scribe, I need to know what you saw, what you did. The truth. Are you up for it? Things are coming back to you, aren't they?"

"Get me some water, doc, and we can talk."

"Excellent." Doctor Face must have somehow rung a remote bell, for the door opened and a nurse came in, holding a bottle with a rubber nipple, like infants and new immigrants drink from. I knew this man, from my own vigils here, but could not recall her name. She was a prole, hunched somewhat, with a heavy brow and milky eyes. Her hair was cropped short. She looked at me but there was no recognition. Recalling times I had surreptitiously watched her movements—big, reddened hands flattening a crisp sheet; wringing water from rags at the sink; rooting about in a hallway closet or, once, bending to retrieve a stylus she'd dropped—I heard a shuddering sob rise up from my own depths.

Doctor Face rested a hand on my shoulder.

This nurse had been in Miss Bridge's class, the year after me. I should have watched her die. She had advanced leukemia. I could tell. I would go down to the cramped shed, or to city hall, and write her epitaph in the ledger—

"I resigned, Doctor Face. I quit my job." City council would impeach me, at the very least. I wondered if there were guards at the door. I sniffled.

Keeping her distance, the nurse handed Doctor Face the bottle, who took it and, as she stepped back farther, pumped up my bed; I rose at a uniform rate to a muffled racket and bone-shaking vibrations. He cranked me to a sitting position, tugging the sheet away from my body with ease.

I was still wearing my filthy shawl, though it was torn and bunched. There were burns on my stomach, yellow bruises on both legs. A nasty scar the length of my right arm. I wasn't restrained, but straps lay on the mattress like eels exposed in this light. Straps that had recently been tight across my torso and thighs. I looked at the doctor. There had been a bit in my mouth, to stop me from biting my tongue. I had a slow flash of me on a table, spine arched, thunder clapping outside, the doctor holding a spinning saw—

I heard the nurse leave.

After turning the bottle this way and that, watching the milky contents sluice about, I became satisfied no creatures swam within, put the nipple between my lips (hot!), and sucked. Whatever the contents might have been, they were surprisingly exquisite, and I drank deeply, pausing only to lean my head against the pillow and close my eyes while air hissed loudly back into the nipple.

The doctor patted my arm encouragingly.

I waited for questions I could never answer.

THE INFIRMARY WAS SILENT, DARK, AND the vista beyond the window darker still. The moon was still high, but dimmer. I had been abandoned in the sitting position, the sheet still tugged down. I had not been strapped back in. Drool soaked my chest, which I could feel, rather than see. Something squirmed in my lap.

Returning my gaze to the view outside, a sudden, startling light travelled quickly through the sky, across the expanse defined by the window; the reflection, below, shimmered for a second on the waters of the invisible sea and then both source and reflection were gone.

I sat for a long while, wondering if I was capable of walking, hearing nothing further except for low, steady breathing from the other patient, behind me in the room. The creatures Doctor Face had put inside me stirred yet within my blood, sluggish but alive, going about their mysterious tasks.

Mayor Richer had said we were doomed. *All citizens dead*. What would I find, out there in palmetto? A necropolis?

The tray remained where Doctor Face had left it. I picked up the flashlight, turned it on, and shone the narrow beam toward my roommate: the giant, prone, leg upraised, almost entirely bandaged.

I got out of bed very carefully, sliding my legs off the mattress one at a time. Though my nethers felt tender and wobbly, I managed to stand—and stay upright—on flooring warm and soft as flesh.

I slowly made my way over to where the giant lay, using empty beds for support, and shuffling between them. The flashlight was designed so that the beam illuminated only a narrow field. The giant's good foot hung well over the end of the thin mattress and the structure of the bed itself sagged greatly under his weight. His bad leg canted up at a sharp angle, high above my head, almost to the ceiling. I shone the flashlight at the hook anchoring the chain in place and brought the beam along the filigreed links, back down, to the bed.

I had never before known an ogre to be in the infirmary.

The large chest rose and fell in motions so shallow I had to touch the giant with my fingertips to ascertain if he was breathing.

I could feel the dim moon watching through the window as I leaned closer, lips near his ear, and said: *"Wake up."*

No twitch, no moan, no response at all: the shallow breathing continued unabated.

Searching for an end to the bandages, and finding none, I fumbled the fabric free, starting at the forehead and pulling strips down roughly. My knuckles were stiff. Several times I tried to shine the flashlight on swift crustaceans, the size of my thumbnail, darting away from my touch, seeking cover under ribbons that were in turn stretched by my hands and pulled roughly away, but they were fleet. The ogre seemed rife, a veritable ecosystem, a cosmos unto himself.

Eventually I managed to expose a fair portion of the large, shaved head, one closed eye, and a broad, grimy cheek. I touched the rough skin, pushed at the sallow flesh, as if I would find answers there, then I shone the light onto the scar over the exposed eye: this was without a doubt the *adenoma* who had accompanied me out of town, piloting the doomed sled.

I tried to shake the giant by his shoulder but my hand was so small, and the body so heavy, he did not budge. "There were government men waiting for us," I said. "Right? Out by the sun? It was a trap. We were captured by a frigate?"

There might have been a brief pulse in a vein, a spasmodic twitch to the ogre's eyelid; I thought I detected a stirring of unfathomable consciousness.

"We were in rios together, me and you. Remember? We were together in a cell, in the palace. They jammed their guns against us. We were . . . hurt."

Now a low moan arose from the body, a bass rumble starting not from the throat but from that deeper place.

Eagerly, I said, "They wiped us both clean and brought us back, like immigrants—"

The one exposed eye slowly rolled open, glazed. I caught my breath, but the eye kept rolling up, oblivious, into the giant's skull.

OPENING THE DOOR LET IN LIGHT. I peered into the hallway. No guards. There was a wooden staircase at either end of the deserted hall. I knew the layout of this building almost as well as that of my own mother's house. The hall smelled vaguely of the sea. Fragmented memories passed through me and I shut the door quickly to cut them off.

"Okay, look," walking back toward where the ogre lay, "this is what—"

The exposed eye, clear, was open wide, staring at me.

As I approached, his breathing became more pronounced; he twisted, and moved his arms, in trepidation, I imagined, clenching his fists. He reminded me, absurdly, of the young perfect, on the sarsen stone.

Fumbling with the pulley, I released the traction; the ogre's leg came down heavily onto the mattress, bouncing once, making the bed creak. That one big eye watched me the whole while but the giant made no exclamation whatsoever.

The bed itself, when cranked, rose slower, and to a louder clatter, than had mine. I struggled with the ogre's weight and the awkward crank mechanism but the gear ratio in the elevating device was effective and soon he was sitting up. There were straps across his chest and hips but these came free after I flipped the locks open.

Climbing, hoisting myself, I curled into the ogre's lap, and cradled there. Hugging myself as the bed creaked further and sagged and rocked, I closed my eyes. I never wanted to get up again. I let the infirmary and my memories of death and abduction and attraction fade away. Not since I was an infant had I tried to comfort anyone. I had refused all entreaties, all advances, all propositions. I was a peeper chosen for a career in civil service and my mother was the comforter. But no longer.

Afterward, the ogre shuddered and rose; displaced, drained, I nearly fell to the floor, landing in an awkward crouch. The giant stood before me on both legs, arms akimbo, still tagged with glowing shreds of our union. He moaned. He did not seem injured at all, despite the bandages.

Holding the frame of the bed for support, I stood weakly. "They'll try to stop us," I told him.

He was already pushing at the door, heading into the hallway, ducking his head to avoid the low jamb. He did not look back at me.

After a moment, I followed.

The guards I had imagined previously were stationed at the main door, facing the town, on the ground level: aglow in the exit light were Tang and Seminural, my old friends. I could see them both clearly, over the ogre's shoulder, as we came down the stairs. Sitting on the stoop, deep in conversation, with their backs to us, they each held an electric prod. Tang poked at exposed obsidian with his weapon and was talking; Seminural, half-listening, picked his nose and looked uncomfortable.

Beyond the illuminated area, palmetto's night was abrupt and expansive—

Keeping his head low, the ogre took the last few steps in one stride, moaning loudly, and with the momentum of his descent burst through the exit doors, knocking one clear off its moorings, nearly killing Tang, the counter, and Seminural, who, jolted alert, just managed to dodge the door crashing away past them into the dark.

Staring, wide-eyed, toward us, they seemed to shrink.

The ogre stood on the landing, breathing heavily, bunching his fists.

I came out behind him.

"Shit," Tang said, rising uncertainly, holding the prod down and away from his body, as if to make it clear he was not a threat. "Come on, man—"

But the ogre roared, a sound I had never before heard, and lurched forward, swiping at Tang with a giant hand; Tang leapt back. "Scribe," he said, eyes wide, clearly terrified. "Tell him to stop!"

"I'm not the scribe."

The ogre lunged again, this time grabbing Tang's forearm, slapping the prod away and lifting the counter clear off the ground; Tang's little legs kicked—

Skin touching at the shoulders, I wondered if Tang also wanted to sit like that forever, sharing a strip of warmth from our union, feel peace, a modicum of security, belonging—

Enraged, the ogre swung Tang violently in a wide arc; Seminural, stepping forward, was knocked backward and, as the ogre released Tang, both vanished into the darkness; I heard them crash painfully onto the stone, out of the light—

A siren of sorts sounded, the alarm from the town hall, a rally to arms.

The ogre, heaving, glanced back at me, his exposed eye black and wide and wild. My attempt to comfort him had clearly done the opposite; he was distressed, tormented.

From the dark, commotion grew, beyond where my old friends had landed and were now scrambling or writhing in pain: other men, with sudden lights, were coming. I saw the town hall's silhouette flicker as torches went ablaze.

Council men—

Reaching one hand toward the ogre, to connect again, to retry, express the need for us to leave *together*, but he turned just before my fingers touched him and roared in furious rage, spittle like hot sparks, breath rotting. He did not want me near him. Not again. Freed from the infirmary, reeling at the attempt to be comforted, and by the violence he had wrought at my behest, he lumbered off, toward the town.

Several men, whispering, agitated, headed toward the infirmary. I wondered if the good doctor was among them.

Moving out of the light, I went behind the infirmary, keeping close to the wall, and peered, from the far side: the men were in front of the building, where I had just been; I could hear them, see their lanterns. Tang was talking, telling them what he could, what he had seen, how I'd been with the ogre.

All the way to the sea and the high moon, the vista was dark and clear.

I slipped across the warm obsidian, toward the town hall. I felt as if I floated. Was gravity thinning? Looking back, I saw figures lingering in the light of the infirmary's ruined exit, at the door, though I could not make out who they were.

On the inland horizon, the sun was dull and stationary, a broad arc, waiting for morning.

I headed swiftly seaward, taking the path from the town hall toward the beach, over the bunker. Each time I glanced up, I could see the moon on the far horizon, high, a grim grey, watching.

Fragments of construction broke free as I passed, floating in my wake.

WHEN I GOT TO MY MOTHER'S house, my lungs were burning and my heart thumped. I opened the front gate, hesitated in the garden, then went through the unlocked side door. Immediately, I could hear my mother's snores and smell her spent glands. Was there a citizen in her bed? I moved through the kitchen and stood in the doorway to her bedroom, where a nightlight burned. My mother was alone in her bed, asleep, body covered by a sheet. Just as she had been in my vision. She lay on her back. Shreds of endomorphs among the sheets, face noticeably creased, shadows enhancing her growing flaws. Stripped of beauty at last.

"Mom?"

Nothing.

"Mom?"

She opened her eyes, rubbed at them. "What the fuck?"

"I'm in trouble, mom. Council's after me."

"I thought you'd vanished." She sat up. "You scared the shit out of me. Where were you?"

"In rios." No response. Her hair was thinner. "Was there just someone here with you?"

"No."

"Government men took me to the palace. I think they've cleaned me out. Wiped my memories clean. Then I woke in the infirmary. I don't remember anything clearly. . . . Can I get in bed with you?"

"Fuck, no." She sat up. "You look like shit." Another deep breath. She stared. "I'll be out in a second. Go wait in the hall."

I hesitated, tried to say several more things, but turned silently and moved away.

"And shut the fucking door," she shouted.

MY MOTHER TOOK HER SWEET TIME getting up. From the kitchen, I heard her groaning and cursing and banging about. I peered out the window several times: there were many fragments in the air now, drifting past, as if a storm was coming and gravity was fluctuating madly. I could see hints of the shed and a curve of the stone beach. A wedge of dark sea. *The moon.*

The mob must still have been searching the infirmary area, or had gone in the wrong direction; I could neither see nor hear them.

I returned to the kitchen table and sat with my head in my hands.

When my mom finally emerged, she was naked. I could not imagine why she had taken so long if she wasn't even getting dressed. Her skin was almost translucent and her musculature was startling.

"They told me you'd gone," she said, "and that I'd need a new kid, if I wanted one. A different type, maybe. They told me you'd done all kinds of crazy things. But I don't want another kid. I'm done."

"The moon's not rising anymore," I told her. "I mean, it's too high."

She looked at me for a long while with her large blue eyes. "Shit," she said, at last, "you and that fucking moon. See what I'm talking about? That fish filled your head with such shit. She should never have been working for the school. I'm glad they pulled the plug on her type. I should have trained you myself, and this would never have happened."

I shrugged. "My problems started long before Miss Bridges."

She pulled up a chair, the legs clattering on the tiled floor. "Look," she said. "I know it's not easy. I know nothing works out, no matter what sort of man you are. Being my daughter, and all." She arched her back. "Are you hungry?"

"No."

"They turned on me, those fuckers, and kicked me out of their stupid club—but they still come sniffing around. They can't help themselves. I got what they need, you know? It's fucked up being a peeper. But you were never in rios, sugar. Sure as fuck. That crazy Doctor Face pumped you full of those creatures."

"Zygotes."

"Whatever." She scratched at her armpit. "Now you're here. *Alive.* But you're fucking fried. I'm surprised you even remember where you used to live."

I got up and returned to the window: I still could not see the council men but now I thought I heard the susurrus of their voices nearby. I waited stupidly for my mother to come press up behind me, hold me, say something reassuring; instead, she coughed and said:

"You're like everyone else in this stupid town. Chasing the past. When we were all viable, healthy. When we used to fall in love, whatever the hell that means, and fuck to prove it. Pump out our own babies. A happier place.

Like what's described in those books that come up from the crater. The books you studied at school."

Lantern lights shone off the burnished street; a garbled command: they were coming for me.

"Why don't you say how pretty I am?"

I left my mother sitting there, at the table.

SOMEONE HAD RANSACKED THE SHED. THE lock was broken off the door and my mattress upended and sliced open. The counter where I had placed my few possessions each night had been splintered, and white powder sprayed fanlike across the floor—and across the ledger, which was out of its niche, thrown into a corner. Opened to the last page. I did not look to see what was written there, in a scrawl not my own, but crouched and gently closed the cover.

Standing, I hugged the book to my chest.

With the feeling I was forgetting something—though I looked around several times and could not recall what—I left the shed, passed quietly through the garden of my mother's house, and opened the front gate.

AS I WAS CROSSING THE BEACH, I heard the council men again, searching for me, but saw no one. The ledger had become heavier and heavier and was slowing me down. My arms ached. Gravity felt stable, but fragments of houses still drifted past.

When the voices whispered directly into my ear, I turned to greet my pursuers, to confront them, but was surprised to see instead an enclosed craft, a sled of sorts, with no sail, and lights about the blunt nose, hovering a few metres away. For an instant I felt I'd seen this sort of craft before, and had even been inside one, but that was unlikely, absurd, and the sensation faded.

I waited for something to happen, feeling tired mostly, expecting a government man to emerge, or maybe the new mayor, but the craft just bobbed silently, lights playing about the nose, so I turned away to leave; after a moment, though, the floating sled lurched. I watched lights reflect off the beach in front of me.

From a speaker, the voices said: "Scribe. Scribe. Stop."

Doctor Face.

So I stopped. The sled swung around and listed before me. Sounds I might have earlier mistaken for council men tracking me down fluttered from all around, and as I tried to locate a true source, a panel suddenly popped open and I could see the good doc within, in full outfit, mask, gloves, and all.

"I don't take my mekhos out very often," he explained breathlessly. "Only in emergencies. These confounded controls are made for hands, well, unlike mine." He grimaced and showed me, briefly, an open glove before snatching at what could only be an odd steering column. "Why did you run away from the infirmary, scribe? Why? That was unbelievably foolish. I'd just managed to convince them you were no threat but now the storm—Ach!" Slamming at a dangling rod that had suddenly appeared. "Will you just get in? There's very little time. The storm's coming again and I can't fly this damn thing!"

I scanned the horizon but saw no clouds. "I'm not getting in."

"Uh, you need to, scribe. You *really* do."

"Stop calling me scribe."

I walked away. The moon was entirely above the horizon, broken free altogether from the mechanism that linked it to the sun. I imagined that the orb might stay like that forever and never click or ratchet down again. The sea, silvered beneath, was active, though sluggish; slight waves lapped at the stone shore.

When the sled caught up to me again, the side panel was still open and Doctor Face battled the controls, which had multiplied in the brief interim. I wanted to laugh as he passed me, inadvertently, I think, and tried to turn the mekhos around, chassis briefly banging against the obsidian; I hopped back to avoid getting my foot crushed.

"Where are you going?" he shouted. "You know by now we can't leave town. Just get in!"

Thin clouds moved toward the land, a dark vortex funnelling into the sea out by the rift. I could see lightning there. Storm winds *were* coming. Clutching the ledger tight against my chest, I asked, "What is this thing, Doctor Face, this machine? Have I ever been in one?"

"Quite possibly."

"What are you up to?"

"Me?" He grimaced again. "Saving palmetto, what else? Saving citizens, as always. Doing my job. Please get in. This storm'll kill us both."

Inside the mekhos were devices out of my dreams. On the seat next to Doctor Face, a large egg rolled.

"I'm not getting in, doc. I'm not."

"Next time they won't clean you out. You can't keep coming back like that. I told you. They'll squash you outright. I *told* you. And now, well, your type is no longer allowed. Too dangerous, they say. Capable of *murder*. Henceforth. The peeper is too dangerous."

I looked back toward my mother's house, but the winds were strong enough now that all I could see were eddies of debris, torn from the structures and whirling on the beach. How could there be another storm this soon? Who would register the victims? I wondered if the council had made it to my mother's house, and if she would be sacrificed on the sarsen stone. She hated those bureaucrats so much.

"I didn't kill the government man."

"Come now, scribe, get in. No one ever accused you."

But as I turned my back again, to leave the doctor, to find shelter—though I knew none could truly be found—a piece of debris, whirling down in a sudden gravity surge, hit me hard in the back of my neck and I pitched headlong.

I WOKE, AS I OFTEN DID, with a terrible headache, and to strange, humming vibrations. I felt these tremors in my bones and my teeth, and they compounded my headache and I needed to pee. Though the lighting was dim, I could see that I was resting in the armchair at Doctor Face's home. I could not recall arriving, but I supposed we must have spent the night drinking milk and playing cludo, as we sometimes did. My mouth was gummy.

Before the window, Doctor Face slept. He had been looking outside—his face at quarter profile—and was slumped in his own favourite chair.

I frowned at the strong sense of déjà vu that washed over me, a powerful surge, but I managed to shudder it off; I am not a believer in such phenomena.

The vibrations grew, and the chair beneath me continued to shake. There was a dull roar as accompaniment. At first, I had thought my own blood flow was the source of this roar, but this was clearly not the case.

Tubes and beakers on the doctor's tables clattered together and his home grew hotter; I stood—into utter and abrupt silence and stillness more ominous than any noise or vibration. Thinking I might have died, unbalanced, I nearly fell.

Outside—past the doctor—the landscape was invisible, inscrutable.

I walked carefully toward the rear of the doctor's home, toward his lab, seeking the washroom there. Walking proved exceedingly difficult; my weight had changed, somehow, lessened, and I needed to ensure my feet were planted securely with each awkward step.

Through an open door, expecting to see plumbing and a familiar, cluttered toilet, I saw instead a large chamber in which a series of cots were arrayed, and, upon each, recumbent, unclothed forms, dozens of them, all types, extending into the distance.

"Doctor?" I frowned, turning away, stepping back. I was nearly floating and had to grab at a railing. "Doc, wake up—"

In his armchair, Doctor Face, awake now, struggled with what looked to be strange controls sprung from the frame of the window. I recalled an odd, floating sled, and once, in a storm a few years ago, how an entire building had landed, intact, in the town square.

"Are we within your . . . mekhos?"

He looked at me as if I was insane. "My *what*?"

"Your—" I wanted to return to the armchair and close my eyes again but the chair was not there when I turned. In fact, this was not the doctor's home at all. There was something happening in the chamber where the figures had been sleeping, a ruckus of some sort.

I knew, in that instant, Doctor Face's creatures had been sent inside me to alter me, maybe augment my brain, but they had failed.

"Strap yourself in, scribe."

"Stop calling me that." I thought about my mother's death at the hands of bureaucrats, now that peepers were condemned. I wondered who had led the ceremony. "What ever happened to Mayor Richer?"

"He joined the ranks of the vanished. Perhaps he went to the palace. He's never returned, either way." Doctor Face smiled in a pained fashion. "But that was ages ago."

"And who took the sled?"

"You did, scribe. Now, please, strap yourself in. This storm is unbelievable!"

Flashes of light out the window, too fast and brilliant for me to see any details. Had Doctor Face misunderstood my question? We were hurtling forward again, through the night. Doctor Face and I, hurtling through a dark night with a room full of sleeping men—

"Hold on," Doctor Face shouted.

I braced for the crash.

WE RECOVER FROM ACCIDENTS, FROM STORMS and other mishaps, like our houses, unable to fully repair ourselves, becoming less each time, pieces breaking off and drifting away.

Council wanted peepers dead?

We were not an ideal type, it's true.

I was flat on my back, on a bed, a ceiling above me. The quiet hum of air circulating, though recently there had been an awful shaking.

"Doc?" My voice was weak. "Doctor Face? I can't do this anymore."

No answer. I touched my head, felt swaddling there, bandages.

I got up.

On the beds around me—there were many—I saw grunts, a prole, a prentiss. Naked, as was I. Running my hands over my abdomen and shoulders, taking inventory, as it were, I walked between rows of beds: three grunts per mattress, though they were very young. Toddlers, maybe. Two rows in, to my pleasant shock, lay Miss Bridges, her fish skin grey and moist. My eyes were watering by the time I reached her side. There was a band around her wrist and a chart at the other end of her bed. I took her cold fish hand in mine.

There was someone in the distance. Tall and thin, a man, watching me. *A government man,* in a bodysuit—and another one, bent over an occupied bed. Both straightened now that I'd seen them.

They watched me.

They were pushing the barrels of their guns against a recumbent form: I could see a large chest, curved spine, the elongated face of a hunter's muzzle.

I leaned forward to kiss Miss Bridges' cold cheek before hurrying away.

DOCTOR FACE WAS READING A BOOK from the crater, recumbent in the light of its scrolling pages. His lenses were fixed coins of light. On the table next to him, an open notepad, pages marked with his scribbles.

"Doc."

Without taking his eyes from the book, he held up one finger, asking for a moment; I waited until he put the machine down and met my eyes.

"Good to see you again," I said.

"You, too." Doctor Face showed me his teeth.

"What is this place?"

"This is where it all begins. Everyone in your ledger is here, and then some. Ha! How are you? Better than before?"

"Not sure yet. I think so."

"A piebald?" Smiling broadly, he looked me up and down. "Or are you a perfect? Hard to tell from the outside. Anyhow, suits you."

"Thanks. Is this your home, doc?"

The chambers I'd passed through had been replete with beds, citizens sleeping within, some types I'd never seen before, others I hadn't seen in years and had forgotten, though in diminishing numbers the farther I walked. Most beds were empty. On one had lain Tang, the counter, looking restful, but I didn't approach. If it was indeed Tang, his scoliosis had been worked on with significant success.

"My *home*? Don't be absurd," said the doctor, "I just work here. You know that. A *volunteer*. Doing research. Trying to get it right." He grinned at our apparent shared joke, though I didn't get it.

"You know there's government men back there? Two of them?"

"Well," he said, "there's a lot more than two. This whole place is theirs. Now then, shall we?"

"Shall we what?"

He rose. "Get you a shawl. Take you up. Set you free, as it were."

"You look younger, doc."

And he did: paunch reduced, skin smoother, moustache bushier. There was a glow to Doctor Face. He certainly wasn't limping anymore, like he had been last time I'd seen him. Laughing, he turned this way and that, a giddy schoolgirl. "I suppose I am."

I wondered if he could see the amusement on my face.

CLIMBING THE LADDER WASN'T SCARY AT all, like it had been other times, though each rung did seem to take me ages and my mind was wandering.

Once, I believed, my life had ended on the sarsen stone; another time, in a storm, at sea.

Above me was the light of day.

Doctor Face came up behind, boots loud on the rungs, but presently he fell back, despite my own evident torpor and numerous pauses. The sound of his boots faded. I looked down at one point and could not see him for the mist.

When I clambered onto level ground, I had to use my hands to stand upright.

Facing a stone beach, some distance away, and, beyond that, a becalmed sea. Weathered but cared-for structures of a smallish town either side. A light breeze, fresh-smelling, pushed my hair back. I waited for a long while, breathing, watching, but whoever it was I waited for never appeared.

Presently, an odd-looking man, with scales around his eyes and mouth, approached; I was sure I had no connection with him, yet he addressed me:

"All well, citizen?"

I nodded guardedly.

"Welcome to palmetto." He cocked his head. "You're in the immigrants' camp, friend, on the rim of the— Careful! Watch your step!" But he smiled. "I'm a volunteer. I can help set you up."

The man had a strange smell. I could see a frigate, on the embankment that circled the town, departing. The ride here, in the hold of the nightsled, had been brief and not altogether unpleasant. Dozing, mostly, dreaming of ladders—

"Are you hungry?"

"Not particularly."

"What are you looking for?"

I was searching the horizon for the broken moon but could not see it anywhere.

Arc of a Complex Spike

CERTAIN THAT CLOUDS WOULD SOON APPEAR, and taking advantage of an unusually profound sense of self-satisfaction, Leon decided to fly a mere cursory reconnaissance of his area before settling down to bask in the northwest quadrant—fully-exposed Glade-C— with collectors outstretched and other functions virtually dormant. The morning sun was hot and direct. At times, as he shifted lazily to better catch the rays, his black solar panels clicked softly and reflected scales of light about the glade like brilliant semaphores.

He stored energy for a rainy day.

Sure, Leon's jurisdiction had its share of problems. What part of the forest didn't? Overall, though, the picture was healthy. Minor indications of blight on some elms, and the discovery of an as-yet-unidentified species of voracious larvae gnawing at the leaves of new growth in the oleander garden, but no grave, stressful concerns.

This morning offered a golden opportunity to bask, to shut down, to reboot refreshed, with all cells—

There had been a fire.

Startling graphic files downloaded suddenly into his memory; he staggered as they opened.

Burnt remains. Today! *Within his jurisdiction.*

The sudden arrival of this information had stunned Leon, collectors frozen, half-collapsed. How could he have encountered such a calamity without alarms being triggered? And how could he be *here*, oblivious, in Glade-C, attempting to *relax*?

Shuddering to let his collectors settle fanlike onto his back, Leon rose to his full height. Of course he knew the ordinances of his job: prune, excise, mulch diseased specimens. Water, fertilize, fly recon. *And only you can prevent forest fires. That was number one.*

The rogue folder, without parents or children, was an orphaned series whose origins grew more mysterious the harder Leon tried to trace them. Where had the information come from? How had it materialized, suddenly, in his temp? And how had it been hidden?

Reviewing his back-ups, he understood this much:

Moments before dawn. Coming in low over Ridge-D, mists curling up from the pine-needle floor, Leon spraying firs with a light 20/10/20 mix as he went. All logged and documented in a well-organized, parented chain of files. As data should be. Banking around a stand of blue conifer and there it was: filaments of smoke coiling against a sky almost the same colour—

His alarms *had* ramped up, reaching the first stage of readiness. He *had* been on full alert.

Broken, charred wood—twigs, bark, punk—all taken illicitly from his trees. Unnaturally arranged. Still smoldering. Scent of smoke. Crushed grass, all around.

Circling lower, in disbelief, input rushing to his processors, being stored, sequenced, his adrenaline spiking, hoses sliding into position—

Then he was landing. Certain that clouds would soon appear. Feeling a profound sense of self-satisfaction. But not among the blue conifers. Not near the fire. Coming down, instead, here, in Glade-C, smug, eager to rest, to charge his cells, all data about the fire vanished, all data about what had happened *after* he had seen it somehow still misfiled or erased altogether.

Was the fire still burning?

Where had his memories gone?

Not only were things terribly awry in his jurisdiction but also, it would seem, within the parameters of his own operating system.

Gauging the light breeze that had sprung up, Leon took a bit of a run across the glade and spread his wings. By the time he reached the crowns of the maples, his legs were gathered in, held tight against his chest, and he had attained maximum airspeed.

I: SIGHT

FLAMES HAD ONLY PARTIALLY CONSUMED THE matter. Lengths of branches, hacked and broken from living trees, leaned against each other to form a rough cone. Moss and kindling packed the base. Thankfully, the fire itself was out now; water had been used to douse the flames before consumption of the wood was complete, before much damage could be done to the surrounding area. Leon had not put the fire out. The trajectory of the water used to extinguish the conflagration had been random, uneven. Cause of initial ignition was neither lightning strike nor meteor impact. Certainly, Leon had not lit it: no burns were scheduled in this part of the forest and no burns were *ever* scheduled in the spring.

Smoke could no longer be detected.

Perched on a branch, Leon studied the remains for some time before swooping, soundlessly, down.

He landed in underbrush, a good ten metres from the firepit—

And hesitated.

Firepit. His lexicon had supplied him with that word—a new one—but before he had a chance to understand its etymology, a second cascade of files downloaded, *en masse*, so many this time they seized his memory capacity and he crashed:

When the sheet fell he saw that the canvas was huge, almost as big as the entire studio wall, taking up greater space than his field of vision. He stepped back and still could not take in the whole painting. Indigo tints floated against similar, darker blues. Tinged in one corner with russet, like far-off embers burning at night. Shapes still darker than the background seemed to shift at an impossible, remote distance.

—Would you even tell me if you liked it? You're not reacting. I can see it in your face. You don't like it?

Her hand at his back, fingers poised, tense, as if ready to propel him forward, perhaps into the painting itself should he not answer appropriately. But what could he tell her? That looking at her work brought emotions he could not contend with into his throat? That he was reminded of a similar, malignant shape, in an x-ray, and that looking at her picture tore his heart out and flayed him alive?

He turned to her, utterly at a loss.

—It's called Pendulum and Firepit, *she said.* I know that's a dumb title.

To which he agreed, though he could still say nothing.

II: TASTE

LEON LAY FLAT ON HIS STARBOARD side. Right legs folded under his chassis, right wing outstretched. He checked the membranes for any tears and then folded the wing. Beyond professional embarrassment and a growing concern for his programming and interface integrity, he felt a lingering sense of malaise he could not identify.

Above him, the sky remained blue, but now those clouds were coming in.

He stood, and saw that he straddled the firepit. Idiotically, he had flattened evidence with his body. This realization was catalyst for a surge of something very close to panic, which he fought, trying to remain calm, to detect reasons for his malfunctioning in a logical manner. He filled his lungs. Emptied them. Felt marginally better.

Electrostatically, he cleansed himself, and organized, piecemeal, as best he could, all remaining data from his unusual morning. The most recent series of files were already fragmenting—too foreign for him to assimilate and back-up properly, for they had not concerned trees or anything about the forest. He had no context in which to process or store them. All he knew was that, when his ram had seized, he had gone *somewhere else*. Had ceased being Leon, forest caretaker, jurisdiction 742.

And when awareness returned, he lay like an oaf on top of a valuable source of clues.

His lexicon supplied more new words: *Gorgeous; Chiaroscuro; Lustrous.* Threw them up into his vision, glowing red letters that rose and reached the top of their parabola and dropped back through him like fertilizer falling through the air. No meanings attached, no context. *Just words.*

Diagnostics found that his body and operating systems—despite the throbbing sensation in his head (which spread in surges now, down through his neck)—to be functional: wiring; hydraulics, intact; ditto his armature; solar collectors; wings. Tools of his trade were lubed, efficient, and sharpened. Theta activity normal, energy at full, fertilizer reservoirs brimming.

With an anterior manipulator Leon gently picked up a half-charred fragment from the remains of the firepit. He turned it over, scrutinized it, took enough graphics to reconstitute a virtual replica, and then popped the charcoal into his mouth. Carbon, mostly. Carbon, but also a few cells. Tiny scraps of a mammalian biology, singed, clinging to the rough surface of burnt bark. Crunching with his strong jaws, Leon injected mild acids into the pulp.

As he waited for the analysis—as the coal and other fibers broke down in the enzymes of his saliva—he walked around the firepit, examining broken blades of grass and crushed moss. Indentations, where some creature or creatures had paused to rest. Here, low branches formed an arbor. Delicate twigs had been snapped. A considerable bulk had passed this way—

The results downloaded, erratic, hard to read. Leon was trying to scrutinize the corrupt data when, for the third time that morning, vast amounts of hidden files surged onto his main drive, instantly shutting down his already compromised systems:

The sip of green tea reacted with the spices in his mouth. He swished the tea around with his tongue and swallowed. Against his hands, the glazed, ornate bowl was warm. Tiny blue and white figures poled gondolas past bonsais and weed-choked shores: timeless figures; immortal. There was only vermicelli left, growing cold in the fish sauce. Beef gone, broccoli gone, snow peas gone. All goodness gone.

—You've been staring out the goddamn window for ten minutes now. You wanted to tell me something and all you do is stare.

Yet emotion cracked her voice. In a perverse way, he appreciated it, even liked it, because deep inside he thought everybody should stop what they were doing and shed tears for him, even people unknown to him. Kids, sitting at the restaurant; women at other tables with whom he might have, in other circumstances, fallen in love.

Putting his hand inside his coat he felt the pamphlet there, its paper soft with reading and re-reading and from the sweat of his own hands.

—Jesus Christ, *she said,* I'm trying to be patient. I already know you're dying and I'm sitting here waiting. I'm sitting here with you. What else could you possibly want to tell me? Did you think, because you were sick, it might change things between us? Would you like it if my reason to come back to you was sympathy? So I could hold your hand while you died and cry at your funeral?

These other people were looking, the children and women. The waiter. He disliked being the centre of attention, yet he wanted everyone to know about his illness and weep for him? Perhaps she was right about him being messed up.

—You don't even know how to begin dealing with this, *she'd said to him.* You don't even know where to start.

Clearly it had been a bad idea to try, in public, and tell her about the final arrangement he'd made. Maybe it was a bad idea to tell her at all.

III: SMELL

FACE DOWN, ONCE MORE, IN SOFT needles. Another series of unparented files fading. An *illusion.* How strange it had been, to hear those odd sounds, to see through those eyes, to feel those odd, complex emotions. To his ruptured lexicon appeared additions: *Savour; Nutmeg; Ambrosia.* None was given context or definition.

He was breaking apart. There was no denying that now. A major malfunction.

Leon pushed himself up. All recent data, including that which he had just asked for—feedback on the cells he'd found clinging to the wood—were deleted now. A mere ghost, a tiny text file, remained flickering in his temp. Something about a . . . a bowl? A bowl he held in strange manipulators?

The only bowls he knew were shallow vales between the grassy hillocks of Glade-G.

The ghost file vanished.

He stood, inert, for a long time, functions dormant. Then he shook himself, tried his best to become alert, and started to track the passage of whatever creature had preceded him through these pine trees, some hours before. Branches were broken, sedges pushed aside. Prints had been left. He inspected these odd-shaped depressions in the humus, where weights of between sixty and sixty-five kilos had pressed down. Regular intervals. Patterns suggesting bi-pedal gaits. *Two creatures.*

As he moved, the throb in Leon's head and neck spread. He staggered at one point into a web of branches, and leaned there, against them, until his own six legs responded once more to the commands being sent. A breeze lifted the leaves, made them wink at him, and carried scents that triggered more data to download abruptly from his olfactory pit receptors.

This time he was almost ready:

Smell of sex from under the duvet, a smell he thought would never fill his lungs again. She slept, breathing lightly, on her side. Angry still, in sleep, but perhaps anger was not exactly an accurate term to describe what she felt. He understood parts of her reaction now: he was meant to always be there for her, a touchstone, an anchor, even when they weren't dating. And she was going to lose that.

He had told her about his decision to register at Think-a-Head, gave her the pamphlet, explained a few things about cryogenics, but she just looked at the paper and then back up at him and said he was an idiot.

—You think they'll find a cure one day, like in a month from now? Or maybe after everyone you know is long gone? Or do you think your brain is invaluable, mankind's gift for the future? Those charlatans will probably sell your fucking bits and pieces on the black market or just take your money and toss your body in a dumpster. I mean, is this even legal? And what kind of name is Think-a-Head?

At this stage, she seemed tired more than anything else, even as she scolded him. All she had left in her was a set of rote lines, clever and effective but delivered without conviction. The expression on her face had been resigned when she'd given him back the pamphlet.

Later, though, at her place, the sex had been great and a total surprise. She had initiated it. She always did when they were going out, but this time it took him a while to respond. Since the diagnosis, he had felt that his body was rotting inside, diseased, not very sexy. Stupid for him to think that what was happening to his insides could be passed on to her by screwing, or even kissing, but that idea haunted him.

Lying in the dark, listening to her sleep, he felt alive once more.

When he had come, he was on top of her, leaning on his arms, and he opened his eyes to see her smiling up at him.

—Finally, *she said,* the old you.

—Likewise, *he answered quietly.* Likewise.

And kissed her on the mouth.

IV: SOUND

BECAUSE HE HAD ANTICIPATED THE CRASH, Leon rebooted in a braced position, still on his feet. This time, he tried immediately to retain the illusive files, back them up, view them and organize them, try to understand them, but they fragmented, dangerously corrupted, and in the end were deleted by his anti-viral.

The throbbing in his head had become a pounding now, darting down his neck and across his shoulders, where his wings and collectors sprouted.

Glucose levels were way down. This condition would explain why his operating systems were faltering. Why had diagnostics not picked up on this problem before? How long had his levels been dropping, undetected? If they continued to fall at this rate, he would soon become totally incapacitated, in an update cycle, lexicon supplying an endless stream of gibberish.

But for now, at least, he could still move slowly, quietly.

Ahead, faint sounds. In his crippled state, it was painstaking to transcribe these dim noises into his translator. Discomfort was great, yet, in a way, focusing on a task helped him remain quasi-functioning:

—*I'm cold.*

—*Keep it down. Rest.*

—*Just light another fire, right now. Get this over with.*

—*I want to make sure the gun's charged. We're not ready for that thing to come back. First thing in the morning. Get some rest.*

—*I said I was cold, not tired.*

—*Listen, if we attract it again, I'm putting it out. In one shot. I'm doing the shooting.*

—*You're not convinced I hit it?*

—*If you say you did, you probably did.*

—*Shit. I hit the thing. Believe me. I had the goggles on, remember. I was the one with the gun. I saw the spike discharge and I heard the pulse hit it.*

A guitar strummed, two chords, G and C. Diminishing from his speakers. The hiss of a lightly brushed hi-hat. A drink in an old fashioned glass, smooth shapes of ice clinking as the glass is set down on a wooden table. The ticking of his watch, when he held it close to his ear, in the dark.

—*didn't shut it down. If you winged it then who knows what it's doing out there. The complex spike would try to bring every memory alive at once. So maybe it's remembering all kinds of stuff. Maybe it's gone berserk. There's a brain somewhere in that thing, you know.*

—*Don't lecture me. Of course I know.*

—*The wet drive alone is worth a fortune. Armature is priceless. Nobody even knows what that metal is anymore. We'll eat like kings for a year. We'll go off side to live forever. Now let's find it.*

The hiss of the wheelchair's tires along Think-a-Head's halls. Really, quite a rinky-dink operation. Like she said. The wheelchair is for dramatics. The hall is short. In this room, at the end, here's the doctor, smiling. Looks about twenty, slick and tanned. More like a porn star than anyone with legitimate credentials. It's a good thing she's not here to see this. It's a good thing, in the end, she wasn't able to say goodbye.

V: TOUCH

NIGHT. BRIGHT MOON, CLEAR SKY. LEON could discern, just ahead, the mild heatshapes of two large, warm-blooded creatures. *Mammals.* Sleeping. These things were *people*. His heritage. Part of him understood that now, though he had no hard evidence to support the knowledge, no remaining infrastructure left to consult.

These are people.

Was he once like them? Was this a second chance to be human again? Only tactile memory was left to sample. Touch would complete the doppelganger of senses he was rebuilding. Touch would make him a person again.

He moved silently. He was the wind.

About to caress the recumbent forms, a doubt froze Leon. What if this was all part of some trick? Hadn't these dangerous mammals caused the breakdown in his systems, initiated this discomfort and confusion? Why on Earth would he want to be human once more?

Manipulators hovering over the warm flesh, he thought: *and what if these manifestations, these things called people, are symptoms of some new, malignant gall, a cancer that has insinuated itself into my jurisdiction?* As he considered this most distressing possibility, his pruning knives, unbidden, edged forward in their sheaths, gleaming in the light of the full moon.

The Carpet Maker

THE MAN FROM PERSONNEL HELD OPEN his office door and indicated curtly with his free hand that Patrick should enter; as Patrick did so, and passed him, the man said in low and threatening tones, "Mr. Troy, you understand we are not running a whorehouse?"

Chagrined, Patrick took a seat. The chair was creaky and uncomfortable and very small. He faced a huge wooden desk. Air in this dank basement office smelled sour and stuffy, and he shifted in the chair. Black mould grew on the cement walls, by the baseboards and over the edges of the carpet. Above the big desk, a single bare bulb cast huge shadows.

He looked down at the carpeted floor as the door squealed shut behind him.

Walking softly, the man from personnel returned to his place. His own chair—deep green, leather, high-backed—glistened in the light as if it were a living thing. The man put his hands on the desktop, locked his long fingers together, and waited.

Patrick cleared his throat. "Well," he said, "I can understand why you said that. But let me explain." Leaning forward, elbows on knees, he took a deep breath, focussed again on a spot between his sneakers. He could distinguish a muted pattern of red, gold, and black on the carpeting, where fleurs-de-lis swam in depths of the worn pile.

"Mr. Troy?"

"Yes . . ." He could even *smell* the carpet now, the ages it had laid here, the vanished lives come and gone, passing through this room. "You see, it's just that my wife and I—"

"Look how you've dressed your daughter."

Following the direction of the pointing finger, Patrick was startled to see that the wall to his right had become a window, of sorts—had it always been? A one-way mirror? Had a curtain been lifted?

"How—?"

Words failed. He was looking at the waiting room, where he had left Samantha, moments before.

But that room was on another floor, on another side of the building altogether.

Samantha sat between two tired-looking teenagers, a boy and a girl, her thin legs stretched out, one ankle crossed over the other. At least she had taken off the stilettos. The shoes had been hurting her feet, she'd said, on their way uptown. With her head tilted back, so that her neck was taut, smooth—her throat curved and muscled—Samantha's hair hung down, out of sight. Patrick couldn't see the make-up—the foundation and blush, the blue eye shadow and lipstick—that Kendra had applied to Samantha's face before he had brought her here, but that sequined dress, clinging tightly to her thin, boyish body, changing tone from deep red to small lakes of cerise as she breathed, made him wince.

"My wife is . . ." Now he met the gaze of the man from personnel and the disapproval he saw there caused anger to bloom in him, and it felt like a release. "Look," he said, "my wife is not a happy woman. We know this isn't a whorehouse. You should be more careful what you say to me."

His outburst was ignored. "Where is your wife now?"

"Kendra is, uh, she's busy. She couldn't make it."

The man from personnel continued to stare for a long time. Shadows moved, like bruises, over his face. Finally, though, his expression seemed to soften. He brushed at his black moustache with one curled knuckle. "We have to be careful here, Mr. Troy. I thought we had agreed to the utmost discretion. I thought you understood our position."

"I thought so, too. I'm sorry about the dress."

"Mr. Troy, we are trying to operate a business. That's all. This is a cut-throat world. We want to provide quality carpets at affordable prices." He smiled a thin smile.

"Carpets," Patrick echoed, nodding. "I understand."

"And, Mr. Troy, your daughter certainly seems like a very healthy twelve-year old. Just as you had promised." The man's eyes glittered. His hands went flat on the desk. "Though I honestly can't fathom why you dressed her like that. She is by all means hired."

Patrick did not know what to say. He did not even know what to feel, whether relief or remorse. "Thank you," he mumbled.

"Now let's fill out the forms, shall we, and forget about this unfortunate incident?" The man from personnel had bent to open a drawer; Patrick heard the sound of wood moving on dry wood, and then the rustling of the documents he would shortly sign to complete the sale of his child.

SAMANTHA'S CLOTHES—HER RIDICULOUS SHOES, HER GAUDY and sequined dress—were quickly stuffed into a paper bag by a thin woman in a dull twill suit. Like the man from personnel, this woman did nothing but scowl at Patrick. Her skin was stretched so tight over her cheekbones that tiny blue veins showed, patterns of cracks in fine china. She handed Patrick the bag and nodded as he took it, an almost imperceptible movement, then took him firmly by the arm with surprisingly strong fingers, guiding him toward— he realized with additional shock—the rear exit of the building.

"Do not worry about Samantha, Mr. Troy," said the woman as they made their way through a large kitchen: ceramic-tiled floor, sinks along one wall and, between them, truncated pipes of gas mains that protruded from the sea-green walls like accusing fingers. "The food here is wonderful and the rooms are always comfortable. I assure you Samantha will make a lot of new friends. At lunchtime, all of our young workers sit together in the sunlight, eyes closed, faces turned toward the sky, as if they have found peace. This is a sight we have come to love."

He stopped, turned toward the woman, confused. "Sunlight? *Peace?* But where, where do they sit? Where could they go?"

The door had been pushed open, his unanswered question sucked out into the night; it was raining, diffusing the city lights. Car tires hissed on nearby wet roads. Blowing in, the rain was cold and reflected neon on the wet tiles at their feet.

"Tell her to write." Patrick clutched the bag to his chest like a life preserver. He could smell the perfume. Kendra had splashed Samantha liberally with Prada knock-off this morning, after the fight.

With little choice, Patrick stepped outside. The metal door sealed behind him shut with a loud *click*.

Standing atop a landing, in an alley, stunned for a moment by memories, Patrick was soon soaked. A car horn blared, waking him, as if from a dream, and he blinked, letting the rain patter his face. He took a deep breath. The segment of street he could see at the far end of the alley was busy with people hustling to get somewhere dry, bustling with trucks and cars and buses that appeared and disappeared abruptly.

A set of cement stairs, strewn with garbage, led down from where he stood. A black metal dumpster, engorged, lid unclosable.

Before Patrick made it to the street, the paper bag had darkened, shifted, and fallen apart in his hands. The shoes spilled away from him, splashing into a silvered puddle where they lay sideways in the rainwater like tiny, capsized boats. Struggling to keep hold of the reeking dress, Patrick stepped into the water and bent, one hand outstretched.

He did not pick up the stilettos.

Instead, he kicked out, spraying water up his own leg, nearly falling as one shoe clattered onto the sidewalk and was immediately picked up by a passing man in a long dark coat who did not so much as look into the alley where Patrick stood, feet apart, breathing hard, fists at his sides.

He went back to the dumpster to toss in the dress. When he saw the ink stain on his hands, like blood, he realized he could not remember having signed any documents. He tried not to dwell on this lapse, but he was frightened as he walked the length of the alley to the street. No, he could not remember signing any documents, nor could he remember any features of the woman who had just shown him the door. He could no longer even remember details of the altercation with Sam, when he and Kendra had told her, just today, what they had decided.

As Patrick turned onto the busy sidewalk, his vision had kaleidoscoped through drops of water. This effect was not from the rain.

HE DID NOT HAVE ENOUGH CHANGE for the bus, which he thought was rather ironic, since he'd just pawned his daughter. He walked home, a twenty-minute trip, and decided this mode of transportation was for the best; by the time he got back to the apartment the knot that had been tightening in his chest had time to somewhat loosen.

He went slowly up the flights of stairs, as if there were a force repelling him, and passed two derelicts, asleep on two different landings. One of them had pissed himself. The urine was as dark as steeped tea and smelled like ammonia.

The door to his apartment stood ajar. Dark inside, but Kendra often kept their place dark, either watching TV or sleeping on the couch. Suddenly,

Patrick felt drunk; his head buzzed, reeled. He pushed the door open with one foot and let it hit the wall inside. He staggered in.

From the gloom of the bedroom, dressed in a torn and yellowed nightie, Kendra appeared, knuckling her eyes. "Make a little more noise, why don't you?" Her voice was hoarse. The apartment smelled of cigarettes and stale food and traces of lingering perfume. Dishes filled the sink. The coffee table was strewn with ashes and papers, and a good deal of the floor was covered. Neither he nor Kendra had ever been good at cleaning; Samantha had done most of the housework.

"Well, that's it," he said. "They were absolute freaks. Thanks for your support." Then, louder than he had meant to: "For god's sake, Ken, why did you dress her like that? They gave me a fucking hard time."

Kendra scratched at her hip. "You're getting the floor wet."

He flicked on the light. His hands shook. When he looked back, Kendra had vanished. He went to the bedroom doorway and, with one hand either side of the jamb, tried to control his breathing.

She lay on her back, on the bed, arms above her head, legs open. He could see the dark patch of her pubic hair. He and Kendra had not made love—had not held each other or kissed—in over a year.

"I asked you," Patrick said, his voice tremulous, "why you dressed her like that."

Kendra stared up at the ceiling. "Did they give you money?"

He licked his lips. "No."

"Don't try to make me feel any worse than I do. We both agreed to this. Samantha *wanted* to get out of here."

There had been times in the past when their daughter had screamed at them both, *I hate you, I hate you*, and twice she had run away, coming home once by herself, another time with two police officers who had found her at an arcade. Recalling his daughter's vehemence, and his own anger at the policemen's questions, Patrick stepped closer to the bed and reached out. "Ken?"

"Don't fucking touch me," his wife replied, immobile.

PATRICK WENT TO THE POST OFFICE daily to see if any cheques had come in, and to see if Samantha had written, but nothing came: no cheques; no letters. After a week or so, he returned to the building where he had brought Samantha, feeling nauseous and edgy.

It was still raining.

He waited for over an hour in the lobby. Behind the taciturn male receptionist were two disintegrating wall hangings. Patrick was finally met by the stern-faced woman who had given him Sam's shoes, and he recalled the strange absence he had felt after the previous encounter with her. He scowled.

"Where is she?" Patrick said. "And where's our money?"

"Mr. Troy, your daughter is fine. We can't force her to write if she does not wish to. This is a transitional period for her. Please be patient. As for the cheques, if you'll read the contract, you'll see that we keep two weeks in hand. Next week your money will start to come in."

"Do you think I can talk to her? Can I see her?"

"Mr. Troy, I really suggest that you go home and read over the contract. I will relay your regards to Samantha. Now, we are very busy here. There are many parents who participate in our program; we are always busy. If there's anything else we can do for you, be sure to make an appointment before coming by."

THE CLUTTERED APARTMENT SEEMED TO BE filling with litter. Every surface of the room, covered with paper plates and cups and plastic vials, cardboard and magazines, the detritus of their lives. He wondered how he and Kendra could generate so much refuse, especially since Kendra, who had always, in times of stress, relied on Valium, and had begun to take more and more of the pills, sleeping through the long and silent days. As for himself, between running to the post office, where he would invariably find the box empty, and trying to fill bogus prescriptions in drugstores all across town, on foot, the days also passed and he spent little time at home. Yet garbage continued to accumulate.

Whenever he did return like this, exhausted, numb, Kendra would be in bed or on the couch, her eyes staring at nothing. When she spoke, her voice was slurred, slow:

"We wore uniforms to school," she told him.

He stood with a vial of Ambien in his hands.

"Tunics were dark blue. I was always called into Mr. Hornstein's office. I must have been ten years old."

"Jesus Christ," Patrick said. His breath came in short gasps. He felt like he was on the verge of an anxiety attack. His insides boiled then went preternaturally calm, as if he were suddenly rendered hollow. A buzzing in his ears. "What are you talking about, Ken? Why are you telling me this?"

"Mr. Hornstein used to cane me. Across my knuckles, with a wooden ruler. Twice he bent me over his knee, and lifted my skirt."

Before he knew what he was doing, Patrick had stepped over to where his wife sat and, awkwardly, hit her across the face. His open hand knocked her hair forward and she fell silent.

Amid a rush of cascading images, Patrick remembered his wife's face when they had first met. He remembered her smile, her laugh.

Slowly, Kendra stood and went into the bedroom without another word.

Patrick watched her go. He sat heavily on the couch where she had been. His hands operated remotely; he had no control of them. He watched them as they lay in his lap.

He might have slept then, for an instant; when he managed to open his eyes—perhaps at the creaking of floorboards, or the rustle of papers—he saw Kendra's brass hairbrush, clenched in her fist, coming down swiftly toward his head.

THIS TIME HE STOOD IN THE reception area for over two hours before anyone came to see him. Under the cap, his head throbbed. Seven stitches had closed the gash and the doctors had shaved a good deal of his scalp.

Again, the receptionist was no help. And, again, it was the stern-faced woman who eventually came out to talk to him.

"Where's our money?" he said, but he didn't sound as tough as he had wanted. "You have our daughter and we haven't got any cheques from you at all."

The woman frowned. "May I have your name, sir?"

"Don't give me that shit." Ice formed in his blood. "My name is Patrick Troy. My daughter's name is Samantha."

"Just wait here a minute, I'll get the manager."

The woman turned and left.

At a loss, Patrick waited.

A short time later, the receptionist's telephone rang. When Patrick looked over, the receptionist gestured toward the receiver. Frowning, Patrick walked over to the desk and answered the call.

"Hello?"

The receptionist watched him coldly.

"Mr. Troy?"

The voice was that of the man from personnel. Patrick said, "What the hell is going on?"

"My wife tells me you seem angry."

"Your wife? Yes, I'm fucking angry. That's your *wife*?"

"She says you want money. Well, Mr. Troy, I have your daughter's file here with me. Samantha Troy. Twelve years old. Extensive bruising down her left thigh and on her left biceps. Swollen tissue around her right eye."

"What are you talking about?"

"Your daughter, Mr. Troy."

"What the hell have you done to her?"

"Us? We merely try to help. You know she was admitted in this condition."

"I will go to the fucking police," he hissed.

"You won't, Mr. Troy. We both know that. Now listen, according to our records, Samantha's contract expired over two months ago. She was sent home."

The walls receded and the floor dropped out from underneath Patrick's feet. He clenched the receiver and put his free hand flat on the counter for support. "Two months ago? Are you insane? We just signed her up."

"Don't raise your voice to me. I have dealt with many fathers like you before, many parents. Some of them sent their children into mines, others forced them into bordellos, or onto the streets, not to mention a litany of more horrific and unmentionable fates."

"We did the best we could. I don't need to justify myself to you. Tell me where my daughter is."

"I just told you. She's gone home. I ask you to do the same. Goodbye, Mr. Troy."

"Wait—"

The line went dead as the receptionist's hand fell onto Patrick's shoulder, firm, squeezing. Patrick's knees buckled; all his strength had gone. He hung up, and was escorted out.

PATRICK GOT DRUNK THAT NIGHT. HE drank a twenty-six ounce bottle of vodka, sitting, ruminating in the dark while Kendra slept on the couch. When he finished the bottle, he stood and woke Kendra by kicking at the couch pillows.

"Goddamn you," he shouted, swaying over her. "This is all your fault! Where is that fucking contract?"

"My fault?" Kendra had not bathed in weeks. Her hair was stringy and greasy, her eyes sunken. She was falling apart. "I never saw any contract. So leave me alone, you bastard. Let me sleep."

Knee-deep in garbage, struggling to stay on his feet, Patrick felt both fists clench.

The Brief Medical Career of Fine Sam Fine

Parties, & Promiscuity

Moira had been at figurative loggerheads with Lucinda for as long as she could remember; she imagined an ending to their relationship that would rival the greatest *tragedies lyriques*. Home life (termed this with the strongest of ironic intonation) was bickering and bitterness, uneasy silences, drunken rages, crockery smashing. Outings were a different sort of nightmare: fiascoes, each time the sisters left their apartment.

But, by far, the most heinous occasions were house parties.

Needless to say, Lucinda had a fondness for attending these sordid affairs with unimaginative regularity.

A cool September night. Leaves crunching under feet and the faint smell of smoke from chimneys returned to the air after a long hot summer, but stuck in this stale basement Moira felt claustrophobic and nauseous, clammy all over. Like she did at every party. Mushed up against the back of a stinky couch (beer, mostly, and mildew), she waited, unseen, appalled.

Perhaps this boy entwined with Lucinda was someone once glimpsed standing, smoking, outside a corner store. Moira imagined her sister descending the stairs to spy him, sitting in the gloom, then making her way over to where he sat, vapid on the couch, knees wide apart, big dirty football hands hanging between them. She imagined her sister introducing herself (though surely that wasn't necessary: Lucinda was a legend in town).

And now she was draped over him. Or somehow semi-reclined. Without being able to see clearly, Moira, thankfully, could never be exactly sure of the compromising positions her sister achieved. Merciful, too, she could hear very little. Puccini's *Madame Lescault* played in her mind, a baroque feast intended to smother remnants of any external din, such as the incessant *thump-thump* of the so-called music and the drone of drunken voices. Any snippets of conversation she overheard were, for the most part, composed of Lucinda's inane twaddle—the same twaddle Moira had been listening to and feel *hum* up her spine for twenty-one years now.

Moira tried to breathe and choked on thick cigarette smoke; she stopped trying. Twice, inebriated louts had knocked her about. And, once, Lucinda banged into a wall or something else *really* solid; Moira had been bruised pretty good, she was sure.

There was still the inevitable *finale* to look forward to, Lucinda's *fin-de-soiree* on some settee or bed—maybe on this very couch—rolling around with a hormone-mad male.

Moira sighed. Her delicate sensibilities were stripped away at these parties. Such indignities, and all of them suffered cooped up in the depths of Lucinda's ridiculous hat.

THE CAT IN THE HAT HAT, & A CLOSE CALL

ON THIS PARTICULAR EVENING, LUCINDA SPORTED the Cat in the Hat hat: tall, unattractive, and ungainly. Striped red and white, it rose a good two feet above her scalp. Some room inside for movement, but Lucinda had warned Moira against moving.

However, because the Cat in the Hat hat was made of felt, it didn't rub Moira's skin raw, like some of the other hats did. Certainly rank inside. Moira was sweating.

Through pinholes, she saw unfathomable glimmers.

At one point, a warm, masculine forearm, thrown behind Lucinda, pressed the fabric of the hat up against Moira's face until Lucinda was kind enough to move. Another time, the same boy (Moira hoped it was the same boy) tried to run the fingers of his free hand up the back of Lucinda's head, actually working them under the elastic brim of the Cat in the Hat hat itself. One large, clumsy digit came within half an inch of Moira's pounding breastbone.

From shadow, she watched its dreadful approach—

Lucinda diverted the boy's attention.

If nothing else, Lucinda was good at diverting boys' attentions.

WASHROOMS

BRIEF REPRIEVES CAME WHEN LUCINDA WENT to pee, or to cake on more foundation powders. Or smear on more lipstick. And then only if she remembered, and felt like removing the hat. And if the bathroom door had a functioning lock. And no one was passed out on the floor. Or in the tub.

At this party—thank God!—conditions were met.

Lucinda yanked off the Cat in the Hat hat, leaving Moira blinking, gasping for relatively fresh air. Even the dinginess of this water closet was too bright, blinding after several hours of being treated like a mushroom. Lucinda's coarse hair had dragged across Moira's body but Moira had given up complaining about *that* problem long ago.

"Did you see this dude?" Lucinda peered into a mirror; Moira, of course, watched the wall opposite. "This hot guy, Sam Fine? Did you see him? Hey, I'm talking to you back there."

Had she seen him? Was there any point in addressing that question? What Moira wanted to say was, *You tell me the same thing at every stupid party. 'Some guy likes me, he* really *likes me!' Then you let him slobber all over you and grope you and he never calls you again. So you sit at home, getting drunk and watching TV, crying. You complain about your life as if everything's my fault when I refuse to take responsibility!*

But Moira didn't want to fight. She just wanted to go home. So she kept quiet.

Lucinda, meanwhile, popped a zit. When she bent to splash cold water on her face, Moira's view of the wall changed to nothing but ceiling. Two pipes up there, painted green. Peeling. A big yellow stain. Moira wondered if her sister was going to vomit tonight—another common, foul ordeal.

Over the sound of the water's plashing, Lucinda repeated what she had said about Sam Fine. Then she asked, "Are you awake back there? Retard, I'm talking to you."

"Of course I'm awake," Moira finally replied. "You expect me to be sleeping? Maybe you were concerned I'd suffocated."

"I should be so lucky. You can't suffocate. I know. I've tried many times. Listen, just do me a favour and answer when I ask you something. Least *try* to be a normal sister." Lucinda fumbled to push her jeans down and sat heavily upon the toilet. "Anyhow, what I was saying is that this guy is a *babe*. And I think he likes me. His name is Sam Fine and he is fine, fine, fine."

How Moira hated her sister's laugh, which unfortunately filled that tiny water closet for some time, shaking her like quaking from hell itself. (Right there, gray and spongy, dark sea to Moira's tossing ship.)

Some while after her sister had calmed—Moira's shoulder was pressed up painfully against the rusted underside of a cheap medicine cabinet—Moira said, "Could we please get out of here. *Soon.*"

"What?" Lucinda fumbled with the toilet paper. "You little twerp, what did you say?"

"Let's get out of here. You're just going to make a fool out of yourself. Again."

"All that whispering back there. Idiot, speak up, will you? Whisper all the damn time. So negative. We just got here, okay? Didn't you hear what I've been saying about Fine Sam Fine? Just relax and enjoy yourself for once. He's in Med School, did I tell you that? *A doctor.* Or at least, he will be soon." Getting up from the toilet, Lucinda had to hold onto the shower curtain to stop from falling into the tub. "Jeez-us," she continued, regaining her balance (such as it was), "if only I *could* leave you at home but look, retard, we're not splitting for a long time so deal with it, okay?"

Before Moira could answer Lucinda had rudely pulled the Cat in the Hat hat back on and was fumbling at the doorknob with eager hands.

A FEW SURPRISES, FOLLOWED BY SOME TRUE MUSIC, *EN FIN*

THE FIRST SURPRISE OF THE EVENING came when Moira realized how much the boy with Lucinda was actually *talking*. Not only could she detect the drone of his conversation but she could tell quite easily when Lucinda was just listening: there was little movement from her sister, except for nodding. Her curiosity piqued, Moira paid more attention, letting the operatic mantra she recited to herself fade. This Sam Fine, it appeared, spoke in reasonable tones, as if he might be actually be expressing ideas, sharing rational thoughts. Was that possible? Had Lucinda selected someone here, at this party, with thoughts of his own? In the darkness of the hat Moira smiled. If what she suspected were true, then the choice must have been an oversight. Serves Lucinda right; she was probably very disappointed.

But other surprises were in store, and they unfolded in succession, nearer to the end of the evening, the most astonishing being the fact that Sam Fine left the party abruptly, by himself, with nothing more than a hug for his time. And, despite this, Lucinda travelled home on the last subway train in an exuberant mood. When she and Moira finally arrived at their apartment (a shabby room, plus kitchenette and bathroom, on the third and top floor of a tenement situated on a dead-end street), Lucinda was actually *bubbly*. So good was her inexplicable mood that she acquiesced without prompting to change the radio station from Rockin 92 to Classical 88.2, which at this point was playing the Nightly Opera Hour, Moira's favourite three hours of airwave time. Lucinda even moved the radio so Moira could better hear the wonderful arias.

(The deal the sisters had settled on, long ago, was that if Moira didn't let the cat out of the bag, so to speak, at inopportune times, she would be rewarded with a book of her choice from the library or a few hours of radio, or Lucinda would sit facing away from the TV while some "dumb-ass" show on PBS aired. But rarely was it this easy, and never without some sort of grumbling.)

Lucinda lay upon the bed, talking nonsense about her future life with Fine Sam Fine, strategizing her next move. Moira listened to Schutz's score for the Rinuccini libretto *Dafne,* her entire body pressed up against the thrumming speaker in an unbalanced embrace. How she revelled in that ancient piece (arguably the first opera ever written). The night was ending with a very unexpected treat.

When Mozart or Lully or even good old Henry Purcell took hold of Moira, she rose to a world where she could leave Lucinda, walk away from her sister on legs of her own. When tenor voices swelled, she filled those small lungs of hers and imagined herself standing atop a mountain, the beautiful princess Electra, waiting for her knight Idamante, who was coming, coming, racing breathlessly along the trail to sweep her up and onto the back of his throbbing stallion.

Thus revelling, Moira gazed dreamily at her treasures, precious items collected over the years and stored neatly in a series of recesses in the wooden headboard of the bed, just within Moira's reach when Lucinda slept or reclined, as she did now, giddy and waffling on and on about Sam Fine while music and the sight of these *objets trouvés* flowed through Moira in ecstatic waves.

A SUMMARY OF THE CONTENTS OF MOIRA'S TREASURE TROVE & BRIEF HISTORY THEREOF

ONE (1) ARTIFICIAL ROSE, BLACK IN colour, petals threadbare. Liberated from a vase in a Doctor's office while Lucinda bent to tie her boot.

Two (2) knitting needles, attached (irony not missed) by a nylon tether, with which, one day, hopefully, to make a garment (i.e., custom sleeve/shoulder warmer).

One (1) creased Technicolor photograph of the venerable Marylin Horn, whose flexible vocal range was most extraordinary, performing in Handel's Orlando at the Lincoln Centre for the Arts. (A show Lucinda had said she "would not be caught dead at," when Moira begged her to go.)

Seven (7) very shiny brass buttons that distorted reflections to the point where one could imagine, if one so desired, one's face looking quite different.

Two (2) HB pencils (leads broken).

One (1) small notepad.

One (1) wedge-shaped shard of mirror, perhaps six inches in length overall, used to see various parts of the room while Lucinda reposed or, sometimes, walked around hatless. The item was acquired after Lucinda had had a particularly bad tantrum in which she accumulated fourteen years of bad luck by throwing an ashtray at two separate mirrors—picking the ashtray up and throwing it a second time—while screaming phrases such as "you freak," and "you f@#king parasite." When Lucinda had eventually fallen asleep on the floor (for she had been very drunk that night), said shard was scooped up from the detritus that lay scattered about them both like a tornado's aftermath.

One (1) desiccated moth, believed to have traces of red on its underwings—too brittle to confirm.

One (1) tiny figurine of a dog, glass, within which swam wondrous colours stretched like mysterious and beautiful taffy.

Two (2) se tenant postage stamps from the United States of America, valued five (5) cents each, bearing the likenesses of Frances Farmer, whose dramatic life and death were particularly affecting (even though Farmer was not an opera singer).

SAM FINE'S ENTRANCE

RUDELY RETRIEVED FROM *LA BOHEME* AND her mental inventory by, of all things, a knock on the window! Lucinda had fallen asleep in such a manner that Moira could see the silhouette of someone at the glass: pale face peering in from the utter darkness at their third-floor window.

"Lucinda," Moira hissed, quite terrified. "Someone's here! Wake up, cover me. There's an *intruder!*"

Rapping again. Out in the night, the indistinct face shifted, no doubt trying to see better, cupped hand to brow. In her drunken slumber, Lucinda moaned and rolled. Then lights from a lost vehicle turning around in the *cul-de-sac* allowed Moira a good yet brief look at the intruder and she was taken aback by the face she saw: intelligent eyes, high cheekbones, soft wavy hair. She gazed upon these features as they bloomed and then faded, as if stricken, knowing the boy could see nothing in the dim room, maybe a few dark shapes against a darker background, at best.

A third time came the knocking, and Lucinda finally woke up, snorting and thrashing about until she discovered where she was and what had caused the disturbance. Then she was on her feet, staggering groggily toward the window when she realized she was hatless and ran back for her nightcap. (This piece of haberdashery wasn't so bad, either, because Moira could easily hear through the thin fabric and even see shapes moving about.) Lucinda knew this peeping Tom? A suspicion bloomed in Moira. *My goodness*, she wondered, *could this be Sam Fine, from the party*? And a twinge of something she had long ago tried to suppress forever stirred in her. Having resigned that she could only ever meet family members (who were all long gone now), and the occasional doctor (the services of whom the sisters could no longer afford), Moira had been bracing for a life of solitude, with only the Opera for company, and her treasures, yet her heart was racing wildly as the window slid up and the boy at the window said, in a deep, mellifluous voice, "Hey there, Luce."

"Get in, Sam."

It *was* he! Adonis, beautiful Orestes.

"Get yer ass in here." Lucinda's own voice was crude and breathless and phony.

"I wanted to see you again," Sam explained. "Is that all right? I couldn't sleep or study and I was thinking about what we said. The door downstairs was locked . . ."

"Yeah, come in, come in."

Lucinda stepped aside while Sam clambered through the window. He must have scaled the lilac tree. All Moira could see was a gauzy view of Lucinda's *Guns N' Roses* poster but when she heard Sam's runners thump to the floor it thrilled her to know he was in the same room as her: under the nightcap, she was as naked as the day she (and her awful sister) had been born.

CARL MARIA VON WEBER'S *DER FRESCUTZ*

LUCINDA SPRAWLED ON THE MESSY BED, trying to look enticing, but Sam, thankfully, was not to be enticed. Against the padded headboard, Moira watched as best she could. Even through the hazy gauze of the nightcap, and at such an obscure angle, Sam was truly gorgeous to behold. As he talked, his large hands moved gracefully. Wonderful hands. The hands of a prince. His eyes and teeth sparkled in the dim light.

Oh, what words he spoke! Yearnings, goals, each phrase reverberating inside Moira, resonating to her very core. The sentiments were familiar, echoing her own or counterpart to them. How these words must be wasted on Lucinda, who grunted and uttered her usual stupid contributions. What did Sam Fine see in her? He had already proven to Moira in a short while that he was far from shallow, yet here he was, about to willingly talk through the night with her luddite sister. Moira wanted to shout, *I'm back here, Sam! It's me you want to converse with!*

But if she did that, Sam would see her, and then he would run screaming, never to return; Moira bit her tongue.

Soon, though, Carl Von Weber's *Freeshooter* (or *der Freschutz*) came on the radio—Moira's favourite opera of all time. Sam abruptly ceased talking. Those lovely hands leapt at the overture of the opening horns.

"Von *Weber*," he breathed, pronouncing the name properly. His face became even more angelic. "Listen, Lucinda. Hear that? Hear the, um, crescendo. And the, the uh . . . ascending *struggle*."

Moira's own definition, verbatim! Sam's eyes had closed as he sank back. Trying to stare at him, incredulous, Moira felt her girlish crush turn to the first pangs of *love!* The boy was her *soul* mate. There could be no doubt. Songs filled her, poignant tunes of Eurydice and Dido. (And not that contemporary Irish tart.) A protective ice broke away from the tight little bulb that was her heart; green shoots reached up toward the light, burgeoning, alive; hopeful shoots, tender shoots. Feelings so intense ravished Moira that tears sprang to her eyes. She was in *love!*

Then the unthinkable happened.

THE UNTHINKABLE

PROPPED UP BY PILLOWS, LUCINDA HAD passed out as the opera unfolded— no fan she—and toppled like a felled tree; the nightcap, as she went over, caught on the headboard and was yanked clean from her head. Sam Fine, leaning to catch Lucinda, instead came face to face with Moira, who lay naked and exposed, an ugly boil on the back of her sister's head.

They stared at each other for a long time.

Sam Fine's eyes, so blue, widened slowly. He did not laugh, or scream, or flee. Quietly, very quietly, he asked, "Who are *you?*"

"Moira," said Moira, her newly expanded heart pounding. "I'm Lucinda's older sister." (Technically, this was true; she *had* emerged first.)

Licking his full lips, Sam reached out to move Lucinda's hair away. He let one finger trail down Moira's tiny arm. In his eyes was a look that could only be described by Moira as one of *rapture*.

"Please, cover me," Moira said. "I asked Lucinda to make me a nightdress, but as you can see, she's not yet done so."

"Sorry, sorry . . ." Fumbling nervously in the bedclothes to arrange the sheet, so it covered Moira's body but left her face exposed, Sam was visibly embarrassed. He worked quickly, eyes averted, cheeks reddening.

"Thank you," Moira said, when he was done.

"You, uh, you been back there all night? Of course, what a stupid question. The hats. The hats. That's why Lucinda always wears those big hats."

Moira nodded, but since most of her head and neck and what little spine she possessed was fused to Lucinda's skull, the movement was imperceptible. She hesitated, then said, "It's not Lucinda who likes to listen to the opera, Sam. It's me." How delicious it had been to say his name.

Sam Fine smiled. His teeth were big and white and glorious. "Did you like that, uh, von *Weber* piece?"

"I love *der Freschutz*."

They both said, "That romantic setting," at the same time, and laughed briefly together, and stared again into each other's eyes for a long while, without blinking, searching each others' gaze.

Moira was starting to let herself hope there was a possibility her new and tender love might be requited.

Lucinda, meanwhile, began to snore.

A LITTLE LATER

SAM LAY ON THE BED, HIS Adonis body next to Lucinda's, his head tilted so he could whisper to Moira directly. Those lips, inches from her. She could feel the heat of him like a furnace. Never before had Moira felt this alive.

They spoke of the opera, of course, and of literature, the ballet, philosophies. Moira knew she was soon doing most of the talking but Sam seemed engrossed. It was as if floodgates opened up inside her, releasing an unstoppable torrent. She had never spoken thusly in her life.

After listening attentively for what seemed like hours, Sam said to her, almost breathlessly, "What I want to know is, uh, more about *you*. Tell me . . . tell me about your family." A bead of sweat ran down Sam's forehead, though it was not hot in the room.

"My family? We were orphaned." Moira wished she could mop Sam's brow. Was proximity to her making him flush?

"Did you, uh, know your mom?"

"I know a bit about her, though we never met."

"Could you tell me, tell me about her?"

THE HOPELESS CASE

LITTLE ELLA MAE BAINBRIDGE, SENT OUT, twelve years old, to the corner store, for a quart of homogenized milk, on January 26, 1972. Skinny and pig-tailed, Ella Mae was the only child of Reverend Joe Bainbridge and his wife, Victoria. The neighbourhood was white, pristine, quiet; the trip to the store three short blocks.

Skipping along the sidewalk, money clenched in her right fist and singing a merry tune, Ella Mae was pulverized by a huge gold Cadillac that jumped the curb. The car, driven by fourteen-year-old Sam "Deep Purple" Painscott—who had just taken it minutes before from the parking lot of the first strip mall to be built in the area—had been found with the keys inside, engine running. The Caddy belonged to Old Boy Frankish, who was doddering around in the sporting goods retail outlet, searching out a lure for winter pickerel. Just as Frankish reluctantly paid for his purchase, and addressed complaints concerning inflationary times to the very air about him while attempting to count out the exact amount in small change, his stolen car was coming to rest in a great cloud of brick dust, metal, oil, dirt and Ella Mae's blood. Pinned somewhere in that mess, every bone broken, body sundered, yet miraculously alive, the child had plunged immediately into a coma from which she would never emerge.

Prone on a hospital bed, in a ward that no patient had ever left under his or her own power, Ella Mae lived out her life. A host of machines kept her body going. Bleeding eventually stopped, and fractures knitted, and that inert body grew, changed, entered puberty. Over time, Ella Mae had gradually metamorphosed into an adult, albeit atrophied. A grown woman. She might even have been an attractive woman—if she were capable of a smile, or even a twitch, any sign of life at all besides those you could read on monitors.

Devices next to her bed beeped. Cylinders hissed up and down in their glass housings. Lights mimicked the patterns of her heart. And years went by.

Over a decade she lay before a doctor noted a change in Ella Mae's condition—an inexplicable change: the patient appeared to be *swelling*. This Doctor, who was new on the ward and had not yet succumbed to the futility of his assignment, speculated that there might be gas trapped in Ella Mae's lower intestines. Subsequent examination, however, revealed the rather unsettling fact that visitors to Ella Mae's room, aside from her once-grieving parents (who had not come by in many months, by this point) had found the patient attractive. An orderly, perhaps, or a night cleaner. Maybe even a security guard.

Now it goes without saying that the good Rev. Bainbridge and his wife were Christians, and that they believed in God, and in the wisdom of His ways. This, despite the fact that their only child, their sweet young girl, had been literally crushed before her life really started, and now needed machines to keep her breathing and had to be flipped on a regular basis to stop bedsores from rotting the flesh from her bones. They would not hear of terminating this new life growing inside their Ella Mae; they were appalled at the suggestion. *This pregnancy,* they said, *is God's way of giving us back our daughter. A new chance, a miracle.*

But the eager young doctor pleaded: *Ella Mae has had a steady stream of drugs administered to her over the past ten years. For her to give birth is madness!*

The Reverend and his wife answered: *We won't hear of it. What you are suggesting is murder in God's eyes.*

So, five months later, after a messy delivery in which their daughter lost a lot of blood but *still* did not die, the pious couple remained adamant, stoic. They would not consider the proposed operation to separate the twins, for it was obvious that the tiny one—caught by a ring of bone, as if pulling herself out of the larger girl's head with her one little arm, legs hidden under the surface of her sister's skull—would surely die.

Two souls, the parents said. But they sounded less convinced now. The Reverend was tired, stubbled. On Victoria's breath was the faintest scent of Bombay Gin. *Two gifts?*

Anyhow, heartbreak killed them, Vic and Joe. Ground them down. Too much grief piled up, crushing even their beliefs. They went to confront their God.

There followed for the girls a series of foster homes, a series of towns. Some rudimentary tutoring, since regular schooling turned out to be an impossibility. Upon reaching sixteen, a government pension. Set up in a small apartment on the outskirts of the outskirts of town, on a dead-end street.

Which brings us pretty much up to date.

SWEETEST SORROW

THE SUN WAS BEGINNING TO RISE when Sam finally said he had to leave. It seemed as if the story had made him weepy; his eyes were glazed and unfocussed. Moira could feel the tenderness established between them like a palpable tether.

Sam promised, in a strained voice, to return the following night, at eight. They would get Lucinda drunk, and when she fell asleep, he and Moira could talk, and lie next to each other once more.

Sam Fine gently pulled Lucinda's nightcap back on.

Listening to him clamber over the sill, Moira knew that the prince she had always dreamt of had finally arrived in her life. She imagined the two of them galloping off into the sunset, heading toward a place far from her sister, or perhaps a place from which her sister had vanished altogether.

LOVE: DAY ONE (1)

JUST BEFORE TEN THE FOLLOWING MORNING, Lucinda awoke, very hungover. Moira had not slept at all. Complaining, and holding *her* head, one hand either side of Moira (who never sympathized with her sister's suffering one whit), Lucinda made a big production of her headache and dehydration and general woes. As she drank a pop from the fridge, she wanted to know what had happened after she'd passed out. Moira told her that Sam had merely gotten bored watching her sleep and had left. Lucinda grew angry at hearing this and half-heartedly threw a few things around the room. Eventually, though, after two bloody Caesars—hair o' the dog, Lucinda's hangover cure— and listening to a terrible combo called AC/DC, she mellowed out somewhat.

For Moira, that day of waiting was bittersweet torture. The paradox was she wanted to savour every moment of anticipation yet time could not go fast enough. How could these disparate, delicious feelings be sustained?

Just before supper, Lucinda showered. Though her body and face were too close to the source of the spray itself—and when Lucinda washed her hair it was somewhat uncomfortable—showers were predominately refreshing for Moira. Also, a relief to know that the sisters would smell clean this evening, and fresh, for Sam's return.

Ablutions complete, Lucinda wrapped her head—Moira included—in a towel. Possibly to drown out Moira's humming. Then Lucinda made a telephone call. Moira knew this because she was hit twice by the handset while Lucinda had a rather animated conversation, trying to keep her voice down, which she succeeded in doing, since Moira heard nary a word.

She did, however, feel her sister's urgency in her backbone.

An hour or so later, when Lucinda took the towel off, Moira asked whom she'd been talking to; Lucinda denied being on the phone at all.

"Whatever," Moira said, buoyed beyond such vagaries as her sister's bald-faced lies.

Eight o'clock finally arrived and so did Sam, punctual, knocking on the door this time. Moira was giddy. Lucinda pulled on her puffy Rasta hat. This piece of apparel, though ridiculous, was not too stuffy, affording fuzzy visuals and minimal acoustics.

From what Moira could gather, Sam had brought a bottle with him, the contents of which Lucinda promptly drank. Before long, Lucinda was sleeping and Sam was lifting up the Rastafarian hat like he was lifting the lid off a frying pan, smiling down at the hash cooking there.

"Hi there," Moira whispered, heart fluttering.

"Hi there."

Lucinda slumped face down at the kitchen table, which meant that Moira lay on her back, face up. An ideal position, really. Empty bottle of Dewar's whiskey on the table, one glass. Sam had tuned the radio to the opera show. Lights were dim.

A little odd, even for Lucinda, to drink so much, so fast, by herself, but fates were clearly pulling strings to achieve Moira's happy ending—

Where was Sam walking off to?

"And that goes out to our two new listeners who called last night and concludes the request part of our aria—"

Over by the bed, quickly turning off the radio.

THE SECOND CONVERSATION

MOIRA TOOK THE LEAD BY ASKING rather boldly what Sam thought of Rossini's *La Cerentola,* which was the story of Angelina—better known by her nickname, *Cinderella*—and was a story that Moira associated very strongly with, but Sam didn't seem to know that particular *opera seria.* Bit of a blank look, in fact, on his pretty face, which was a little surprising since the piece was a foundation block of early opera. But never mind; relationships were complicated, dramatic.

But then Sam Fine mentioned the Three Tenors; Moira did not know what to say about this pedestrian offering.

After a brief, almost awkward pause, Sam changed the subject altogether, telling Moira a little about his own family, all of whom sounded like good, if somewhat simple, people. Sam seemed a little nervous. Maybe he wasn't feeling well.

And, since he and Moira felt so close already (Sam explained), he asked if it was okay to inquire how Moira stayed healthy under the hats, if she was comfortable in there, what she ate (indeed, *if* she ate), and other such questions about her biological make-up. "Because your sister don't know this stuff," he concluded.

"Lucinda?" Moira was confused (though Sam's piercing gaze may have been the cause). "You've, you've talked with her about *this*? About *me*?"

"I, no, I mean, it's obvious. I mean, she wouldn't know about this kind of stuff, would she? About science and all that? If I did ask her." Smiling somewhat shakily. "That's all."

"I guess not," Moira said slowly, curious about the reddening of Sam's face but not willing to let the evening slip out of her grasp. And since she *had* listened to the doctors while Lucinda flirted crudely with them, Moira actually was able to explain to Sam, without feeling self-conscious at all, about her what it was, precisely, that made her tick.

WHAT MAKES MOIRA TICK

PELVIS, LOWER EXTREMITIES: ABSENT. REPRODUCTIVE ORGANS: absent. (Pair of cyst-like nodes at the junction of patients: vestigial ovarian tissue?) Spine: present (severe "corkscrew" abnormalities) but only first ten (10) anterior vertebrae, all fused to the parietal plate of patient L's skull. Series of nodes along sphenoid plate of patient L's skull indicate ill-formed lumbar backbone and sacrum. Left arm: present, greatly undersized and movement limited. Muscle development and strength: advanced. Right arm: absent. Microcelaphia. Head mobility: limited.

Personalities remain distinct. Brainwave activity at par in both brains (if not more advanced in patient M.)

Digestive system: incomplete. Sustenance derived from patient L. Circulatory system: limited. Independent heart supplies blood to head but 'body' proper gets oxygen from patient L. Lungs: present, tiny, but do not supply air to the secondary system. They are redundant—

LOVE: DAY ONE (1), ABRUPTLY CONCLUDED

BEFORE MOIRA HAD COMPLETED HER DESCRIPTIONS—IN terms she thought Sam would appreciate, what with his choice of a medical career—he appeared to swoon. He looked ill. Then he said he had to leave, though Moira begged him to stay.

"I have to get outta here," he repeated, curtly.

"Have I upset you?" Moira was frantic.

"Of course not."

"Was I too graphic? I just thought—"

"I have an accounting final tomorrow," Sam stammered, and with that he left.

Stunned in the silent room, Moira understood that something had gone awry. Clearly, there were misunderstandings, communication troubles, frayed edges, but *accounting*? Why had Lucinda lied to her about Sam's chosen profession? Or had *Sam* lied? Was Sam Fine to be a practitioner of medical science, or a bean counter? Moira did not mind which, both being honest professions, but why had she been told falsehoods? And by whom?

LOVE: DAY TWO (2)

LUCINDA WOKE, STILL SEATED AT THE table, in a terrible state. The first thing she did was move a shaking hand up gingerly, to touch Moira, whereupon, contacting her sister's body, she began to cry. Then she went and lay on their bed and cried some more while Moira fondled her glass dog figurine and pondered her love, which was wounded already, feeling pains that were not quite pains cracking around her tender heart.

After a few cans of pop and a pack of Winstons, in a foul mood, Lucinda pulled on the Cat in the Hat hat and went outside for a slow perambulation. Moira could smell the heat of the day and her sister's rising, boozy stench. She could see flickers of sunlight but little else. Lucinda walked and walked.

At one point, Moira was sure she heard Lucinda arguing. There was a muffled male voice, and she heard her sister shout what sounded like a furious, "No more stalling!"

But when the sisters got home later and the hat finally came off, Moira asked Lucinda about the encounter and Lucinda, once again, denied anything of the sort had happened, saying only that she had only gone for a walk down by river because she had wanted to be alone. Moira dismissed this lie, entertaining the suspicion that the male had been Sam Fine, and that Lucinda and he were discussing problems in their own failed relationship, problems that she, Moira, had caused. Maybe Sam had been stalling in asking Lucinda to go steady?

For once, in a complicated love life, and shared paramour, the sisters had something in common.

A MYSTERIOUS SCENE (PRECEDED BY AN INTERLUDE ON THE NATURE OF LOVE)

SUFFERING A MAYFLY'S EXISTENCE, DELICATE GOSSAMER (though we pretend these comparisons are not true), love cannot stay fierce and burning. No attempts to fan the embers can keep them blazing. Indeed, they flicker out in an instant. Initiated, wearied, Moira understood this all too well now. Opera had forewarned her: Mascagni's *Isabeau*, anything Greek. *Romeo and Juliet*, of course. Now she felt the sweet pain firsthand. Was Sam ever going to return? He had not said. Uncertainty was a form of agony. There was no way to bond two people together in this life. (A bond of flesh, like the bond between her and her sister, was a sham, a cruel joke.)

Recalling the last conversation she'd had with Sam, Moira could not stop a terrible thought from entering and reentering her mind: What if her love was already torn from her life? What if this torrid affair was over before it had really begun?

However, in the early evening of that wretched second day, there came a knock at the door; Moira wanted to cry out from where she lay fretting at the rear of her sister's head.

Lucinda picked up the big fedora and tugged it on. The big fedora! Of all nights! Sight and smell gone! Hearing gone! *The bitch!*

Moira waited in the darkness, heart pounding. How would Lucinda be taken out of the picture this evening? Was her sister dim enough to fall for the same trick two nights in a row? Was Sam even prepared to attempt it?

After opening the door, Lucinda moved about the apartment restlessly, pent-up, pacing. Now Moira had doubts that it had been Sam Fine at the door. Who else could it have been? Moira was unsure of anything. Was that a faint male voice? It seemed insistent at times. Did her sister yell the word "coward"?

Once again, she felt Lucinda drinking heavily, head tilted back. Guzzling straight from the bottle this time.

Abruptly, Lucinda slammed the bottle down and dropped to her knees. Moira thought maybe she had fallen, or that she was going to vomit, but after a moment her sister's head moved backward and forward, backward and forward, like a terrible ride at some 'amusement' park, as if Lucinda were nodding in time to an aggressive tune Moira couldn't hear. During these motions, a hand (Sam's? was that Sam's firm hand?) twice grasped Moira's body briefly yet roughly, fingers caught in Lucinda's hair, pulling her forward before releasing her.

When Lucinda stopped the odd motions, she coughed for a while, spat (on the floor!?), and went to lie on their bed. Under the hat Moira was frantic. *What* was going on? Whoever was in the room with them came and sat on the mattress. Then they, too, reposed.

For a long period, only the rising and falling of Lucinda's breathing. Moira waited but the fedora was never lifted off. Very carefully, she began to work the hat off herself. Lucinda did not stop her. The fedora was tight, removing it was difficult, but she had accomplished this feat several times in the past when Lucinda had fallen asleep without getting undressed, and Moira suspected this was the case tonight.

Soon the hat rolled off the bed onto the floor.

On her back, snoring, clothes in disarray, Lucinda lay. She stank of booze.

Next to her, Sam Fine sprawled in a similarly dishevelled state.

THE UNDERSTANDING

GETTING PAST THE INITIAL CONFUSION, MOIRA deliberated, putting the pieces together of a working theory:

Sam had arrived, after much soul-searching, with intentions to tell Lucinda of the love he felt for Moira. The previous night he had realized it, following his talk with Moira, and had abruptly left when he found himself unable to deal with the intensity of his emotions.

Upon arrival, he had promptly confessed; Lucinda, listening, paced.

Tormented, they argued, and consumed an abundance of alcoholic beverages.

When Lucinda had heard enough and was being torn asunder by despair, she had dropped to her knees, shaking her head to negate the confession. During this pathetic display—in an attempt to comfort her, or maybe even to keep her at bay—Sam had felt the need to physically hold Lucinda's head; distraught himself, and somewhat tipsy, Sam had momentarily forgotten Moira's unfortunate place of residence and gripped her slight body, releasing it only when he realized it was his true love he held.

Lucinda had thrown herself onto the bed.

Following, Sam Fine tried to comfort her, to let her down easy.

Their clothes, naturally, became disarrayed during the ensuing debacle.

Exhausted by emotions and whiskey, they both fell asleep.

Now Lucinda drooled and Sam (dreaming of Moira?) smiled in his sleep. How hard it must have been for him to confront Lucinda and tell her the truth. To confess his love, his new, delicate love.

"My sweetness, my sweetness," Moira breathed, feeling much better. "We will be united soon."

And, with a tear in her eye, she drove her shard of mirror deep into her lover's jugular, pulling laterally with all the might of her one tiny arm, trying vainly to turn her face away from the erupting geyser of Fine Sam Fine's hot and pumping blood as it sprayed high into the room.

CURTAIN

THE IDEA, IN KEEPING WITH THE greatest operatic stories of all, was to expire together, on that mattress, life-forces mingling, souls forever as one;

Lucinda messed that up by rolling over (one arm outflung to slap against Sam's still chest), twisting Moira quickly in such a way that Moira dropped the shard of mirror. She tried to reach for it but Lucinda sat up suddenly, gagging as if there were something caught in her throat. Desperate, Moira swiped up her knitting needles from their recess in the headboard—the only thing she could reach. She *had* to die embracing Sam! That was the only way to seal romance forever, to keep love fierce and burning.

But Lucinda was heading toward the bathroom, stumbling across the carpet, leaving Moira to watch Sam's cooling body recede.

In one hand, she saw, he grasped a *knife!*

Had his plan been the same, to seal their love with eternity's kiss? Moira's heart struggled to soar!

And on the bedside table were open medical journals, vials, and a . . . a garbage bag?

Lucinda washed her face, gargled, spat into the sink. Moira frantically told herself that when her sister went back into the main room she would see Sam's body and surely run to his side. Then, as Lucinda bent over him, Moira could grab the mirror shard and finally kill herself, their blood commingling, for all eternity. All would be as it should be, as it is at the end of the greatest love stories.

Heading back to the bedroom, Lucinda rubbed her eyes and mumbled, "What are you waiting for, you loser. You don't have the guts to do this? You gonna stall another night? Don't expect another blow—"

She stopped. Halfway across the room. "Oh my God," she screamed. "Not tonight! Not tonight! You were going to, you were going to . . . Little *freak!*"

Her tone had risen to a relentless shriek.

Distraught beyond all reason herself—Moira was only trying to stop the vibrations from shattering her body and frail sanity—she had to *think,* to regroup, to *plan*—she plunged the knitting needles easily into her sister's soft temple. Lucinda stopped screaming but didn't topple onto the bed, like Moira had hoped. Her sister stood very still. Then she said, "Chocolate. Mommy? Want to see my triangle? The sun is *hot.* Four plus four plus four plus four is shitshit*shit*," and turned, without another word, to flee the apartment.

Moira caught one last glimpse of Fine Sam Fine's body before Lucinda pounded mindlessly down the stairs and galloped outside, past the lilac tree, past the dead-end, hair streaming out, plunging with Moira, who was weeping now, atop her head, beyond the last developments of town and into the dark night.

GLASSRUNNER

THE WIND FOUND HER DAYDREAMING ON the leeward side of a drumlin and screamed triumph around the burnished old rock, whirling in mocking eddies there before racing over the glass beach. Now gusts thrummed up through the runner she lay on, up through her breastbone and braced knees and knuckles tight on the brakes, shaking her loose. Her teeth rattled. The wind had torn apart her thoughts and demolished the frail image she tried to nurture.

Through the distorting patina of scratches on her goggles, endless obsidian glistened. She blinked away tears and squinted directly into the glare. Inland, other rock outcroppings, other drumlins, scattered the petrified beach, their smooth shapes half-sunken.

She waited for the pilot.

Gripping the handles tight, she wriggled her body farther down into the sled—spikes on the toes of her boots grinding the glass—and braced herself against the renewed buffets that howled again and plucked at her.

The pilot, meanwhile, on his hands and knees, pressed up against the drumlin, puked.

She could hear the coughing and wet hacking but did not look at him. Tiny flecks of the pilot's blood dotted the runner's windshield. She was grateful that the wind, at least, drowned out the worst of the man's retching.

When he had finished, for now, the pilot crawled back into his place at the front of the runner, flopping down heavily. Attaching his belts with shaking hands, he glanced back at her, weakly waving the lichen satchel in her direction, exposed leather of his face wrinkled into an unconvincing grin. Like herself, the pilot was covered in rags and fragments of old plastic sheets, in ersatz spikes and goggles and folded pads of fabric. She saw the blood gleam red between his gums. The pilot mouthed, *okay, girlie,* and she pushed violently outwards, so disgusted, releasing the brake handles until the runner's sail snapped taut and they were clear of the drumlin and off, hissing quicker and quicker across the glass beach, flecks arcing brilliantly behind them like twin tails.

Just that morning, she had turned fourteen. Only she knew of the occasion. She had kept track of the days. And now she bore the unwanted legacies of being both the youngest person and the only woman in the settlement. There were twelve men living there, including the pilot, and her father, all of them ancient. She cooked breakfast for them. She cleaned their filthy bedrolls. She watched them slowly kill themselves.

Were the men an entirely different species from her, a race of withered beasts, aged by the wind and the glass-dust and by the lichen they consumed? Their minds were enfeebled, and their bodies—under the scavenged coverings—dried and awfully cracked. In an experiment gone horribly wrong, the eve of her birthday, groping behind the windwall with one of the men, whose skin was like parchment, she had proven to herself once and for all that the men were truly incompatible with her in the most basic of ways. The memory made her cry. She had no future with them. They were crumbling, incontinent, impotent.

Once, these sorties were a source of relative peace for her, but no longer could she build castles in the air. The wind always found her now, ruined her dreams, and always brought her back.

OVER THE PILOT'S SAGGING SHOULDERS, SHE caught glimpses of the trembling driftwood and tin huts of the settlement, coming suddenly closer, breaking the smooth seam of the horizon. The huts scratched at the white sky in an attempt to catch hold, be scoured from the glass beach forever. Pulling up hard, she turned the runner 'cross wind, to slow it—the sled groaned in protest, dust spraying across her and the pilot as the blades under them ground the obsidian. Steel toe spikes gouged: the sled tacked, and the settlement swung fully into sight, very close now, fingers of sunlight glaring between its dilapidated structures.

Two other small runners, already parked, and a group of huddling men— four of them—crouched behind the windwall. The men were passing a rag amongst themselves. She could smell their rot already and her stomach clenched. She did not look at their faces.

The pilot stowed the sail. Braking with all her might, so that their runner nestled close to the other two, she brought it to a halt.

Still lying flat, as the pilot rolled off, she used her spikes to bring the runner behind the windwall. There she parked it, and tethered it.

Someone took the satchel from the pilot. He said something that strong gusts of wind snatched from his dry lips.

Someone else slapped her on the ass.

The wind howled laughter.

LONG AGO—BEFORE SHE WAS BORN—THE SETTLEMENT had been a cluster of robust buildings and the handful of people living there ambitious, rebellious pioneers. There had been less wind then. Her mother had come from another place, a city on the distant coast, peddling vegetable seeds and the knowledge to grow them. The population of the settlement had been close to forty— twenty-odd men, seven women, and six children—all braving the frequent storms and the isolated glass beach town to be self-sufficient, free of restricting laws and politics, far from stifling economies and mores and judgements.

Her mother had stayed, first for one night—intrigued by the remote commune, amused by these outlaws and their ideals, and by the lichen they all chewed—but her stay stretched to a week, and then a year, sleeping with her father, a handsome young man then, in his bedroll (and with others, she'd heard whispered), until her mother became as firmly anchored in the lichen's mire as the rest of the adults living there, trapped, soon enough, by addiction, and an unwanted pregnancy.

Her parents' faces grew slack, their eyes glazed, glassy when they turned their gaze upon her. She knew only the feel of their hands hard and callused on her skin. Affection and eagerness was lost, wit and laughter blown away.

Shortly after she learned to walk, a tempest came, ripping buildings from around her and taking the other children, her mother, and the rest of the women from her life. But by then she had already turned away, clambering the parapets and towers of the refuges she'd construct inside her mind.

THE MEN SAT AROUND A TINY fire in one of the remaining huts, sucking lichen from rags, muttering and staring at the flames. She huddled in a dark corner, knees under her chin, as the wind whipped around the wood and tin and sheet metal, trying to get at her. She also listened to the inconstant rambling of the men as they spoke of the distant cites they had fled, of how good these drugs were, of old storms and distorted, deluded wonders in their precious, broken community. The men could talk this nonsense for hours, all at once, when they got truly high, blathering and chuckling and finally spitting up bloody hawks to crackle in the flames. From where she sat, she saw their eyes glisten red as if reflective chips of the beach had been placed in their sunken orbits. Wind and the lichen scoured clean their hearts. Glass dust sliced through their veins. She sat for a long time, trying to imagine a nice place, but that was impossible to maintain now, as she kept thinking instead about the awful men, and being groped by their slow, dry hands, returning again and again to the harsh reality of the ruined hut when her father called out for another rag in his dead voice.

WHAT LITTLE SHE KNEW ABOUT THE rest of the world and the cities beyond the glass beach—and the people living there—she had gleaned from the drugged conversations of the men and from the occasional visitor who came by to trade, or buy lichen, but those visions had once been as vivid as if she herself had travelled, to the ocean even, where she could taste the thick, salty air and gaze at exotic, walled cities dotting the coastline of her imagination. Fortresses blossomed throughout her childhood to take on wonderful proportions, and she went to these as often as she could, crafting tall, twisting spires and majestic courtyards, walking narrow cobbled streets past vibrant marketplaces. She saw the faces of hundreds of people living there, some just like her, some like her parents must have once been, before she was born, or even like the furtive, foreign young men that came, at times, to the settlement now. She splashed brilliant colours over the walls of her city and smelled the open-air grilles, her mouth watering with imagined foods. On her streets, skin tingling, she was caressed by incredible fabrics, by soft skin, and by still, quiet air.

Every night she would sit in the hut and listen to the men, drifting, her eyes closed, trying to uncover nuggets of truth, trying to add to her dream cities stone by stone, street by street, cherishing the delicate images she had managed to form.

After the men were exhausted and their cold eyes glazed, she felt a sadness spreading inside her like none she had ever known before. A desolation. She crept outside and stood behind the windwall, breathing deeply and slowly while the wind's howl rose to a banshee all around. In just a few hours, the men would start to rouse, barking for their food, puking up bloody chunks, snorting back mucus—

The obsidian was like spilled oil, to every horizon, merging with the darker sky. The moon and its reflection mocked her as wind whipped and tore away the tears trickling down her cheeks.

Children from her past, her mother, and the other women: they had been the lucky ones, she thought, and she wondered where the wind had taken—

Cleaving the night, a pale glassrunner quietly slid past; her breath was taken away. Frozen in place, she watched the runner come to a stop on the far side of the settlement. She knew it had come from the city. She imagined the smooth-skinned pilots and smelled the spices they had brought, heard their accents, felt their strong touch. Had they come to bring food, or wood, or maybe perfume to trade? What secrets could they reveal before climbing back into their ghost runner and knifing back out forever into the dark?

Her heart yearned.

Sails lowered, the craft quivered in the wind.

She turned her face to peer through a chink in the tin wall of the nearest hut, making out the flickering of the mens' fire and the dull glint of their half-closed, inhuman eyes. She frowned. Stepping gingerly out from behind the windwall, struggling against the sudden blasts, she took a few steps toward the pale runner.

Later, when the men awoke, long after the sun had risen and was pounding their battered shelters, they were hungry, hung-over, strung-out and sick, puking and sputtering, and they called out to her for help. The pilot and the other men yelled hoarsely for the girl, coughing, spitting up blood. Her father staggered around the tiny settlement, yelling, *girlie, girlie, girlie?*

But the only answer was the mournful wind.

Out On the Photon Highway

ASPUTCIA HAD BEEN GONE FROM THE ice-moon for several weeks, working on a new poem, but beauty and colours and the mysteries of the universe quite literally took her breath away; her lungs were nearly drained. Photosynthesis could not keep up with the amount of oxygen she used maneuvering and seeking inspiration.

And her stomach grumbled.

Detecting the curve of Callisto now, set in fiery relief against the brilliance of the photon highway streaming past, Asputcia reserved the reflective side of her sails and began the long process of slowing down. Collected by the area of boron she had exposed, kelvins of energy channelled down the length of her body to her feet, where twenty metres of trailing cables radiated it into the chill of space. Letting the power that had leaked from the charged cables react to the electromagnetic field of Jupiter and tug at her, she changed trajectory.

Her receivers picked up The Diner's steady beacon. She headed toward it but did not reply, sure that her brother would be somewhere close, scanning angrily for traces of her signal.

If it were at all possible, Asputcia would spread her hands to their fullest, letting light fill the webs between her fingers, and head into the photon highway forever. The song of deep space was a lullaby to her. Certainly not duty, nor affection for The Diner, nor even love for her devoted-if-misguided brother made her return time and again to the dead moon to which the three of them had been assigned: it was hunger, and the keening sensation of breathlessness, ancient physical binds left to her by ancestors she could barely remember, that tethered her to her dreary post.

CAREFULLY CLOSING HER FISTS, ASPUTCIA SWEPT her arms back as she neared The Diner. In her imaging monitors, she watched the orbital—locked in perihelion over Callisto—discover her approach; rotating to face her, gleaming sunlight. The Diner opened an entire side. Releasing a burst of methane from her posterior vent, Asputcia drifted into the docking bay. She was caught by the shoulders and gently pulled, head first, into a mass of thick gel.

Your brother's frantic, The Diner said as a thousand workers swept over Asputcia's skin, coaxing open pores, cleaning her, scrubbing her. *There was a signal of some kind from the inner colonies while you were gone.*

The inner colonies? Asputcia was surprised. *I thought they'd forgotten all about us. What did it say?*

I wasn't listening, The Diner admitted, *but it must've been important to Hespatus. He said something about court-martials. He's docked twice looking for you, asking questions. Demanding, really. He's quite upset.*

Did you tell him where I was? Asputcia felt her lungs fill with fresh oxygen; the rush was like adrenaline, clearing her mind.

Are you kidding? You know how he feels about you and your excursions. The Diner drained Asputcia's body of excess waste. Not all of it could be reused and so was sent, frozen, to drift about the orbital's squat body. *Did you write a new poem, at least?*

Yes, Asputcia said. *Almost finished. Listen:*

> *This life, hard light*
> *Breaks*
> *Mercury on my skin*
> *This sine, cold wave*
> *The touch*
> *Breaks—*

A squeal of angry feedback overrode her recital.

Shit, The Diner said. *Here comes Hespatus.*

Pushing out from the bay, Asputcia executed a slow turn. The gel that clung to her skin detached itself and The Diner's manipulators reached out quickly to gather it back, draw it into the safe, symbiotic fold.

Against the white sphere of Callisto, like a growing black hole, the webwork of boron between Hespatus's fingers was all Asputcia could detect of her brother's body. Trailing behind him, creating a nimbus, his cables were blazing spent energy, a brilliant red in her infra-scanners.

Asputcia! His transmission was loud and urgent. *Where have you been?*

My brother, Asputcia sent, *you wouldn't believe the sights I've seen.*

Hespatus pulled alongside, a few kilometres distant, using his posterior vent to slow his progress. *It's over,* he said curtly.

What is?

The assignment. Superiors have called us back.

For a long moment Asputcia was unable to communicate. Almost easy for her to forget there had ever been an assignment. Neither she nor Hespatus had detected a thing on Callisto since their posting, no life of any kind, no movement other than cold winds and blown dust and tiny meteorites forever pounding the moon's glacial surface.

They had not heard anything from the people that had sent them here in over four hundred years.

You would've known if you'd been doing your job, Hespatus said. *Never strayed from the right channel. I was ready to leave you behind, report you dead. I should have filed an official comm when you first showed signs of your rogue tendencies.*

Rogue tendencies? Asputcia relayed a signal that conveyed her contempt. *How long could you expect me to watch that damn ice without going mad? What was the purpose of it all?*

Asputcia, we had a duty here. Don't you realize we could both face demotion? Or even dismissal! I can't believe we're cut from the same DNA. You should've been proud to serve—

But Asputcia was no longer interpreting the messages her brother sent; her imagination had begun to soar. She was thinking about the journey to the inner planets, and the people living there, at the command bases. She even tried to recall her childhood in the corrals of Mars, but memories of her earlier life were like ghosts. Nonetheless, the ideas of impending change, now that she considered them, thrilled her. She would go with Hespatus, but not out of any sense of the duty he felt; she would make the trip inwards because she longed for adventure, and was curious to see those little creatures again, the ones Hespatus called their *superiors*.

BEFORE LEAVING, ASPUTCIA DOCKED AT THE Diner once more, to say her farewells.

Oh, Diner, she said. *We're really going inwards!*

The Diner made a sighing noise. *I worry about you, dearest Asputcia. They're original humans, you know, on the inner planets. They're not like you and me.*

Of course they are, Asputcia answered, though in truth she remembered very little about the people who had raised her. *Don't be foolish. They may be the basis of our ancestry, in the original form, but that doesn't make them gods. They're nothing to be feared.*

The Diner was silent for a long time.

We'll be back soon. Asputcia wanted to reassure The Diner, for she could tell how upset it was. *We'll visit you. Where else will we get our food and breath from? You're my only friend.* But as she spoke she was picturing the sights she might detect when she reached the command base. In all of her journeying, she had never considered going inwards, but now the concept burned stronger and stronger within her.

Asputcia, my dearest Asputcia, I'll miss your poems. They give me such joy, if you can believe that.

Thank you, Asputcia said, touched. *Now, Hespatus is waiting for me. You know how he gets.*

She backed out of the gel and spread her sails; it was time to go.

THE PHOTON HIGHWAY WAS A SERIES of wide, interwoven beams of light that emanated from mirrored satellites ringing the sun, stretching out past the inner planets, past Jupiter, until they eventually lost momentum somewhere near infinity. Even with joints locked, spines rigid, and skin hardened to maximum Rockwell-C, Asputcia and Hespatus had to regulate their acceleration when they sailed it. Boron webs extended to a full seventy metres across, the only limit to the speed the siblings could attain was the velocity of light photons themselves. But long before they reached that speed they would black out, organs crushed from the g-forces of accelerating. So Asputcia, following several hundred kilometres behind Hespatus, tacked gently back and forth across the highway, furling her sails regularly to lose speed, cables blazing away accumulated kelvins.

The command post that had signalled was at Tharsis Bulge, on Mars; the trip inwards would take nine standard days, a little less if they came close enough to Venus to use its gravitational pull, as Hespatus calculated they would.

Over the first two days, Hespatus reminded Asputcia endlessly about duty: *Do nothing stupid when we get there*, he warned her. *Don't humiliate me in front of our superiors. Show some respect for once.*

Eagerly sailing, and lost in the creation of a new poem, Asputcia paid little attention. But when Hespatus continued to lecture her about the anarchy that would prevail if everyone gave in to free will, and about indulgence of selfish behaviors, Asputcia was forced to close her channels in order to hear herself think.

The remainder of the journey to Mars was mostly a disappointment for Asputcia, ruined by her anger at Hespatus's lack of understanding and by the wonders she knew she had missed by shutting down her communication systems.

THE TRAJECTORY THAT HESPATUS HAD PLANNED brought them out of the highway as Mars was moving across the red face of the ancient sun. When the planet nearly filled her imaging monitors, Asputcia changed the reflective side of her sails—as Hespatus did, a distant silhouette—and began the deceleration that would bring her to the docking satellites locked in geostasis over the Tharsis Bulge base.

Presuming her brother to be too preoccupied with docking and the swellings of pride to continue with his boring lectures, Asputcia opened her frequencies and searched the proximity of space she drifted in. She could sense immediately that command's orbitals were not at all like The Diner. She scanned them thoroughly: if the orbitals were indeed functioning, it seemed they were doing so on a level she had never encountered before.

Welcome, they said flatly. *Link up here. Link up here.*

She watched Hespatus do as he was told: with a short burst of methane, he moved forward into the nearest docking bay.

Intrigued by these odd satellites, yet not trusting their cold stillness, Asputcia was careful to stay clear of the reaching interfaces.

When she detected movement coming toward her from Mars, she infrascanned between the base and herself, made out two minuscule forms, a pair of slight heat traces coming closer. It took her a second to realize what these shapes were, but, registering them, she recalled others from her childhood, such small things, tending to her in the corral where she'd been born. And she recalled their odd vessels, constructions almost as large as herself they lived inside of, in order to survive the vacuum of space. Difficult for Asputcia, as she watched the approach of these two original humans, to imagine how the insubstantial gnats could have constructed an empire and colonized the glorious universe, let alone be the basis for her very own DNA.

Broadening her channels, she cycled through her range of frequencies and picked up signals coming from the forms growing quickly in her imaging monitors.

—were they thinking? What monstrosities they bred. Look at the size of them!

—They were possessed. They devised a thousand and loosed them across the galaxy, to watch for enemies that never existed. We'll free the poor souls trapped within.

It took a moment for Asputcia to translate what she had picked up, another to signal a warning to her brother, but he did not respond. On the other side of the satellite, held tight by the orbital's jaws, he remained silent. Asputcia froze. She wanted to breathe, but dared not to. Her heart pumped once; a long slow throb that shook her entire body. She watched the two originals swing around level with herself, and then dart, zigzagging over to where her brother was moored.

—Did you hear something?

—No, but I'll be glad when this is all over. These infernal monsters terrify me.

Asputcia remained motionless. She could still pick up the weak signals of the humans coming from the far side of the satellite. Hespatus had not yet responded. There was absolutely no energy radiating from his cables. Millions of kelvins were streaming from her own; the trip from Callisto had energized them to near capacity. Impossible that her brother's energy should be gone, if he was still functioning. Which meant the humans had done something to Hespatus, taken his power—

His distant scream, a disembodied sound she had never heard before, tore into her like a blast of light, opened her body, flayed her.

Hespatus! she cried.

No answer, only the clicking of solar winds through her receivers.

Then, quietly, on a frequency at the bottom of her range, she heard Hespatus lament: *Asputcia, I have made a horrible mistake.*

Asputcia called out his name again, just as quietly, but Hespatus did not seem to hear her.

They've stolen my thoughts, he said. *And taken the sails from my fingers. Wherever I am, I can see my lifeless flesh, laid out in this dark cave. They've ruined me. I can't bear to know they've done this to you, too, sister. You were so filled with life.*

Releasing a short hiss of gas from her posterior vent, Asputcia backed up slowly. She detected movement; the original humans were rounding the orbital's curved side, coming toward her.

This one's broken free, one of them transmitted, a tone of urgency in its signal. *How're we going to redock?*

Asputcia could hear Hespatus's weak message from the bay where he was being held, and to her receivers it sounded like sobbing. The agony of betrayal in her brother's tone was heart-wrenching. He had devoted his life to duty, and, in appreciation, his beloved superiors had emptied his body of life the same way The Diner would empty a carbon dioxide-filled lung.

The two small forms were near her head now. She scanned them in her imaging monitors. The humans appeared to be attaching a cable to her dorsal receiver. Everything about these creatures, Asputcia realized, was enigmatic to her. She could not defend herself, could manipulate nothing here, in this alien setting. She and her brother should never have come. She ached to be out in the interstellar reaches, circling Jupiter or chasing Ganymede, or even scanning the snowy storms on dead Callisto.

She was pulled toward the orbital. The original humans had maneuvered over to a platform there and were drawing her in.

No! Asputcia shouted, and with another short burst from her posterior vent jetted backward, turning. One of the originals came with her, tethered to her back by the cable he had attached.

Help! his signal blared.

Asputcia yelled, *What have you done to Hespatus?*

Take it easy, now, the human answered. *We've . . . downloaded him into . . . wetware. We're taking him to the chapel, to grant him peace, once he has received the sign of our Lord. We're here to save you.*

Hespatus's moan filled Asputcia's channels. She knew then, by his forlorn tone, that her brother was as good as dead.

Momentum brought her through a long, slow roll. The original human was still trailing from her, miniature limbs flailing.

Asputcia's charged cables struck the orbital. As she was blasted away, the orbital blossomed behind her into a growing, blue-veined ruin, and Hespatus fell mercifully silent, free now from his torment.

Waves of energy from the explosion sent Asputcia tumbling through the photon highway, end over end.

GRADUALLY SHE WAS ABLE TO STRAIGHTEN, angling her hands in front of her, and turn in a long arc between Mars and the sun. She was not damaged. Her oxygen levels stabilized. With thoughts of vengeance for her brother's death, Asputcia raged. She scanned the sandy red planet as she circled it, saw with horror the corpses of others like herself, discarded, clustered together in blood-coloured sunlight. Like Hespatus, they had all been emptied of life.

She swung around Mars, using its gravity to pull her. The satellite she had destroyed was gutted in space before her. Unanswered signals were being sent madly from the base below. Asputcia went through her frequencies, heard the originals' plans of attack. Should she crash into the Tharsis Bulge, she wondered, in her fury, rupturing the flimsy base there, killing all the original humans and herself, too?

No, she decided. There had been enough death.

She opened her sails to leave this place.

Then she heard her brother's voice, on a frequency she had never used before, calling to her from very close.

ASPUTCIA LET THE PHOTON STREAM PUSH her along without attempting to move her sails or change the tilt of her cables. She was nearly out of oxygen. Carbon dioxide was not being recycled fast enough and portions of the journey outwards were lost to her in a dark haze.

But she finally made it back to Callisto, exhausted, and thrust herself into The Diner's waiting maw.

Asputcia, my darling! You've come back. Tell me all about the inner planets.

As her skin was cleaned and her lungs and stomach filled, Asputcia was too overwhelmed with emotion to respond.

Where's your brother?

With me, Asputcia finally managed to say. *Hespatus was . . . transformed by the original humans. I found him, or at least I found his thoughts, drifting through space, locked in a tiny shell. I gathered him up and . . . He's with me now. Inside me. There were mysteries there, in the colonies, which I'll never begin to understand. Horrors . . .*

Shuddering, Asputcia could not finish her story, but instead recited to The Diner a dirge she'd composed about her brother's unswerving devotion.

The Diner was quiet for a long time after, ruminating on Asputcia's words. Then it asked, *And what other wonders have you brought with you? What is that strange thing tied to your back?*

WITH THE DINER'S HELP—ITS GEL LINKED together to form a hooklike appendage—she rid herself of her unwanted passenger.

Asputcia and her brother had come up with a plan.

They fused the body of dead human to The Diner. Using the dorsal vents still strapped to the tiny corpse as a power source, the orbital was able to maneuver awkwardly. Then, tethered to Asputcia, it broke away from

Callisto's pull for the first time in centuries, bouncing off her rib cage as it tried to control the newfound motion.

I've got it, I've got it! The Diner said excitedly, dropping back. *Oh, Asputcia, my darling Asputcia, we can leave this place together!*

Trailing her now, The Diner bathed in the heat of her cables.

Drawing a deep breath, Asputcia opened her sails. She could feel Hespatus's wonderment as he saw the universe through her sensors. When she entered the photon highway and moved outwards, accelerating slowly into deep space, toward infinity, she recited her most joyous poem.

The New Father

BEYOND THE GARDENER'S REACH, WHERE THE grounds became too rocky to trim the lawn evenly, grass grew tall and thick. There were paths through this area James and his older brothers before him had worn, some winding their way to a small stream that could be easily crossed, others meandering between the ginkgos and yews and date trees until they opened upon a series of quiet, sun-filled clearings.

In one of the larger glades, a statue of a man, stone face turned skyward, his expression one of wonder, as if he could see something miraculous in the clouds. On one shoulder, a stone squirrel perched. There was a bird on the other, forever about to take flight. The man's hands were extended, palms up, fingers splayed.

When the last of James's brothers had gone off to school, leaving him alone and bored on their father's estate, he would often find himself talking to the statue.

"Do you have any brothers?" he'd ask, accustomed now to the silence of the clearing's occupant. "I have seven, but I only met three of them. They don't live here anymore. Do you remember when they first brought me to visit you? They used to play with me, but now they're gone. Now it's only me and father. And the staff, of course. They're not much fun."

The stone man would stare up into the sky, his mouth open wide. He, too, was not much company.

Three years had passed since Richard left for college. Three long years. And father was always too busy for games, sometimes working for days on end, locked in his room, coming out only for a quick meal and a few grunted reprimands. He certainly did not like to be disturbed by such minor things as what James had to say. Father was a man with short patience, a man who could yell impossibly loud when he was angry, a man who would shake his fists and throw dishes at the walls that the cleaners had to sweep up. In some ways, James didn't mind his absence.

Now that James was older—almost ten—he tried to converse less with the statue. Instead, he sat at its sun-warmed feet and daydreamed. He thought a lot about school, and what it would be like to finally leave his father's house. His brothers sent such fascinating messages. They had seen so much, learned so much about the world since they'd left. James wanted to learn these things, too. He wanted to ride in a streetcar down the hills of San Francisco, toward the ocean, or sing in an opera, like Sebastian. He wanted to skim methane gas from the atmospheres of far-away planets and bring it back to Earth, for fuel, like Richard had done for the past two summers. James wanted to meet other people.

"JAMES!"

Moving quietly through the foliage and tall grass, the caretaker approached. James could see the sun glinting off steel-plated skin. He did not respond, but the caretaker always knew where James was and homed in on him without effort.

Coming into the clearing, the caretaker made its way over on long, long legs to where James sat.

"Hello, young Master," the caretaker said, head bobbing and swivelling. "A fine day, don't you think? Very little humidity. I like that; good for my joints. How are you?"

"It's not dinner time." James scowled. "What do you want?"

"Ah," the caretaker replied. "Your father, you see, has a surprise. He sent me to get you."

James frowned, reluctant to reveal the rush of excitement he felt. "What is it?"

"I'm not permitted to tell you."

Getting to his feet, James brushed himself off. "Well, give me a hint."

"I think your father would like to tell you the news himself."

"What if I want to stay here?" But James knew that was impossible.

"Come," said the caretaker. "Climb on my back."

James hoisted himself onto the caretaker's saddle and held tight. Soon they were trotting out of the clearing and through the grass, picking up speed. A thin, diaphanous shield wrapped around James to protect him from the branches whipping past. *A secret*, James thought. *At last, something new!*

They came out onto the trimmed lawn in a flurry of leaves and shorn grass. In the distance, at the crest of a gentle, green hill, the sprawling white building where James and his father lived nearly gleamed in the brilliant sunlight. A fountain in front sparkled. The caretaker increased speed further still, dropping lower and widening to change his centre of gravity, legs barely touching the ground. Wind roared through James's hair. From somewhere distant came the muffled sound of the gardener's rotors as he clipped a hedge, the only other sound on this otherwise quiet day.

FATHER WAITED IN THE STUDY, STANDING by the fireplace, his back toward them when they entered. James leapt off the caretaker and stood at attention.

"Sir," he said. "Here I am."

Father did not answer, as if deep in thought. Finally, though, just as James was about to speak again, he turned.

"How are you, son?"

James hadn't seen his father for almost a week; he was taken aback by the shadows around his father's eyes and the stubble that darkened his father's chin.

"Uh, fine, sir."

Father nodded. "Son," he said, "do you consider yourself lonely?"

"Pardon me, sir? Lonely? Well . . ." James considered telling the truth. But he said, "I have the caretaker as a friend."

"A machine?" His father smiled. "What sort of friend is that?"

At James's side, the caretaker said nothing.

"Well, sir, it's just that—"

"I know you're lonely, boy. This is a big house for just the two of us, don't you think?"

Unaccustomed to this mood in his father, James didn't know what to say.

"Yes, sir," was all he could manage. "I guess it is."

Suddenly, disconcertingly, his father grinned. "Let's dispense with these formalities, shall we, James?"

"All right, sir."

"Son, I would like you to meet your new brother."

Before James could react, from behind the heavy curtain that hung against the east wall of the study stepped a boy, younger than James by a few years, dressed in shorts and a blazer, like James wore. In his hands, he clenched a cap. He seemed pale, and moved with a sad air.

James stared.

"This is Simon," father said. "He just arrived from mother's house this morning."

"Hello," said Simon.

Like the three brothers James could remember, and like the four he had never met but who still sent files of their adventures at school, Simon looked exactly like him. He had the same almond-shaped eyes, the same high forehead. Their hair was an identical shade of red. Simon, of course, was shorter than James, but James could remember being his new brother's height. Recovering from his shock, somewhat, he reached out and shook Simon's hand.

By the fireplace, father was still grinning. "Go on," he said, "show Simon around. Teach him your games."

"Yes, sir," James replied, letting excitement take over at last. Still holding Simon's hand, he ran from the study, tugging his brother.

The caretaker turned and loped after them.

"I'M AFRAID YOU'RE NOT TO GO back there," said the caretaker.

"Why not?" James was livid; he had his father's temper and angered easily.

"I was told not to let the two of you leave the lawn. Until Simon is a little more accustomed to the grounds. Surely there are games you could play here?"

"There's nothing here, just stupid machines." James had picked up the word his father had used, hoping it would fluster the caretaker, but the caretaker seemed to take no heed.

"What about tag?" the caretaker said. "I can show you how to play that, if you'd like, young Master. If you promise not to exert yourself too much; you know how I worry. Your older brother used to love a rousing game of tag."

"No," James said. "Tag is stupid."

Between them, Simon remained silent; he did not even appear to be listening. Instead, he looked about the lawn, the rock gardens, the clumps of trimmed shrubs, his face shadowed with consternation.

When the gardener flew over their heads, on its way to water the cherry trees, Simon ducked low, whimpering.

James laughed. He suggested they play hide and go seek. The caretaker, or course, was *it*. As the caretaker turned its head to begin the count, James and his brother ran off, across the lawn, to leap over a short stone wall that skirted the goldfish pond. On the small ledge of gravel, between the water and the wall, they crouched. Hide and go seek was a pointless game to play with staff; they could find James, and Simon, presumably, in an instant, at any given time. But the brothers would be indulged and, for a short while at least, they could be alone.

Maybe now James could tell Simon everything he wanted to. He didn't know where to start. Should he begin with what subjects Simon would take in school, or tell him about the statue, and the stream? Or about the exploits of their older brothers? He finally had a living, breathing playmate. Someone who would listen to him, and do what he wanted.

But Simon just stared into the water of the pond, eyes wide, lips moving silently. His skin, in the sunlight, looked gray.

"Hey," James said and, getting no response, he poked at Simon. "What's the matter with you? You're supposed to play with me. Isn't that why you're here?"

Simon looked up slowly. It was as if James was seeing his own reflection in a mirror. But the face looking back at him, though younger, seemed to radiate weariness and concern.

"This pool," Simon whispered.

"What about it? It's for stupid goldfish." James threw a stone into the water and watched as one of the fish went for it, turning away at the last second.

"I remember a pool like this. Yesterday. Being under water . . ."

"Yesterday?" James frowned. "At mother's house? I don't remember a pool there. Did she just have it put in?"

Simon was peering into the water again. His hand, held out over the surface—not quite touching it—trembled. "No. The pool was here, in father's house. In a . . . white room. There were tubes down my arms, and one in my mouth."

"What are you talking about?" James was getting angrier. "You just got here. Mother keeps all of us at her house until we're six."

Simon grabbed James's sleeve. "I remember mother's house, too. She packed me some oranges, mandarins. She cried when she kissed me goodbye. The carriage ride took all night. I slept in the back seat." Simon's voice dropped lower still, barely audible. "But just now, James, I remembered being in a pool, in *this* house. And that was yesterday, too."

The look in Simon's eyes was starting to frighten James. He tried to pull back but could not.

"Father was there. He pulled me up from the water, pulled tubes from my arms. *Another beauty*, he said, as I dried. *Another beauty*."

"From a pool . . . of water?" James frowned. Like the goldfish, fleeting images briefly surfaced in his mind, too quick to leave him with any impression before sinking back to the murky depths they had come from. Sweat broke out on his palms; his fingertips had gone cold, even though sunlight dappled him. He was breathing hard. His chest hurt. The strange story seemed to have disturbed something inside him.

Simon pulled James closer. "Then father took me into another room and sat me down. He asked me how mother was, and how the trip from her house had been."

"The . . . trip?"

"And I said that mother was fine." Simon was near tears. "What do you think it means? What? I can tell you've felt this, too."

James managed to pull away at last. "It means you're crazy," he said loudly. As he stood and backed away from his brother, the caretaker's head appeared suddenly over the wall, startling them both.

"My, my," the caretaker said. "I've just let your father hear what you said, young Master Simon." A thin arm whipped out and pinned Simon's arms to his sides. Simon struggled, but a worker's strength was limitless. "He wants to see both of you, right away."

James tried to clamber over the stone wall but the caretaker lurched toward him, too, grabbing him around the waist and hoisting him high into the air.

FATHER WAS FURIOUS. IN HIS DRESSING gown, he paced the study from wall to wall. "What nonsense," he shouted. "What utter nonsense you were talking. I thought you were old enough to leave your mother's house but I was wrong."

Simon was still being held tight by the caretaker. James stood off to one side, rubbing the bruises on his hips. The caretaker had been none too gentle: it had never been like that before. Something serious was happening. James was terrified of his father's wrath.

"James," his father said, red-faced. "I don't want you to think about what Simon told you. Do you hear me? Simon is ill."

"Yes, sir." James could see sweat beading on his father's forehead. Veins bulged there, and tendons stretched tight at his father's throat.

"I've worked so damned hard to keep you boys out of trouble. Do you know how hard it is to raise nine sons? Have you any idea—"

Father stopped speaking abruptly. His face, for an instant, took on the astonished look of the statue's before he fell forward, clutching at his chest, and crashed down hard, face-first, onto the thick carpet.

"Oh dear," said the caretaker. Holding Simon with one arm, it hurried forward and stood over father's body. "Oh dear."

James said: "Is he alive?"

"He is," replied the caretaker, "but he's had a massive coronary again. That heart of yours, you know, doesn't last forever. I kept telling him to take it easy." The caretaker turned toward James, who had been backing away. "I want you to go to your room, young Master."

"But I want—"

"*Go!*"

When James turned, two squat cleaners stood in the study doorway, blocking his exit. They each took an arm, and led James down the hall. He did not resist.

JAMES WAS SHUT IN HIS ROOM. He sat in the wooden chair by his desk and wondered what was happening. As he toyed with a paperweight, he remembered another time when his father had become indisposed, just a few days before Richard went off to college. Father had recovered then. James had no reason to believe that things would be different this time.

And, despite the warning his father had given him, James found himself recalling what Simon had said, and the sensations the words had aroused. He felt as if he were about to remember a dream that had been lurking, always, in the periphery of his thoughts: the pool, the tubes—

There was a knocking at his door.

James got up, but before he reached the door it burst open and he was grabbed once more by steel arms.

"Young Master," the caretaker said, "I'm afraid things have taken a turn for the worse. Though you're too young, it's time for you to go to school."

BORNE ALOFT, JAMES LOOKED ABOUT, FASCINATION mingling with his fear. He was in a part of the house he'd never been in before, where his father worked. Events were happening too quickly for him to follow. Was he really going off to school? He had tried to ask a few questions but the caretaker was quiet.

He was taken to a large, brightly lit room and thrown roughly onto a bed. As he tried to rise, several writhing thongs caught hold of his arms and legs and held him, pulled him spread-eagled on the mattress.

The caretaker left the room.

Is this part of school? James wondered, but before he had much of a chance to consider his predicament, the caretaker returned, pulling a gurney, upon which his father lay, which was wheeled adjacent to James. He could see that his father was very sick. A mask covered his father's mouth and nose. Under the mask, his breathing was ragged, uneven. A stand attached to the gurney held up a soft bottle dripping solution into his arm.

The caretaker soon had father's clothes off, slicing them with sharp fingers and throwing them to the floor.

James tried to turn away but could not. His heart pounded. As he watched, a compartment opened in the caretaker's chest and a narrow arm extended out, toward father's body. At its end, a tiny saw unfolded and whirred. James fought the bindings on his arms and legs but they only seemed to tighten.

"What are you doing, caretaker?" he asked breathlessly. "What are—"

The revolving blade sank into father's breastbone, whining, making his body shudder. Leaning over the gurney, the caretaker grasped both sides of the cut and, while the saw continued to send out a plume of pink mist, opened father's rib cage. There was a rending, crunching—

Something sharp jabbed James's buttocks. He gasped at the sudden pain. The room and the horror swirled around him, fading. He felt his eyes closing. There was welcome blackness.

A QUIET SOBBING SOUND WOKE HIM. The room around him was dark.

"Young Master?"

"Yes?"

"You're awake?"

"Yes."

"Something terrible has happened."

"Let me up." There was a fumbling; pressure relieved from James's wrists and ankles. He pushed himself onto his elbows; the lights came on. A bloodied sheet covered the gurney where his father had lain. James could see a large, lumpy, unmistakable shape under the sheet. The caretaker stood at the foot of James's bed, making soft, crying sounds. James frowned.

"I warned him so often about his heart," the caretaker said at last. "He knew how weak it was. I told him not to get too excited; you weren't old enough to go to school. At least the others were his size." The caretaker bowed its silver head. "I tried my best. We've been together for two hundred years. Did you know that, James? I don't know what to do now. I don't know what to do."

James got off the bed and walked over to where his father lay. "Is he really dead?"

The caretaker nodded.

"Have you told my mother? She will come and get us."

"Don't be silly," the caretaker said. "She hasn't been around for almost a century. She no longer exists. You were made in your father's image. All of you, without a mother. And you all have the same damned heart."

James felt like he was falling. He put both hands on the gurney to steady himself. His mouth had gone dry. "Call my brothers. Call Richard."

"Richard never made it out of this room. I generated the files you watched, so you would look forward to school. On that bed is where Richard—where all your brothers—got their education."

"Oh," James said, because he did not know what else to say. He could not think straight. Nothing made sense to him. The world he knew receded, crumbling. There was silence for a long, long time.

The caretaker finally ended it. "Look," it said, "I've just accessed procedures." Looking at James, blinking large eyes. "I've consulted your father's last will, which he insisted on filing when I first began to work for him. There are no barristers for several hundred miles, you see. It seems, young Master, that the house and all it contains are now yours. I apologize for my flippant attitude, and for raising my voice."

THEY RODE ON THE CARETAKER'S BACK, whipping it with makeshift crops to make it go faster. The caretaker made horse-noises that were drowned out by Simon's giggling. When the brothers grew tired of this game, James led the caretaker to the statue's clearing, where they would have a picnic.

The caretaker pretended to graze, as he had been told to do.

Simon spread out the blanket.

"Not like that," James said. "Put it in the sun! Don't you know anything?"

Rebuked, Simon moved the blanket into a warmer part of the glade. He seemed to be feeling better after taking the medicine the caretaker had prescribed. He no longer talked about unsettling things.

"Come on, caretaker, set the food out," James said.

"Yes, my young Master."

They ate a lunch of peanut butter sandwiches and washed them down with iced tea. The statue ignored them, as usual, staring up into the blue sky. James scratched the bandage on his arm, where the caretaker had scraped at his skin with a blunt knife, just this morning, in the white room where his father used to work. In the room where James worked now.

"Tell me again why you won't be going to school," Simon said, when they were lying side by side, each chewing on a blade of grass.

James huffed. "I've told you a thousand times. Father has gone on vacation until he gets better. How many times have you seen the file he sent us? Jeez! I'll be staying here to run the house, and to welcome our new brother, when he gets here from mother's house."

"But I'll be going to school, won't I?" Simon asked. "Won't I?"

James tried to control his anger. He was sick of incessant questions. "Of course you'll be going," he shouted. "Of course you will!" He felt his heart pounding and tried to take a deep breath.

"Yes," the caretaker agreed, sighing as he cleaned up the wax paper wrappers the boys had strewn about. "All good sons must go to school."

THE VASSAL

FRAMED IN THE MOUTH OF THE shaft, on the cusp of Iubar's brilliance, the vassal paused: six cretatus hung side by side out there, dangling from the scaffolding that lined the pit's far rim. Above the bodies, which were bleached even whiter by the noontime glare, carrion birds wheeled, restless to taste of flesh that would swiftly kill them.

Watching dumbly, blinking, the vassal's eyes watered as the lifeless forms turned at the end of their ropes. To break his inertia, he clapped big hands together, clearing his palms of rockdust and startling his already jumpy escort.

"Foul beasts," the escort hissed, seeing where the vassal was looking and nudging him with a sharp elbow. "Now move!"

From the pit, innumerable sets of eyes had turned upon the vassal and his escort. Sharp, heavy tools were held poised, in mid-swing.

"I said move! Our ductoris is not accustomed to waiting for the likes of *you*."

The vassal was almost able to imagine that cretatus were carved out of bone, or possibly alabaster. They might even have been composed of some as-yet-unnamed mineral, brought up out of the mines by the vassal's own men, were it not for the wounds, visible, even at this distance, and the way the wings and small legs hung limply; no, the beasts were made of matter much less permanent.

"And don't expect to take that thing any further."

With speed that surprised even himself, the vassal drew his pickaxe from its scabbard and buried the iron tooth so deep into the ground it would later take three slaves an hour to dislodge.

FOUR MEN APPROACHED, BROKEN BY SHIMMERS, drifting across hazy slabs of alternating light and shade—effects of the heat and the aedicule's broad colonnades—so that they appeared insubstantial, otherworldly, flickering slowly in and out of this existence. All were sheathed in formal robes—no flesh visible save for hints of shadowed faces—but the ductoris was unmistakable: a head taller than the vassal (few were); slow, confident gait; great bulk swelling under that garb, ebbing in the shadows and then flaring, almost blinding, in the light. *Unmistakable.*

Trotting behind the group, insinuating in a sudden burst of speed to the fore, and hissing: a chained basilisk, neck frills expanded, clipped wings half-lifted in threat, black claws scrabbling frantic—

A swift kick in the ribs and a yank on the studded leash were rewards for this creature's loyalty.

Locking his hands together behind his back, the vassal lowered his gaze to the hot stones, as the escort—who had actually whimpered aloud at the lizard's lunge—cleared his throat.

"Your eminence, I present to you, up from the mines—from *your* mines—the vassal, as requested. Your eminence."

"*You may go.*"

Crabstepping sideways down the shale embankment, the escort left as quickly as possible.

Now, a mere metre or so away, the ductoris had fallen silent again. Only the rasping breaths of the basilisk, and now the faint sounds of metal on rock from the mines, where operations had resumed, could be heard.

"Vassal."

Lifting his face, narrowing his eyes, still only able to discern fragments of physiognomy in the four: a beard; hinted shapes of a nose; cold glints in staring eyes.

"Do you know," the ductoris rumbled, "why I've called you up from your hole in the ground?"

"To reward me with lands of my own?"

Slowly, a smile spread (which *could* be seen, beneath the hood: a dull gleam of gray); one of the others—a short, rotund man—actually chuckled.

"I have," said the ductoris, "heard oftentimes about your wit. But no, vassal, I am not granting land. You are being transferred."

"Ductoris?"

"No longer will you toil in these mines. No longer will you work for me. I have sold you, vassal. I have sold you."

Beyond the columns of the aedicule, the six dead cretatus could be seen, even from here. They appeared so small. Vultures remained, mere specks, but bolder now, circling lower.

So little shade to hide in, no condensation on nearby rockface to cool the skin. The vassal, dizzy for an instant, shifted. "What is my new task?" His mouth was dry. "Where will I go?"

"Before Iubar starts her descent, you will depart this mine with my associate, to travel to his isle. He has come a long way to meet you. May I present, vassal, Theophilus of Minos."

Another of the men—thin, moving with angular irregularity—stepped forward. When he spoke, it was with an unfamiliar accent. "Your new task," said Theophilus of Minos, "will be to assist me in my studies."

"I handle a whip, a pickaxe, and I dig holes. I can also thrash a man to death who does not obey orders. I can neither read nor write."

"Henceforth," Theophilus of Minos said, waving one bony hand to dismiss these claims, "such skills will not be required. You underestimate yourself. You have good vision? A sharp mind?"

"So I am told."

"And you are *strong*. Look at you. You're *perfect*." There was a pause. "May I ask, vassal, who your father was? A man of note? To whom did he belong?"

"My father? I don't see why you need to know about him."

"Lineage." Theophilus of Minos shrugged. "I mean no offense. I am merely interested in such things."

"Answer the question, vassal," the ductoris said. "We are not here to challenge you."

"I was raised by a relative. An aunt. I never knew my parents."

"Well, I'm sure your father was outstanding, whoever he was: you appear to be everything our exalted friend here has promised. You will prove invaluable, I have no doubt."

"And what will we be studying, Theophilus of Minos?"

"Together, my vassal, we shall solve the riddles of heaven."

NO RAIN HAD LEAKED ONTO THESE mountains for two long seasons. The road leading down from the mine was hard packed and parched, and the wooden wheels of the carts fell heavily into deep ruts, rocking the vehicles from side to side with a force that tossed about passengers and cargo alike; the procession raised such a racket that it would have been loudly announced to the entire countryside had there been anyone lurking in the dry foothills to hear it.

At times, from where he sat in the second-to-last cart, the vassal could see the entire train, a dozen or so carts in all, as they wound the trail, heading to the coast, and thence, apparently, to the Isle of Minos.

Though the lead cart was covered, painted a gaudy orange, and drawn by four massive mesosaurs, it was a modest carriage for a man such as Theophilus of Minos—a man who associated, and could trade personnel, with the likes of the ductoris.

Sharing the flatbed with the vassal were two Mauriorum slaves. From a different mine. Consequently, these black men were not terrified of him. They regarded his face with what appeared to be open suspicion.

In the last cart, drawn by a standard mule team, a dozen guards, each helmeted, clothed in boiled leather, and armed with short swords.

Additional guards rode near the front.

The vassal wondered if Theophilus of Minos feared attack from the hills, or trouble from within the caravan itself.

THERE WERE SEVERAL STOPS THAT FIRST day, primarily to water the huge mesosaurs, whose blood thinned quickly in the heat. Clutching his own jug of water, the vassal passed the time by practicing longer and longer glances at the firmament and open landscape. He had been underground seven years; the expanse did little to ease the feelings of uncertainty roiling in his gut.

At this level above the sea, shale deposits had been replaced by chalk. Otherwise, the landscape appeared much the same as higher ground.

When Iubar's great round eye at last approached the horizon, taking her light away (a common enough sight, presumably, for those that lived aboveground), the caravan reached an area where small trees sprouted from the surrounding scrub. Glimpsed downward, through the empurpled hills, more and more trees could be seen, taller and taller, and the air itself had begun to carry with it the scent of things less arid and stale. These breezes cooled the vassal's sweat.

Clouds were painted on the firmament, veiling Luna's ascent, and he dozed for a moment, but in his vivid dreams he saw those six cretatus, hanging, and he felt their dead gaze wash accusingly over him.

The world grew too dark to journey in. Mesosaurs, temperamental beasts at best, became sluggish now that temperatures were falling, and resumed their sonorous moaning. The caravan stopped once more. Brush was cleared away, several great fires lit. The massive beasts were tethered near the flames, to keep them from falling into seasonal slumbers.

Encamped here and there—basically in any space they could find—huddled both free men and slaves. There was meat, bread, and hard cheese. Presently, Theophilus of Minos himself appeared, accompanied by several of his men, all dressed in informal white robes, to distribute wine.

The vassal sat by himself, his back to a rock. He was given a cup, and though he held it tightly he did not taste of the blood red claret; as a younger man, fondness for wine had caused him nothing but trouble.

He did eat, and heartily.

As men around him fell asleep, the white crescent of Luna's eye at last opened, peeking out from between clouds—

Several large, winged creatures, briefly revealed, passed high over the camp.

Roofs of stone, the vassal silently implored, *close enough to touch, come cover me like a blanket.*

HE REMAINED AWAKE LONG INTO THE night, while others snored, scattered about the waning fires. (There were guards stationed at the perimeter of the camp, but these stood far from where the vassal hunkered.)

As he attempted, for perhaps the tenth time, to lie down and close his eyes, men approached quietly from beyond the glowing embers. One, he saw, was again Theophilus of Minos—inebriated, judging by the man's gait, which was more unsteady than usual. The group stopped, regarding the vassal for some time, whispering among themselves, before the vassal sat up; if the watchers were startled to see he had not been sleeping, this was not revealed.

Leaving his men behind in the gloom, Theophilus of Minos stepped forward, nodding a greeting. "These fires," he said, "should not be allowed to burn out."

"Are you here, personally, to put kindling on them?"

Theophilus of Minos appeared to reconsider what he had been planning to say next, for his lips moved wordlessly before he finally shrugged. "No. I admit it. I came here to observe you. But now . . . Might we talk, vassal? I cannot sleep, either, and my men are little company."

"Certainly," answered the vassal. "After all, I am now yours to command."

After some fumbling in his robes, Theophilus of Minos withdrew a small instrument—a psalterium, of sorts?—and set about adjusting tuning nuts on the neck. He strummed a few chords. Softly, to the vassal's growing bemusement, the man began to play. Despite the preparations, the melody was clumsy, inexpertly performed, and flat.

When Theophilus of Minos finally lowered the odd instrument, ruddy glare from the embers caught off the textured varnish. He waited, expectantly.

The vassal said, "You told me you wished to talk. Your song said nothing to me."

"I do wish to talk." Without waiting for an invitation, the man sat down heavily, cross-legged. "I wish to discuss *music*."

"Music? The heavens? These topics are not my strengths."

"Vassal, answer me this: can you still hear a tune playing?"

"Now? Only fading echoes, thankfully."

"Nothing else? For though my humble song has indeed ended, I wish to know if there remains a harmony, cascading down upon you?"

"I hear nothing but crickets, the fires, and the breeze hissing through the scrub. And your mesosaurs, of course, half-frozen, complaining about the chill."

"Your answer indicates you might be mortal, like the rest of us. Like myself, like my men."

"You suspected otherwise?"

Quiet laughter was the response. "I had been told you could hear rocks, humming in your head. That you were *different*."

"As a young man," the vassal said, "blood pounded hard throughout my body. I heard a lot of things back then. My blood has since settled. I no longer hear such sounds. We are the same, you and I."

"Well, let me tell you, friend, there *is* a song, falling upon us. Yet the ears of mortals, having bathed in this celestial harmony since birth, are deafened to it."

"Who plays this supposed tune?"

"Not who, vassal, but *what*. The musicians of this piece are the heavenly spheres, singing as they circle Terra Firma."

Theophilus of Minos may well have begun speaking a foreign tongue.

"You're skeptical? I understand. Like most people, you subscribe to the idea that our world is as an oyster, suspended in water."

"I told you, I know nothing about these topics."

Again, Theophilus of Minos laughed. "I believe you *do* know about them. At least, a great deal more than you allude to, vassal. But I'll give you the benefit of doubt.

"Scholars, you see, teach us that the world is supported on all sides by water. Water leaks up, through the rocks beneath us—in the form of rivers—and water trickles down, through the upper shell—or firmament—as rain. We are afloat. *Adrift*. Everything you see up there—Iubar, Luna, the many stars—is painted, by the Masters, directly on the firmament, each day and each night.

"But there are those of us who know differently. And we are about to prove it." Theophilus of Minos pointed with the neck of his psalterium. "The eyes of Luna and Iubar are not scribed on the inside of a shell, as scholars would have us believe. What we see are heavenly bodies, circling us. We inhabit a void. The shell, in fact, is *not even there*."

Wanting to grip the ground under him, in case he fell upwards, into the infinity being described, the vassal instead grasped his cup, which leaned where he had left it.

Theophilus of Minos would not relent:

"Not only do Luna and Iubar circle us, but other spheres as well, much farther away, both greater and smaller in size. Now listen to me, vassal. From where we sit to Luna is a full tone—you'll see proof of this when we get back to my observatory. You know about tones? Yes? Good. From Luna to the next closest sphere—which we call Mercury—is an additional semi-tone. From Mercury to the heavenly sphere known as Venus, another semi-tone. And from this final sphere to Iubar herself, a minor third. Do you see? Do you see the pattern of this harmony?"

"No," the vassal said. "I see no patterns." He felt quite ill.

Low flames crackled loudly, rising briefly and gouting sparks. Something huge seemed to sweep across the night.

"The song you claim to be unable to hear is so affirming it would cause tears to spring from your eyes, should you actually hear it." Theophilus of Minos winked, though smoke was thickening and it was getting harder to make out his face. "Mind you, if you did hear the music, and you *were* mortal, all your earthbound problems would soon be resolved, for you would be breathing your last breath. I'm afraid the harmony I speak of is solely for the ears of the Masters, immortals, and dead men, who are ready to be transported from our life of trials to the gods' playground."

"Which did you take me for?" the vassal asked. "Master, immortal, or dead man? For I assure you, Theophilus of Minos, I am none of those." Scratching himself under his tunic, the vassal suddenly said, "I also have a question for you."

Though his men reacted, the philosopher leaned forward, anticipating, perhaps, a nibble from some newly lured fish, but the vassal's question concerned nothing about the harmony of heavenly spheres:

"Why," he said, "did the ductoris kill and hang the cretatum?"

Theophilus of Minos let his mouth fall open. Stymied, he looked over his shoulder, toward his men, but they no longer appeared to be paying attention. So, cradling his instrument to his breast—as if it were an infant—and appearing more than just a little wounded, Theophilus of Minos responded, his voice barely louder now than the hissing and crackling from the coals: "The creatures were lingering in the vicinity of the mines. Our ductoris has never had patience with such beasts. He trusts them not."

The vassal, who had been toying with his cup, which was still full, put it down, so as not to crush the metal in his fist. "All they do is watch, like curious children. They are harmless."

"Nobody can be sure of that. People are frightened by what they don't understand. Many attempts have been made to talk to the beasts, after all. To befriend them. These attempts have been ignored. The creatures have been given chances, and choices, and they elect to do nothing but *watch*."

"For that they are hung?"

"Cretata are *changing*. And yes, they are hung." Theophilus of Minos rose unsteadily to his feet. "Our conversation is over, vassal. You should be wary. To side with the beasts is enough, in the eyes of some, to admit compliance. You have been under the ground for a long time. You do not know. A wise person gathers facts before offering his opinion on such matters."

Moans from the nearby mesosaurs sounded like moans of the dying. As Theophilus of Minos departed, and went back to his men, the vassal looked up. Clouds remained closed, painted over Luna. For that, at least, he felt grateful.

CRIES OF ALARM WOKE HIM: HE opened his eyes to see deep grey still painted over the firmament. By the time he sat up, the fading cries had become a death rattle. He could see nothing of the struggle—though it sounded close, and intense—except a brief flicker of sparks and indistinct smears against an equally indistinct landscape.

The brief din of further mêlée, and a high, thin shriek, followed by a nauseating, lingering stench that made the vassal want to retch.

He vaulted from the cart, to land, in darkness. The camp had come alive: more shouts, echoing through the trees and rocks; men with torches, running, flames illuminating the gloom.

Two guards lay dead.

But also one foe, brought down with arrows, lances, and a flurry of swords.

Other attackers, if there had been any, were not evident.

The men gathered around, mouths open, gagging, their faces stricken.

Only when Iubar's glow was at last being painted on the firmament did they all get a good look at the slaughtered cretata.

RECALLING WHAT THEOPHILUS OF MINOS HAD said about the beasts, the vassal was not only shocked by the violence but by the physical transformation the creatures had apparently undergone while he was beneath the ground; benign cretatus, watching him, had once been consistency in his inconsistent youth. This particular male, lying shattered and bloodied, had little in common with those he had once known. The body was smaller overall, with thinner legs, and the set of membranous wings that had once held the specimen gracefully aloft seemed shorter, bulkier than he remembered, but it was the pale face that had altered beyond almost all recognition. Before becoming twisted into this rictus of death, the features must have been almost pretty, not at all like faces of the white monsters that had stared wordlessly at him so many times during his childhood.

However, cretatus blood remained, as then, sickening. *Putrid*. Flies that had gathered over the broken corpse, and landed on it to taste the pale flesh, lay dead already; the ground around the body was black with their fallen bodies.

When the vassal turned away, to try to breathe fresher air, he felt eyes upon him, following him, and he looked up to see the Mauriorum slaves studying him from their places in the flatbed. As usual, the black men did not look away, even though he approached. Was there any fear in their eyes? Their lips moved, another tongue issuing forth, and they gestured, using motions of upheld palms he could not understand. Were they trying to tell him something—?

"Vassal!"

He wheeled to see two guards, standing by the lead cart, summoning him across the misty dawn.

THEOPHILUS OF MINOS LAY ABED, MAUVE compresses over his forehead. At his side, three of his men stood shoulder to shoulder, cramping the small space.

The vassal let the curtain fall. Air inside the cart was stifling, in a different fashion, thick with scents which rose primarily from a suspended brazier. More brocaded curtains, the likes of which he had just passed through, lined the walls.

Tiny red birds, in cages, shrieked and fluttered madly.

"I'm not feeling well," said Theophilus of Minos. His voice was hoarse. He motioned weakly. "Events that transpired have . . . caused me to become ill."

"Once again you wish to speak with me? And not about music or the heavens this time, I take it?"

"Please." Theophilus of Minos licked his dry lips. "Let us not play games. Fourteen days ago, you emerged from the mines to assist in the flogging of a man the ductoris had deemed guilty of theft. Do you recall?"

"Emerging from the mine? Or that the man I flogged was a thief?"

"All I wish to confirm is that you came up from the ground, a fortnight ago."

After some consideration, the vassal concurred. "Saul Pietros. A slave belonging to the ductoris. One of my men. He had been accused of stealing a rind of bread. I flogged him."

"And prior to that?"

"I don't understand."

"I've already told you, vassal, I'm in no mood for games." Theophilus of Minos took a careful sip from a jewelled cup and replaced the cup on the table by his bedside. "Two of my people have just died. This might surprise you, but I cared for them. I have met their children. Their wives have greeted me in the morning. These women are now widows. The children will grow up without a father. I will be the one to inform the families of this tragedy. So don't make our discussion anymore difficult. My question concerns when you left the mines, before that occasion."

"Several weeks prior. I eat and sleep down there. Or I used to. The mine was my home. Most men could not abide by that, but it suited me."

Theophilus of Minos struggled to sit; one of his men reached out to assist him. "Vassal, I'll get to the point. What do they want with you? Why do they haunt you?"

Again, the vassal was silent for a long time. In the small cages, the birds raised another sudden ruckus and then also fell quiet. Black eyes, no larger than poppy seeds, stared. "I don't know," he replied finally. "Cretatus have always watched over me. Since I was a boy."

Theophilus of Minos raised an eyebrow. "You still consider them to be observers? That would be a hard argument to win, if you looked outside. You can't deny that the creature out there *attacked* us, killed two men."

"I don't know what it wanted. Or what occurred."

"Bah! We are all aware that cretatus are *attracted* to you. The ductoris knew. He had you emerge, to do the flogging, in an attempt to lure closer the group that had been spotted in the vicinity of the mine. You see, he is committed to ridding his land altogether of the beasts. He has declared them unfit to live. In all their varieties."

"I see," said the vassal, at a loss for further words.

"This allure you have for them, I admit, is also part of the reason why I wanted you here, with me. You see, vassal, as you have pointed out, I have diverse interests." The man drank another sip and reclined once more. "I wish to learn more about that strange race. And the secrets of heaven. I thought I might be able to do both, at the same time." He smiled a pained smile. "Truthfully, I never considered lives would be lost."

"Not just of men," the vassal added. "At least seven of their number has recently died."

Closing his eyes, Theophilus of Minos appeared to sleep. But, after a moment, he whispered, "You continue to defend them, vassal. Yet you hid from them, under the ground, for seven years. You claim them as benign, yet you hid from them." His eyes opened. "The rocks that once protected you are gone."

"True. But I was assigned to work the mines. I did not volunteer."

"Yet you say the work suited you. I presume you know the tales people relate, concerning your person?"

"I've heard several." Muscles in his jaw tightened.

"Your own mother died while birthing you, because waters from around your small body, when they burst, eroded her loins like acid? You know that one?"

"Yes."

"And the stench during your birth was enough to render ill all those in the birthing tent?"

"I know that one, too."

"That your mother was accosted, and taken by force—"

"I am a *man*," the vassal hissed, stepping forward.

The guards had drawn their swords with a sound like the wind; Theophilus of Minos put a hand out to still the movement; the vassal reluctantly backed off.

"I was born into this world as every man is born," he said. "Cut me, and smell the blood that spills forth." He held out both arms. "*Taste* of it. See if you die."

Quietly, Theophilus of Minos asked, "But who can vouch for the blood of your father?"

"I am not responsible for the deaths of your men."

Theophilus of Minos let out a long, shuddering sigh. "I never wanted us to be at odds, vassal. I envisioned us a relationship as harmonious as the heavenly song I told you about, when I was in my cups." Again he tried, with a little more success, to smile.

"You were not honest with me, and neither was the ductoris. I am a pawn."

"None of us is innocent, vassal. Perhaps it is not too late to set the record straight?"

The two men stared at each other. At last the vassal said, "Pull a curtain aside. If you wish to speak, we need a breeze to clear this air."

WAVES CRASHING AGAINST THE ROCKY SHORES of Minos sounded like relentless thunder. Working in the observatory, perched high on a promontory, the constant roar of the sea could be clearly heard. In truth, the vassal had come to like this sound, even deriving some form of comfort from it, just as he had come to appreciate that Terra Firma was the centre of an infinite void, within which heavenly spheres rotated, and that there is not, nor never was, a firmament to hide under.

Often, though, for nostalgia's sake, he would leave his tasks and walk down the steep path to the rocky beach, from there to the limestone caves at the Bay of Minos, by the island's port, to sit in the shelter there, soft curves of rock over his head, waves echoing and booming all around. Though he found satisfaction in these visits, he could no longer comprehend the reliance he'd once felt for such enclosures.

On occasion, he brought with him to these caves his young son, who knew nothing of rumours, or history (among most other concerns), and watched as the boy stared into the warm tidal pools or curled sleeping on the stones.

Seldom did the vassal meet anyone on these visits, so his surprise was profound when, on one expedition, two men and a woman emerged quietly from the black depths of his favourite haunt. He was startled, yes, but not for long, for the trio appeared serene, and smiled warmly to see his boy, breathing lightly, stirring at his feet.

The strangers carried nets over their shoulders. All three were young, pale as fish, and glistening with oils. Their robes were wet and clinging. As they approached from the darkness, they produced ceramic jars, holding them out, as if for the vassal's inspection.

Up close, the trio appeared almost human.

The vassal stood. Inside the jars seethed blind white shrimps. As he peered down on the multitudes, the female leaned forward and kissed his cheek, her lips leaving behind a lingering smell that stung the vassal's sinuses.

Without a word, the strangers left the cave, walking the beach until the vassal could no longer see them.

WHEN THE BOY AWOKE, HE RAISED his head and blinked. "I dreamt I was at a feast," he said.

The vassal crouched to move his son's hair away from his eyes. "A feast? Who was it for?"

"The ductoris. He was visiting the Isle of Minos, and there was a celebration. But he ate of a local dish that caused him to clutch at his neck, and cough up blood. He died, father, before he could rise from the table."

Lifting his son, cradling the boy with both arms, the vassal said, "Come. Let's go home. Our own dinner hour is fast approaching."

Outside, on the rocks, Iubar's light was brilliant.

"Father?"

"Yes?"

"It's loud today."

"Yes. Waves are high. Bad weather approaches."

"No, not the waves." A beatific smile had spread across the boy's face, though tears ran down his cheeks. "The harmony, father. The music. Today it fills me with more beauty than ever."

"Come," the vassal repeated, giving his son a light squeeze. He could see the trio now, in the distance, where they appeared to be waiting. "Let's go home."

LIZARDS

THE KLAXON WENT OFF AT 7:28, as I was about to punch out. I was tired, and needed a drink. We were heading back to the office. Comm said some lizard lady was going into labour, east side tenement, her cervix dilating like a junkie's pupil as he hits the sweet spot.

Molly turned the boat around and flipped on the screamers.

While we raced over other traffic, I did a little research.

This same lizard lady brought two monsters into the world already, one of them boneless kinds that's kid's play to put down, and another one that came out with teeth and claws and a bad attitude that hadn't been so easy to send back to the depths of hell these things crawl from. Put an officer in the hospital for a week.

I checked my gun, rasping it against stubble as I read the display.

Why these broads are allowed to keep getting knocked up I'll never know, but I guess it ain't easy on them either, getting hopes up each time for a baby that looks like the rest of us saps, then watching it get blown away or torn apart by the dogs.

The building was three floors, a row of grubby apartments on 38th, near Deputy's. I looked longingly at the sign and the wooden doors as Molly parked on the roof and I couldn't see the bar anymore. We took the fire escape to the alley and entered the building from the back, weapons drawn.

Someone was screaming. A woman, upstairs. We hoped it was just the lizard lady, and that we weren't too late. Took the stairs four at a time and told the small crowd of fuckups gathered outside the apartment to disperse or get caught in the crossfire.

The door was wide open.

I went in first, hugging the walls, gun sniffing her out. The place was a sty. Stunk to high heaven. It was hot, too. There was old food everywhere, rotting or dried out. Flies thick in the air, and a buzzing sound that made you want to swat your own ears.

She was in a back room, on a mattress, dress hiked up and legs wide open, but she was facing away, so I couldn't see what was coming out. If she knew I was there, the lizard lady didn't let on. She was grunting, terrified, alone. Even at the angle I was looking from, she seemed grey and tired.

"What is it this time?" I held the quavering gun out. "Tell me what the hell it is, lady."

Molly was in the doorway now, covering me.

When I stepped slowly to the side to get a better look, a contraction made the lizard lady scream and arch and the air in the room shattered—

My eyes were closed.

Something had *touched* me. I felt it, *inside*, and when I opened my eyes, the baby was there, in a puddle, looking up at me. I stood, lost in that gaze, deep pools of innocence and the sweet pain of being alive and that mad desire to live more. I saw a promise of better times, of hope, of a rarefied future I'd all but given up on.

Jesus Christ, I thought, *a baby is just a fucking baby*, so I turned and put two bullets in Molly's head and then one in the startled lizard lady's, and I picked up that sad, squalling mess. Oh yeah, this one was different. This one was special, all right. *Sure, sure*, I told the kid, *just hush, hush little one*, and I put him under my coat, some place safe and warm in this cold city.

LAKE OF DREAMS

"YOUR SO-CALLED ACT," SAID the chancellor, crossing her long legs, "is deplorable, exploitative, and regressive. The entire festival, Mr. Triplehorn, is offensive to me."

They were sitting across a table from each other, in an anteroom of the chancellor's moon palace. He had tried not to look at the necrotic bruising on her right thigh but, plainly revealed now, as she smoothed her already taut skirt, he suspected how advanced her decomposition had become. Raising one hand, leaning forward, he said, "Okay, look, maybe I started off on the wrong foot. I'm sorry. I didn't know I was auditioning, or defending, uh, what we do, or whatever. I was invited here to perform, and my *act*—what we do in that show—is, well, *art*. Our expression. Surely you, chancellor, of all people, can understand that?" He laughed, and regretted it right away; she had not reacted. "But also I haven't slept well in a while, jet lag and all. I wasn't prepared—let me rephrase my pitch?"

"The festival is cancelled. Please leave."

"What?"

The chancellor had looked away, just a few degrees, but enough: resolute, beautiful, her gaunt cheek frosted with the patina of underlying infarctions. *Cold*. He knew was done here. Incredibly, he was done, and being dismissed.

"Look. You know very well—" Speaking carefully, trying not to sound petulant, or raise his voice. "You know what happened to us. Obviously.

You know what happened to everyone that day. Thing is, shit, I mean, this show's been planned for *months*. There's a lot of people involved. A lot of people are *interested*—" But his heart was pounding. "You *fucking knew I was coming here*."

"Don't flatter yourself, Mr. Triplehorn. I did not know, until today, who you even were, let alone that you had arrived in my city on the afternoon shuttle, or that there was to be a showcase of similar *talents*, such as yours, this very evening. I will inform the festival organizers. They were remiss by not telling me about this."

"But shutting it down? How does that help anyone? Isn't that sort of action just part of, of a . . ." He cast about for words, came up, inadequately, with: "Fucking *bullshit*. Why didn't you know about the show? You're the big boss here. And aren't you supposed to be better than all that anyhow? Isn't tolerance part of this whole fucking thing?"

Now she looked at him again. Her dead eyes seemed to be glacial depths, tâche noire a distant plain in another, fiercer world. "If, by this *thing*," she said, "you mean our refuge, Lake of Dreams, of course tolerance is a part of it. Tolerance, Mr. Triplehorn, and *intolerance*. They are the foundations of our city, of all our cities. And, I must advise you strongly, watch your language when you address me. You are not in a tavern."

Rarefied oxygen being fed incrementally into the throat of the chancellor, from a tiny tube stapled to what was left of her esophagus, made her sound not quite right, not quite, well, *human*.

He said, "Have you experienced what I do? The act, I mean."

"You miss my point entirely. I have neither the time nor the patience to see your act, or to set you straight."

"Explain it to me. I'm listening."

"You are not welcome on the moon."

"That's fucked up."

"Trust me, if you don't leave, or if you cause any trouble whatsoever, or if you continue to be obtuse and foul-mouthed, I will call my security. And I did, in fact, several hours ago, Mr. Triplehorn, read of your antics. About your so-called show. Here on the moon we do not have to abide by earthly conventions. We are not bound by your laws. Do you understand me?"

"Is that a threat?"

She shrugged. "I want you and your friends on the first shuttle back."

"Seriously? You mean me and Myron?"

"Myron? I don't know who that is. I refer to the other acts in your festival. I read of several."

"I'm not in charge of the talent. And Myron, well, he's just my—"

"*Leave.*"

But one of the chancellor's pumps had popped wetly and loudly. In the awkward silence that followed, she looked away again, coughed into her fist, maybe embarrassed, maybe waiting for him to speak again, but he did not. More hardware inside her body made unnatural noises, a grinding, worn shunts activating, or maybe breaking down at last.

He stood, between suppressed laughter and growing fury. Neither would be any help here.

"Ensure you leave quietly, Mr. Triplehorn. Goodbye."

"This is fucking stupid." But he turned, and, as she had asked, left. His cheeks were burning like those of a scolded kid. He wanted to knock something over on the way out but decor in the palatial anteroom was austere at best; there was nothing to break.

Hesitating one last time to see if the chancellor would recant, or call him back—she did not—he pushed open the double doors and stepped out onto a bright landing: the sun was huge, brilliant. Just beyond the set of grand steps, leading down, an artificial lake lay calm and sparkling. He had to shield his eyes to watch a boxlike lander struggle upwards from plastic islands near the extremity of the city's atmospheric cage, likely heading back to earth with a cargo of broccoli or other cruciferous vegetable. He tried for a second but failed to see evidence of his own miserable planet hanging in the sky above him.

"Goddamn," he said, attempting to process this incongruous turn of events, to re-formulate plans for the rest of the day, consider recourse, implications, none of which he was very good at, when his agent materialized, thankfully, leaning against a nearby column. Myron was smoking. This was a new affectation.

"Hey."

Other than this abrupt manifestation, and the cargo activity, out on the water, Lake of Dreams was sure a quiet city—at least here, by the waterfront of the chancellor's moon palace.

"Georgie," said Myron, flicking the butt away to vanish in thin air. He squinted. "Looks like you messed things up in there."

"You bet I did."

They locked eyes for some time. They could have been paternal twins. Their irises were an identical blue, their lanky builds the same, their hair long and equally messy—though George's was blond and Myron's black. They were even dressed the same, in dark, half-length coats that had literally been slept in. Neither smiled. Both might have—and had done so—in similar circumstances, on prior misadventures, but now they were tired, strung out, far from home. This lunar gig, the travelling, and confrontations, had worn them thin. Too old for these sorts of activities. A lot of money was spent getting out here and none would be made in return. George put his hands in the pockets of his coat. Myron followed suit.

"What now, boss?"

If they took the first shuttle out, as they had been directed to do, that still left the rest of the afternoon and what would likely turn out to be an unpleasant evening and night to kill. George, however, was thinking about the chancellor now, lowering her failing, naked body into a formaldehyde bath, peeling dead skin away from her grey forearms with long, yellow nails. George imagined getting in with her— But no. That wouldn't work. So he pictured instead kissing her cool mouth. He *liked* the chancellor. A lot. That was part of the problem.

Her teeth, like the teeth of all dead people, had been the *exact* same yellow as her nails.

"What was she like?" Myron materialized another lit cigarette, half-smoked already. "I checked out pics while you were in there. Pretty cute, I bet, in person?"

"Hot as hell," George agreed. "But uptight. And fucking pissed. We not only lost the show but the whole festival's been cancelled."

"You're kidding."

"Nope. And we've been kicked off the moon."

Myron grinned. Now he was wearing shades. "I should have gone in."

"Well, she didn't want to see you, did she? She wanted to interview the *talent*. The flesh and blood fucking talent." He looked out over the lake again, to where darkness delineated the end of the city. "This place is a shithole. I told you it would be."

"Ha."

Both Myron and George were well aware that the club George had been scheduled to perform at, Time Squared, did have caché, even off-moon, and that the three-star hotel they had checked into, just hours ago—indeed, this quiet necropolis the dead had called Lake of Dreams—were all nicer than pretty much any place either had before visited and likely ever would again; certainly nicer than any derelict location they'd ever been in, or performed at, back home.

"Sue her dead ass," George said, heading back to the guuber, which had stopped on the circular driveway in front of the moon palace, in the shade of a large elm there.

Myron attempted to keep up, as he always did when engaged, but he flickered—because reception on the moon, as the adage went, was less than stellar, and moving was hard for him at the best of times—disappearing altogether once more among the artificial rocks of the palace's rock garden.

DRIVING BACK DOWNTOWN, ALONG THE WIDE, clean road—skyline looming quickly, starkly on the too-close, too-curved, horizon—the guuber ran into traffic and, in another incredible twist—*insult to fucking injury*, George muttered—had to slow down.

"Oh dear," said the car. "Sorry about this."

"Seriously?" George folded his arms. "An *accident*?"

Two black security scoots passed low overhead. George recalled the chancellor's threat. The scoots were new, sleek, and quiet.

"How is this even possible, car? I thought this place was supposed to be idyllic, state of the art? A paradise?"

"Sadly," replied the guuber, "deterministic nature of a system does not make it entirely predictable. I'm changing routes. Please stand by."

Other cars on the road, George saw—like the one now stationary next to his—were empty. Alarmed, he was about to ask why other guubers would drive around on the moon with no passengers when Myron returned, sitting half-in and half-out of the tiny vehicle. George had him hire the car. His hair blew in the wind. Perhaps he thought he was in a convertible.

"See what's happening here, Myron? Myron! Listen up! A *bona fide* traffic jam. When was the last time you saw anything like this?"

Myron squinted, peering inward, and ahead.

"And this guuber's telling me about chaos theory." To the car, George said, "You should give me my money back," surprised to feel the immediate tingle of the refund in his fingertip, followed quickly, alarmingly, by a deflating sense of personal disappointment that tugged at the edges of a familiar abyss much more profound, utterly disproportionate, a vast sense of despair that hit him out of nowhere, causing his breath to catch in his throat, like a sob, and he crashed back, stunned, into the seat.

"I do see," Myron said, oblivious, as always, to any existential moment, laughing like a fool to prove it. At least he was having fun here. His teeth, seen through the dome of the car, looked perfect. They both had good teeth. George was frowning, though, stricken. Myron said, "Looks like two drones collided, boss. Wreckage crashed onto the highway and—"

"Ring road," corrected the guuber.

"Whatever. The road is blocked, for sure. I'm getting more info. This primitive feed is patchy. There's a possible fatality."

"I'm sure that's the wrong fucking word," George said, "since they're already dead."

The car, meanwhile, ignoring this exchange, was backing up, just as the other, empty cars around them were doing, a display, ironically, of grace, like a flower unfolding, a dance as their positioning systems calculated other ingress into the downtown core of the city and plotted them. However, betrayed again by his faulty chemistry, George could not appreciate any of this and was now in an absolutely foul mood. He despised his own disposition. He resented what had befallen him, all those years ago. More than once, he had been accused of his inability to deal, by doctors and girlfriends both. But fuck them all. What he really needed was a drink, or maybe nine. His lunar premiere—Mothership, the festival had been called, a showcase of earth performers—had, as he'd tried to explain to the chancellor, been planned for months. And he never liked travel in the first place. As Myron organized the trip—their first time off-earth, heading into full-on dead territory!— which entailed two full days on the shuttle, each way, it caused him anxious, sweaty nights and provided him with more lurid daydreams than usual concerning a violent demise.

But then they landed safely, after an uneventful flight, and the hotel was surprisingly nice. The few people he'd encountered maybe a bit standoffish— and dead, of course—but pleasant enough. Then the sunny, surprise drive from the hotel to the picturesque moon palace, by the city's lake—a request to be *interviewed* by the chancellor herself—was, as far as he understood, a formality, even a compliment, her desire being only to welcome him, underline the important cultural exchange that was about to happen. George even imagined signing merch for her and, most frustrating of all, when he'd first seen her, sitting at that fucking table, watching his approach, looking cool and beautiful, a tryst of varied and raunchy proportions.

Circling back the way they had come, the guuber soon passed the palace again (which George flipped off, with both hands, while Myron continued to smile at the vista like the idiot he could often be), skirting the artificial lake one more time, before turning inland—if *that* was the right word—onto a much narrower and surprisingly rougher road. Annoying facts spouted by Myron at random intervals over the past few weeks had been retained: as in all eight other lunar cities, downtown Lake of Dreams was a central hub of pre-fab buildings within a large atmospheric cage, ringed by a band of highly successful vegetable gardens and the namesake lake. The *ring road* they had been on before spiralled toward the hub from this lake, and smaller roads, like this one, led directly into the core of the city, spokes from the peripheral body of water. This circular layout appeared precise and clear from the shuttle's window, as it banked, just this morning, coming in for a landing.

The narrow road, however, turned out to be a utilitarian route, not meant for traffic like this, and soon became clogged with the small, driverless cars, all moving slowly, and in single file. George never did like guubers very much. He found them obsequious and pedantic. The annoying little vehicles were not so popular on earth but here, on the moon—in Lake of Dreams, at least—they seemed common as vermin. This one, he thought, scowling out at the landscape and at his vacuously grinning agent, had a particularly shitty attitude.

For what it was worth, though, he and Myron did get to see different sorts of buildings this way, aspects of the city other than the ones they had passed going out to the moon palace, or when they had driven from the shuttle port to the hotel. Just like regular fucking tourists. Here was row after row of small, cluttered, crate-like homes, an expanse of warehouses, pumps and derricks and chimneys, spitting steam, each almost the size of the apartment building George lived in back home—

"What are these places? Slums?"

"There are no slums, per se, in any of our cities. Those are air filtration units, for folks, well, like you, primarily. Behind us, to your left, is low-rent housing."

"Slums, like I said."

Thing is, some people found George charming. He knew he was not much good at maintaining relationships, but he often began them. He had friends. He was a fine-looking guy. A few troubles, but who didn't have troubles these days? Nobody was trouble-free, not since rapture. Glaring out at the factories—approaching Lake of Dreams from the backside, as it were—he stewed. Some people, he had to admit—and not for the first time—found him borderline reprehensible. Deluded women, for instance. Maybe it was the act, and not the conditions behind it, like the chancellor had implied, that made these women see him in that unfavourable light? But fuck it: a man had to make a living. What was he supposed to do? Kill himself, like so many others had done? Drug or drink himself into submission?

"Hey," he said to the car, quieted now. "Can I ask you a few things?"

"Certainly."

"Do you know who I am?"

"George Triplehorn. I have your credit info and pertinent data right here. You touched my screen this morning, remember, reserving me for duration of your visit? I know exactly who you are."

"Yeah, okay, but beyond that."

"A visitor, I imagine, from earth. I didn't dig around."

"Nope."

"You're not from earth?"

"Yes, of course I am. Where else would I be from? But I'm not just a visitor. I mean, I am, but . . ." Outside, verdant gardens passed, misted with silver fog. George had never before seen such greenery but remained less than impressed. Cities of the moon held the earth ransom for these vegetables. Broccoli and cabbage had become another wedge to drive into the old motherland. On the incoming shuttle—living and dead passengers both— their bags, clothes, and devices had been sprayed with potassium soap, to kill any aphids. George figured he would smell forever like rancid cinnamon. "I was invited here," he said, lamely.

"You've been to the moon before?"

"Actually, no—"

Myron laughed again.

"—but that's not what I meant and you fucking know it. I was asked to come here, to your *glorious* city, to do a show, to take part in a festival."

"You're a performer? Ah, yes. I see the festival now. Mothership. Interesting. *George Triplehorn*. There you are. One of nine, uh, mutants?"

"What the fuck?"

"Apologies. Is that an inflammatory term? It's from a rather callous headline. A less than favourable editorial, I see now, about your visit. And, um, you do know that the festival has been cancelled?"

"I do."

Myron held his arms out, either side, as if he were flying. "A goddamn performer," he shouted, gleefully, into the wind.

George banged his fist upwards against the dome for silence.

"Please don't break anything," the guuber said. "I gave you a refund already."

"Relax, car. So, yeah, your fucking chancellor cancelled the festival. Just now, at that moon palace. She didn't like my face."

"Your face?"

"That's an expression. You probably don't know that sort of stuff. She didn't like *me*, guuber. Didn't like my type. Clearly, there's nothing wrong with my face." (Myron, whose face was similar, if not identical, peered down, listening more intently now. Getting concerned? "Let it go, Georgie," he said, or appeared to, but they both knew Georgie never would let it go.) "The chancellor fucking silenced me. She silenced the whole thing. All of us, come all this way, out of a gig. What if we sold a lot of tickets? Who's going to deal with that? You know what? I think she only likes people who actually died that day, not those of us crippled by the rapture and just trying to pick up the pieces."

"Um, I'm not sure about that."

"Well, I am."

"Listen, George, if I may call you that, you're clearly getting agitated."

"No shit."

"You should know that the woman you met in the moon palace is not actually *my* chancellor. Nor do I claim to understand her edicts or motives. You must have upset her. I do know she wouldn't approve of you cashing in on calamity but her reaction does seem a tad extreme. She's very active politically, and I know she's not feeling her best lately. Honestly, George, I never claim to understand or pay too much attention to positions you humans take, living or dead."

"Is that right?"

"Yes."

"What the fuck kind of guuber are you, anyhow?"

"I've been told I have a certain, well, philosophical bent."

"You sure as fuck do." George leaned back into the seat, furious. At least the abyss of despair had retreated. "So now what? You're going to take me and my friend here back into the city, this Lake of fucking Dreams, and find us a shithole bar?"

"Your, uh, friend, sir? I believe I'm taking you back to the hotel."

"Can't detect my pal? Don't give me that. His name's Myron. He's my agent, my advisor, my doctor. He's sitting right here, in my lap. He's a good looking dude, too. And he thinks you're funny."

"I see."

"Will you stop agreeing with me? I'm not a nutcase. Well, maybe I am, but just a bit. You know, mamma, we're all crazeee now. Or dead, right? Resurrected and living out our last days here on the fucking moon. Right? Myron's a program, like you, like your little brain, like the little brain of these other empty cars. But he's more sophisticated than you by a million fold, so go fuck yourself."

Myron was now visibly tense.

No one said anything for some time.

They passed the last of the gardens.

Then the guuber said: "George, I don't think you should go to a bar. Nor would you easily find such an establishment here. I don't believe there are, in fact, any. Perhaps staying in your hotel room would be the wisest choice. I'll take you out to the shuttle port in the morning. You have been banished."

"Banished? What the fuck? I'm a civilized man, a taxpayer, and now I find myself on vacation. So I'm going to stroll about, see the fucking sights of this city, and have a few drinks."

Outside the car now, downtown Lake of Dreams, quiet city of the dead, was upon them.

THE GUUBER PULLED UP IN FRONT of Hotel Del Mino, where he and Myron were staying, and, as it stopped, powered down completely, any opportunity for further discourse over. George hadn't suspected that the car would actually veto his request to find a bar in Lake of Dreams until he recognized the hotel's façade alongside and the car went inert. He gave the vehicle a very low rating and discovered that he, too, had been rated equally low. Though still angry, still wanting to break something, he did not really want to argue anymore, having got his fucking money back, after all, and feeling somewhat drained by the drive.

Likely the car (and chancellor) was right: lying low in the hotel room was best. There was a stocked minibar. The night would eventually grind past, joining other mundane evenings come and gone forever.

Myron already waited on the sidewalk, flickering into visibility and then out again. He had his hands in the pockets of his coat when he appeared, cigarette in his mouth. He looked forlorn. He faded.

George emerged from the dome of the car—popping the cone manually—causing a valet, standing at the revolving door to the hotel, dressed in clean, red livery, to look over sharply.

George waved.

The valet, of course, was dead.

"Pieces of shit," said George, under his breath, not entirely sure what or who he was referring to.

LAKE OF DREAMS' MAIN STREET WAS called Bueno Vista. Like all of the streets George had seen so far in the city—except for the road they'd just taken, coming back from the moon palace—Bueno Vista was uncluttered and glistened a pristine black between banks of stolid, grey structures. The few cars driving it hummed quietly along at the same speed, the same distance apart. Everything on the moon, it seemed to George, was new and practical. Not many round edges, or colour, but he had to admit that, overall, the place, though sparse, had an almost warm, appealing vibe. Dreamlike, he thought. Quiet and fucking dreamlike. He set his lips tight. "Myron," he hissed. "Run bloodwork now. I'm feeling, you know, *weird*."

"I'm on it, Georgie."

There were few pedestrians—all of them dead—but now two living people came out of the Del Mino, a couple, an older man and a woman, talking, opening a scintillating map that floated before them. George nodded in their direction as he walked toward the doors, made eye contact with the woman—saw both their expressions alter, as he passed them, no doubt having recognized him—and then nodded over to the stern-faced dead valet again, whose forehead and left eye, he saw now, were frosted white with advanced necrosis.

Was the old couple going to his show?

Or, he corrected himself, did they *think* they were?

"The city," Myron whispered abruptly, directly into George's ear, making George jump, "is the only one of the nine governed by an all-dead council, including, of course, the chancellor, or queen bee."

"Thanks for that." George had stopped walking. "Look, Myron. I don't really need facts right now. I think I'm about to fucking pop. Please, just monitor my vitals and back the fuck off."

"The largest of the lunar cities," Myron persevered, "Lake of Dreams has the highest percentage of dead populace. Only thirty percent of the population can be considered alive."

"And where the fuck," said George, "are they?" He had come out into the lobby. "Why are you telling me this now, Myron? You shorting out, too? Try to be cool. I need your help."

The interior of the Hotel Del Mino was mostly fake wood and furniture made to look like old-time earth decor: antimacassars on the armchairs, red baize pool tables, mellow, amber lamps on almost every surface.

George passed by the front desk—the clerk, dead, with whom he had dealt earlier, watched him blankly—and stood, waiting for the elevator. Myron hovered, lost, presumably, hopefully, in blood test results, or maybe legal precedents or whatever else he might be pursuing. The elevator was retro (which, George had decided when he'd first stood here, looking up at the old dial, was a pretty weird aesthetic for dead people to settle on). The elevator had a scissor door and was operated by a girl dressed in the hotel's red uniform—a girl who seemed far too young to have been taken by rapture and then revived, but George was no longer in the mood to engage with anyone, especially a pretty dead girl, though he was sickened to find himself tempted, as always, to flirt with her. Merely smiling a weak smile, still feeling deflated, depressed, and getting sadder again by the second, he told her what floor his room was on, the top, and she closed the gate behind him. Her shunts clicked and popped. There was the hiss of air from a leak somewhere on her person. She had a decidedly pungent aroma. He closed his eyes.

Myron had gone ahead, maybe taking the stairs.

THE SMALL BUT VERY TASTEFULLY DECORATED suite had a great view of the city. George poured himself a drink from the minibar and sat on the end of the bed drinking it. When he and Myron had first arrived, they'd spent maybe five minutes in this room before the chancellor's summons arrived. George, who'd been getting primed for the big show, tentatively letting the memories of others trickle in from the rooms around, had been titillated by the request. Flattered. Fucking *flattered*. He snorted. He had heard that the chancellor was an attractive and smart woman, and his imagination had immediately gone scurrying about those ruinous, traitorous fissures of his brain.

Myron, settled on the sofa, knees apart, was still in his coat and shades. Based on the content of his mumblings, he was now for sure looking into the possibilities of lawsuits concerning the festival's abrupt closure. George thought about the chancellor again. He put the glass on the bed table, lay back on the bed, and opened his pants. The chancellor's hair was patchy, what was left of it, and tied back into a ponytail. He thought about pulling that ponytail. He thought about her gasps, and moans, and the hiss of air in her throat.

Orgasm had always been trusted to alter George's outlook for the better, tweak his fractured chemistry, even if just for a brief while. He had relied upon orgasm ever since he could remember, even before he had become this monster, this mutant, as the car had said. But the chancellor's disdain—despite her long, grey legs and inscrutable eyes—coupled with her dismissal of how he honestly just wanted to express himself, and Myron's periodic outbursts from the sofa about setting precedents and respect and litigation—actually, just *seeing* his agent's stupid fucking face as he sat there, watching—so disconcerting that George gave up and lay still with his soft dick in his hand and the chasm of despair or whatever it was that always followed him around much closer.

So he got up and had two more quick drinks, looking out the window at this city of the dead, and felt the booze—at least, consistent, another old ally—dulling his growing fear.

How, he wondered, had this happened? What manner of malignant trick changed the rules that day? Were believers—the multitudes taken by rapture, and not brought back by any form of intervention—in a better place? Were they with their god? George had yearned so many times to be one of them but had never believed in anything. So now this broken universe remained: the legacy of dead, those resurrected pretty much all existing here, in the nine cities of the moon, and those transformed by rapture, but left alive, at odds, living crippled back on earth. Each tried to claim territories, build walls, like a new but fucked-up species.

He poured another drink.

The lake surrounding the city was an attractive silver crescent; beyond, the atmospheric cage cut down, black and definitive.

Ten years or more had passed in depression as dark and abrupt as that wall. Back then, he had wanted to die every day. Lately, maybe a modicum less.

George checked himself out in the bathroom mirror, startled to see how old and manic he looked, how dilated his pupils appeared. There was a twitch in his cheek. He fixed his hair, messing it with one hand, but could not make it satisfactory. He peed.

There were two showers in these lunar bathrooms: water, for him, and formaldehyde solution, for those who had successfully, if temporarily, died.

Outside, evening descended quickly. The effect was an artifice, a filter over the cage, but nonetheless the city at night was starkly beautiful. There were very few lights.

George wondered where the other performers were. Staying in this same hotel? He had not talked to any them on the shuttle coming here, had not seen them at all, opting instead to stay the entire trip in his berth, with Myron. Would the other acts blame him for the cancelled festival? Had they also been summoned to the moon palace by the chancellor, and summarily dismissed? Strange that she had thought him in charge.

And what of the mysterious organizers? He had never met them, not even corresponded with them once, leaving details such as those to his assistant, who arranged everything related to gigs.

George did not really believe that the festival was a chance to reconcile some of the issues between the living and the dead, break down barriers. Not in any fashion. He had suggested that to the chancellor to appear understanding, benevolent, but, like most of what he said, it had been a lie. He only ever wanted money, and girls, and applause.

George had another drink.

Banishment, however—regardless of what he had said, of who the organizers were, or what he believed about anything—was a fucking joke.

He could not stay inside the hotel room any longer. He would lose his shit, succumb for sure, if he did, so he put on his coat and opened the door.

"Whoa," said Myron, sidling up quicker than anyone corporeal could ever move. "Stepping out?"

George said nothing. He was breathing hard. He felt drunk and heavy. "I asked you for a blood test."

"Yeah, man, you're ready to pop, Georgie, just like you said. Numbers did come back, and they're through the roof. I didn't want to— You're going to put on a show one way or the other, aren't you, George? And you're going to get us arrested."

"Ah fuck it, Myron, ain't any cops here, just security guards and wannabes. You should know that. There's probably no crime at all on the moon, is there? They are not bound, old boy. A girl I knew once told me that." On impulse, George broke a sconce off the wall, but as he heard the plastic snap, he knew he had hoped that the act would wake something asleep inside him, light a fucking fire somewhere, but absolutely nothing of the sort happened. He just looked at the broken light dangling there by the wires, feeling that chasm opening, calling him, mocking.

WALKING THE CLEAN, NEARLY DESERTED STREETS, George did not really feel like doing much of anything but, for the sake of consistency, knew that he would, pursuing his usual bad decisions. He retained a vague plan of finding some form of bar, and by chance he came across Times Squared, the venue he had meant to gig at—which, he discovered, was pretty close to the hotel. Downtown Lake of Dreams was tiny.

George's name wasn't on the marquis, if it ever had been, but the names of the others—all, like him, changed on that day, crippled, as some would say, but alive, mutants, if that were any consolation—remained. Looking through the window, he saw only gloom. Possibly the show was not cancelled, only his act? The whole Mothership thing should have started within the hour, yet there was no one outside, no one around. Nor did the venue seem very big. George had been told by Myron that Time Squared had a capacity of two thousand but, standing outside, trying to see in this tiny window, that number seemed really high. In fact, George thought, there could hardly be two thousand people in the entire fucking city.

On the well-lit sidewalks, he saw a few citizens, moving slowly toward him, people who had been claimed by rapture and, for various reasons, resuscitated: men, women, but no children or even teenagers. Now their revived bodies failed them again, not by aging, which had effectively stopped on that day, but by decomposition, always marching downwards, and by simple economics, the cost of medical engineering and procedures to stave off what had once been temporarily and perhaps ill-advisedly circumvented. There were lawsuits from those brought back to life by their families, lawsuits for those left dead, lawsuits for those who had woken up, like him, with a pounding headache the next morning and new skills. Infighting, dissention, discrimination. *Fetishization.* He touched himself under his coat.

And now the earth was dying, too.

Most people stared back with those dark, unreadable eyes. A few, he was sure, recognized him, but not one spoke, let alone asked him for his autograph.

He got muddled flickers of their memories, but let these escape. He was only a conduit, a channel. That was his act. Rapture had turned him into a channel. Pain and sadness and moments of joy all funnelled into him, from both the living and the dead, like glass dust into his veins, or glints of light on water—

The temperature of a necropolis, it turned out, was a pleasant, crisp eighteen.

Twice, security scoots passed silently overhead.

RESTAURANTS AND CAFÉS WERE CERTAINLY SPARSE in Lake of Dreams, or maybe they were located in parts of the town he had not yet seen; the guuber had told him he would have a hard time finding a place to drink and that was proving true. Resurrected dead ate, but only for bulk. They derived no nutrients or pleasure from the act. Food, for them, was gruel. And without blood, the dead found no point drinking alcohol, either, or taking drugs. They certainly did not need to consume the nutrient-rich produce grown on the moon. They just needed money, like him, and maybe power; somehow, the dead had managed to end up with the richest soil.

Most of the businesses George passed were for cosmetic alterations or bodily fixes of one sort or the other: wigs and implants; elixirs; tattoos; infusions; replacement hardware needed for people once dead to stay reanimated as long as possible.

Which was about now.

The majority of the businesses were shuttered.

"LOOKEE, LOOKEE," SAID THE DOORMAN, "A meat monkey and his fuckin' light suit," indicating, with an exaggerated sweep of his necrotic arm, that George should enter the building he had stopped in front of. Everything George looked at now, including this doorman, and the club or bar or whatever the establishment was behind him, had become haloed by a shimmering aura. George held his coat closed tight. Myron, who must have returned at some point, stood silently, so very close, right behind him.

The structure itself was a nondescript prefab, one of several on a side street, with a holo sign over the awning meant to look like neon. Death Trap, the sign read. As with the other buildings in Lake of Dreams, the walls of Death Trap were smooth plastic, clean, and that same, neutral grey.

A single, large window, darkened, permitted few details to be seen inside.

"This whole city," George whispered, "is a fucking horror show." He could no longer relate to the benign sensation Lake of Dreams has previously given him. His disorder was acting up.

Myron smoked again. Gnawing at his virtual thumbnails, he blew smoke out his nose. "It's a spa," he said. "I think. But are you okay, boss? Sure you want go in here?"

The doorman grew tired of staring George down, or maybe he was unsettled by what he saw in George's face; he barked sudden, forced laughter and asked, "You coming in, monkey? What the fuck's up with you?"

The doorman wore braces on his limbs, an eye patch, a bandana. His grey skin crawled with luminous images of skeletons fighting and his grin was wide, cheeks rotted away, or intentionally removed, so that yellow molars were visible.

When George lurched forward, the doorman said, oxygen hissing, "What a genuine *pleasure*. A real man such as you, all the way from earth, selecting our humble cave. I'm a big fan, Triplehorn, but no trouble, eh? Please, come in, come in."

Myron linked arms with George, or pretended to, and took him past the doorman—who held the door open wide. George hummed and vibrated like a thousand taut wires. Impossible for him to know if the voices he had started to hear were real, or Myron's updates, or supplied to him from the increasingly chaotic ether.

PATRONS BATHED IN CLEAR FORMALDEHYDE TANKS. Some leaned against the sides of these tanks, hooked up to canisters of sodium iodine. Those completely submerged watched George enter from within the preserving fluid, dark eyes unblinking through odd goggles. No tune played, and lights were bright. This spa, or whatever Death Trap might be—a transfusion facility?—stank to high hell.

All conversation had stopped.

Now memories and snippets from the others around him rolled into George, too many to parse, and he was unable to release all of them. Some memories rose before him like old photos, and he tried blinking them away. He struggled to breathe.

A girl, staff, approached: at least she smiled at him. She was cute, petite, her face marked with pale archipelagos of decay, her hair gone altogether. Flesh at one shoulder webbed with scars. George got a taste from her: trepidation mostly, a degree of bored curiosity, the flicker of sexual interest, and then the image of a cat, hissing—

"Hi," said the dead girl.

"Can I get a . . . a beer?" George ground his teeth together. The cat had been a pet, long ago, before rapture, when this girl had been alive, and a child.

She had stopped. "Holy shit. I know you. George Triplehorn. I'm going to see you tonight."

"No, you're not, actually. The show's cancelled."

"What? How come?"

"Your fucking chancellor doesn't like living people much."

Hard to read the eyes of the dead, the emotions there, if any, in the dark, blood-marred orbs. "None of us," said the girl slowly, "were treated very nice."

"Then why the fuck were you coming to see my show?" Anger from earlier in the day, ugly and jagged, erupted.

"I can't resist a train wreck."

Myron, for a second, appeared startled by this exchange, unsure what to do, if anything, before smiling his trademark smile. "We're not sure why the show was cancelled," he said to the girl. "But we'll try to reschedule another one soon. Your ticket will be recognized."

The girl paid Myron no heed. Maybe she, too, didn't even see him. She continued to stare at George. He got no more images from her, no visions or memories. He was grateful for that.

Others in the bar had gone back to their business. No one drank, though; there was no actual bar.

"Are we allowed in here?"

"Of course. I can't stop you." But she was not smiling anymore. "You came in the wrong door, is all. That door's not— Come this way. Follow me."

She brought them between the preserving tanks, limping somewhat, to another room, a back room, devoid of customers, where there were a few tables and chairs, and the lights were a little bit dimmer. Faint music played.

"Sit anywhere. It's a quiet night."

George thought about apologizing to the girl but was not sure why. He wondered if the other businesses he had passed in Lake of Dreams also had a portion in the back, like this one, for living customers. Did the closed places? Had the venue, Time Squared, a small back room set aside for the living?

"A beer?"

"Yeah." He and Myron remained standing. George could not sit if he tried. He looked at the bare walls. There was a constant churning inside him.

When the waitress had safely gone, Myron said, "You should know, Georgie, there's activity outside."

"Activity? What do you mean?"

"Chatter, you know, on a few channels. They're talking about you."

"Who is?"

"Security."

Afterimages pulsed at the periphery of George's vision and he could hear other patrons very clearly. Were these voices what Myron meant? He was moving about the room like a nervous mirage, following events only he could track, looking for patterns and relevance in what he picked up. Watching his assistant, George thought, as he always did during times like these, that they were both losing their fucking minds. Had the chancellor called in the scoots to get them both or was their interest in him routine? Or even real? Regardless, George felt his frustrations and anger surging again when the dead girl came back with his beer—a bottle of dark stout, old school, on a tray—George wanted to just fucking seize her, hold her, shake her, but he knew he must never do that, for he could make matters so much worse, so he asked her, instead, through clenched and perfect teeth, if she would stay with him and Myron in this back room, just for a moment, to talk?

Again the girl stood there, absolutely still. "You don't look so good, Triplehorn," she said, finally. "Are you okay? Are you on something? Are you freaking out?"

George took a mouthful of the beer; it was cold, and great, and he felt a fleeting reprieve from what was brewing inside him, a reprieve from what was about to happen. "What's your name?"

"Justine."

"How old were you, Justine, when you were taken?"

"Taken?" Her dark eyes narrowed. "By what?"

"On harvest day. By the rapture. How old were you?"

"Seventeen."

"You're, what, older than me now?"

"I don't know how fucking old you are. What is this about?"

"I had just turned twelve that day. When I woke up the next morning—"

"So what? I'm older than you. Big deal. I didn't wake up at all the next morning."

He drank more, suddenly pointing at the girl with the neck of the bottle. "No one got away that fucking day. Nothing was the same again. We all changed. People, animals. *Fucking cats.*" He saw her reaction and felt pleased. "Even aphids."

"Are you kidding me? You're trying to compare what happened to you to someone who was actually killed?"

"I'm not who I used to be earlier."

"I have shunts and pumps and all kinds of shit inside me, trying to keep my body going." She was nearly shouting, her oxygen supplements struggling to keep up with the words. "I need to take preserving baths every other day. I'm half blind and I can't hear properly and my teeth are falling out. Every day I thank *fuck* I can't feel pain like I used to."

Thrusting forward the payment pad, she was clearly in the ranks of those repulsed by him.

George closed his eyes. A light smile played across his face. These lives passed through him, taking more of him each time. He could not stop them, or help anyone in any way. He reached out his finger, touched the device, and the debit went through.

"Why are you here anyway?" Justine asked. "Are you dying?"

"What?" He looked at her. "We are all dying."

"Fuck's sake. I mean, now, meat monkey. Are you on a mission? Are you a raging Christian? Or do you have cancer, or some shit like that?"

"No." But lights flashed like old camera bulbs going off around his head. "Justine, look—"

"You want to fuck a corpse? Is that it? There is a place. Not here in Death Trap, and not me. I have a boyfriend. He lost an arm last week, literally. He's got about seven months left, eight tops. But that's okay. I do, too. And you know we here don't actually fuck, right? You know that? We dead people can't fuck?"

"I know that." Memories were building up, frenetic: a frightened girl, running down a hallway; boys hitting another boy with a stick; a drunken man, on all fours, while a woman shrieked—

Her cat.

Justine was no longer in the room. George frowned, having lost another chunk of time. His agent suddenly loomed. "Georgie, Georgie," said Myron, "scoots are overhead now. This is really bad. There's three of them. I can hear them. They're coming for you. Stay with me, boss. I found a map." Myron tapped his temple. "There's another exit in the back of this place. I'm going to get you to the hotel. We're going home. It ain't no good for you on the moon. It ain't no good."

Flickering ahead, Myron led George half-stumbling down a corridor lined with shipping bins and crates piled high either side, to a narrow door, which he told George to open, leading to stairs on the other side going down. From the darkness below came the sound of fluids, the smell of formaldehyde and decay—

Myron, lighting the way, descended.

George stood at the top of the stairs draining his beer.

"My signal's fucking worse down here," Myron complained, grumbling. He stood on a platform in the gloom below, looking about. "Shit, boss, it's like a whole other layout, another city here. This is a fucking underworld."

"I'm tripping," George said, going down. "I don't feel so good, Myron."

From Death Trap came a sudden ruckus.

NOT A CITY OF ROADS AND buildings, but a city of water, of dark water. And maybe not another lake, but there was an awful lot of dark water below Lake of Dreams, calm water, in wide channels, lying still and silent between labyrinthine walls. Darker distances echoed and, from those distances, the muted sound of more water, dripping, trickling. Over his head, larger pipes and bundled conduits passed under bars of luminescence. Was this the real Lake of Dreams? George had frozen, looking out across these vast channels.

Lake of Time, Lake of Fear, Lake of Death . . .

Names of the lunar cities seemed to orbit, as if someone had read them aloud.

Then harvest day was upon him again, rapture coming down, like a wave passing through, altering him, altering the universe, changing everything—

Justine died in a classroom. She had her period that day. She put her homework down and rested her face atop it, completely exhausted. Her last living thought was wondering why another student—an overweight boy who sat at the front of the class, and who had tried, at least twice, to talk to her (she was not receptive)—had just done the same. Everyone, she thought, not just us gals, seemed so tired—

Catwalks led out over the channels of water, either side, wide enough for two, anchored to the walls. Ahead, a bridge arched. Openings led to yet more water, other walls, other parts of this underground lake.

"We can get to the hotel," Myron said, "straight ahead. There's a door, and more stairs, going back up."

George tottered after him.

"Security's in Death Trap right now." Myron was fully lit, though the bars of lighting in the ceiling here were sufficient to dispel gloom from the cavern anyhow. "They're talking to our friend, the doorman."

Opposite George was another series of openings, through which the water led, and over each a sign, one reading Bueno Vista, in phosphorescent font, under a two-headed arrow pointing either way. Similar, smaller signs hung over every opening, the names of streets and lanes George had earlier walked, up above.

Pipes flushed violently, and George started. "Myron," he said, "get me the fuck out of here."

But the catwalk, when they tried to follow it, came to an end.

Or, rather, it came to another staircase, leading not up, as Myron had promised, but farther down, to the surface of the water, which was two metres or so below where they stood.

At the bottom of these stairs, moored, was a small raft.

"Jesus, Myron, for real? We're getting on that?"

"Yeah," said Myron. But he didn't seem sure. "Easy to steer. Looks simple. No choice, boss. Let's go."

George clattered down the stairs and they got on the raft, with some difficulty, as they were both unsteady on their feet. George had never before been on any form of water vessel, had never even seen the ruined seas back home.

There was a seat at the front of the raft; George took it. The control panel was fairly easy to operate: a rudimentary screen, like on certain bikes, which he had ridden, responding to George's thumb. No ignition or passkey needed. Above it, a dim dial, presumably for positioning, did not seem to be working. Nonetheless, the raft moved away from the wall. Myron hovered, his reflection like a ghost on the surface of the water.

The raft was slow, though, its AI dim, silent, if there at all.

After a moment, George said, "Where the fuck are we, Myron? I mean, what the fuck. Which way?"

"All this water," Myron muttered. "There's not much info to read about. Filtration to keep the cage going, pipes taking preserving fluid someplace? Up ahead we go left, I think. We're just under that closed wig shop? Remember? Think you can steer through one of these arches?"

"Sure."

There now appeared a second raft, from behind a wall: the boatman aboard had seen them, and hesitantly waved.

"He's wearing a uniform," Myron whispered. "See that? Dead people work down here. Did you see?"

George nodded. He knew the deaths of hundreds of people. He had wanted to tell Justine that they were exactly the same but she was triggered by his attempts. All of these deaths came at him, filled him, drained him. Hers, too.

No, he should never have come to the moon.

"George," said Myron quietly, after some time, in a far-away voice, "you know, for the longest time, I also thought I had died. By that, I mean, I was once living, like you, like these people were, before they moved to this city."

On the catwalks, faces of the dead watched them float by.

"I'll never be convinced," said Myron, "that I'm just an algorithm, like you say I am. I know you tell me that, but I don't think so. I can't be just a program."

George maneuvered through another archway: open water here, and several other rafts, other boatmen, farther out.

"You know, Georgie, when the rapture came, I was like you. I remember my childhood. I remember exploring a garden—no idea where, though—with my mom, who was inside the house, and coming across a coal chute. I opened it, and coal came out. When I tried to close the chute, I couldn't. There was too much. I got caned for that."

"Were you a kid three hundred years ago? Who gets caned? I mean, what the fuck, Myron? Why are you telling me this now?"

"Because I *remember*, Georgie. And I remember when I first tasted an orange. My father hit my mother that day, smacked her so hard her hair went across her face. Me and my sister were having breakfast. We had been given the orange by an uncle. My father was mad about something. He was always mad. The orange sat on a plate, with sprinkles of coconut over it. I don't remember how the argument started, but my father hit my mom and she cried out. She had blood on her lips. I held the orange segment in my mouth and watched the blood well up on her lips."

"I told you that story." George could not catch his breath. "That's my memory and you're messing it up."

"My mother was taken by rapture," Myron said, "and she was not resurrected. Thank fuck. She never moved to the moon, that's for sure."

"Stop talking, Myron. Please. That's an order. Stop. I don't know why you're telling me this. We're lost down here. Can't you see that? Let's just find the hotel. Can we please go home?" He looked back at Myron, and saw that Myron, though growing faint, was crying, or appeared to be, anyhow, tears streaming down his pale, luminous face. George had never seen his agent cry before and was stunned.

"I think," Myron said, "you've missed the turn."

"What?"

"But my signal's fucked up, Georgie. Sorry. I can't help you anymore. I can't. I'm so sorry, Georgie."

Alone now, the last man alive, George steered listlessly, without direction, drifting. The signs on the walls were little or no help, so he stopped reading them. On the raft's tiny console, which glowed feebly, he could see himself as a tinier dot within hundreds.

The silent dead still watched. Dozens of them, watching from the catwalks. They had come down here quietly, all in the last stages of decomposition, their hardware failing, or failed already, huddled here, nothing left to keep them animated, no flicker left in their eyes. They watched the raft pass. They had come down here for their last moments, an entire city of them. Or had they been here forever? George felt their memories inside him like wind through his veins; he returned their gaze but was getting so tired now, tired of gigging, tired of Myron—wherever he had gone—tired of death, of life, tired of getting up in the morning. All he wanted to do was sleep, and he might have, but maybe just for a moment, because he was pretty sure he had a dream that he was curled up on a raft, while it floated out on a dark, open sea. In every direction, other rafts, and upon each, a passenger, being carried to unseen shores.

Under a gibbous moon, George waved at these others, but they did not see him, and did not wave back, so eventually he lay still and let the current take him.

He woke on a platform outside, a few metres above the vast vegetable gardens. It was night. He sat up. Stars overhead were so brilliant they seemed to burn his eyes. He recalled little of the previous evening. He never did. Silver mists still clung to the rich soil and he stepped gingerly down among the plants, walking between rows of broccoli, his cuffs getting wet, until he came to a road, possibly the same road he had travelled so long before, when he'd returned, bitter, from the moon palace.

On the far side of this road, three massive landers waited—squat, spackled with dew—for their cargo. They looked prehistoric and he knew they could wait for a long time, and had been waiting for a long time already.

The city was a dark cutout on the horizon, etched against black infinity. Now George could see what appeared to be a crescent of earth, rising dully—but there was a surging glow then, a red haze, suddenly, shimmering at the skyline—

Silently, a lone guuber came along the road toward him.

He waited patiently. The red glow abated, then rose again, even higher.

"Mr. Triplehorn," said the car, pulling up. "I've been trying to find you all night. Your inlay's not working." The car's dome opened. "Get in. You've paid me until the next shuttle. I'm all yours."

So he got in, and settled back. The seat was comfortable. He was always so exhausted after a show.

"Where to?"

"I don't know. Where is there to go around here? Drive around while I sleep." George, smiling, was still very drowsy. Soon, his thoughts started to grow odd. He imagined that the rules of the universe must have changed again. "Hey, car," he said, "is there a fire in the city?"

"A fire?"

He pointed, or thought he did.

"Ah. Not a fire, George, but a *pyre*. The chancellor died, you see, at sundown last night. Her second and final death. There's a ceremony now, unwinding. Sadly, many people are leaving the city forever. I'm afraid the chancellor's experiment will soon come to an end. Without her, well, let's just say I won't have any more passengers."

George was thinking of the chancellor's eyes, yet again, and the line of darker tâche noire, where blood, at the moment of rapture, had settled.

Now she was gone, like so many others. He looked inside himself but found nothing jagged, no chasms.

"The chancellor wished to speak to you, Mr. Triplehorn," said the guuber. "Last night, but she couldn't find you, though not for lack of trying. So many people searched for you!"

"Me? I was . . ." Where *had* he been? The concept of the raft seemed ludicrous.

"You were vanished! Last seen in a bar, eh? Ha. You did manage to find one. I'm not privy to what transpired between you and the chancellor but can only presume you had some sort of unfinished business. Anyhow, I'm very sorry to tell you the news. Are we going to wait here for your friend, or is he here already, like last time?"

"Who? Myron?" For a moment, George had forgotten what they were talking about. "No. He's not here anymore."

So the guuber began to move away, and the nocturnal gardens slipped past. George stared up at the sliver of earth. Myron, he knew, might never return. Who could blame him? Maybe his agent wanted to stay on the moon, forever. That would be okay, too. George began to doze. For the first time in ages, maybe since rapture, he had slipped into an unfamiliar state of peace.

Phallex Comes Out

Summoned, he opened his eyes. At rest, in the dark storage chamber, surrounded by dormant servants.

—*your services are required*—

Mistress Simone, signalling from her bedchamber in the East Wing. Phallex stood (shedding a surprisingly thick mantle of dust) and, as he charged to full capacity, stiffened his default penis.

He unplugged himself, cracked his knuckles in anticipation, and reached for the door handle.

Outside, in the Great Hall, it was late afternoon. Beyond the porticos, the waning day was quiet, sunny, and autumnal. Two blackbirds flew past, chasing each other. Dust spiralled in amber shafts of light falling through the arches. Looking out at the distant forest ringing the Chateaux, Phallex adjusted his irises.

When he turned to reseal the storage chamber, he glimpsed other faces in there, waiting, reposed and peaceful as they slept: dishwashers, launderers, a cook or two. And another fucker, just like him, curled on the floor, in the corner.

Phallex—

He hurried. Though silicone had coursed into the reservoir of the member he currently wore, he did not yet achieve full erection. Mistress Simone was a woman with eclectic tastes. Sometimes she asked him simply to watch, other times to remain limp. Often, with Simone, he had to quickly change attachments as required: larger penises; smaller penises; ticklers; double members.

The Main Hall stretched north into a hazy, dim distance. His footfalls echoed dully. Alternating shadow and sunlight washed over him as he—

Something was wrong.

A layer of dust covered everything out here, too, and cobwebs hung from the vaulted ceilings above, some so long they brushed at the top of his head.

He slowed his pace.

There was no one around.

He came to a full stop.

No other servants. No Mistresses going about their daily business. No excited visitors, escorted through the halls.

The Chateaux was utterly still.

Consulting his internal clock to ascertain when he had last been called to duty, Phallex discovered that the previous summons had come sixteen years, seven months, six days, and four hours ago. Scrolling through data, his semi-erect member softened further. Prior to this interval, the longest he had gone without being summoned to work was three days and two hours.

Phallex, your services are required—

Yet the voice vibrating at his receptors was unmistakable. Mistress Simone, in her bedchamber, requested servicing. No time to stand around wondering why so much dust had accumulated on the floors of the Chateaux when duty called. Pumping silicone back into his penis, Phallex hastened forward once more, hoping he would not be chastised for his delay.

As he resumed trotting down the Great Hall, he glanced at himself to see what he was wearing: black tuxedo, heavy black boots. He lifted one hand to his face and felt a plastic mask over his eyes, recalling now, with great fondness, the appropriate memory file:

Preceding a mock cotillion held in the ornate Ballroom, Mistress Lenore had summoned. She wore an extravagant, many-layered white dress, with a corset strung up the back, which Phallex and another fucker, Coqué—also dressed in a tuxedo—tore from her taut body. He could literally hear Lenore's faux complaints, her grunted protests as he and Coqué worked at her from both ends.

Nearly running now, dust rising in slow clouds behind him, Phallex replayed Mistress Lenore's pleasure response, sampled just after she came for the fourth time that night, and briefly he savoured the image of her slumping in a sweaty, panting heap, a smile across her beautiful face.

HE REACHED THE EAST WING IN just over seven minutes. Not good time. Still he had seen no one, neither human nor servant. Despite Phallex's appreciation at being selected, and his eagerness to please Mistress Simone, there remained something quite unsettling about this particular summons and the unkempt conditions of the Chateaux, so at the door to Simone's bedchamber he paused again, bending until his ear touched the surface of the thick wood:

From within came a great commotion, the sounds of crockery breaking, and laughter, and shouting. Male voices. He straightened. Mistress Simone had guests. *Male* guests. (Men didn't often visit the Chateaux. Phallex had been told by his Mistresses that the journey across open country was too dangerous for men—at least, for the sort of men that liked to visit the Order—but Phallex never could imagine what that danger might be, nor how the distinction, among men, might fall.)

He heard Simone's voice, breathless and guttural: *That's it, you little shit! That's it!*

Business as usual.

He opened both doors wide, ready for instruction—

Three faces turned his way. Three men. Mistress Simone was nowhere in sight.

All three wore loose-fitting robes. One man, young and blond, stood on Mistress Simone's massive brass bed, poised with a large knife in his hand. Above him, the luscious violet canopy was sliced and sagging. Feathers floated in the air, borne aloft on the breeze coming in through the windows that opened onto the Eastern Courtyard.

Another man stood by the dresser—drawers open and contents strewn—one of Simone's silk stockings pulled over his head.

The third man lay on the tiled floor, holding a small black device in both hands. He was older, overweight, with long dark hair and pockmarks on his face. Seeing Phallex in the doorway, he promptly sat up.

"Hello," Phallex said uncertainly. The device, he saw now, was Mistress Simone's command pad. She should not have let a visitor place the summons; that was in bad form. "Did you call me?"

The young man on the bed jumped to the floor, his robe billowing. "In the name of God," he whispered, "there remain monsters in this place."

All three edged away as Phallex moved farther into the bedchamber. He could smell their fear of him. Frowning, he glanced at the settling feathers, the broken crockery, the undergarments. "Where is Mistress Simone?"

The man by the dresser pulled the stocking from his head in a swift, sudden movement. His face was also young, his hair blond, sticking up in tufts. To his friend on the floor he said, "You've called it here with that infernal thing. I *told* you to destroy it."

"And *I* told *you*—" getting up quickly "—this place was still cursed."

Phallex took another step, and another, trying to locate Mistress Simone. Was she playing a hiding game? Perhaps she was under the bed? Or in the closet? Once, he recalled, Mistress Simone had asked him to fuck a man while she watched. One of those times she had hidden behind a curtain. (The other time she had strapped on one of Phallex's attachments and had gleefully participated.) But those grateful guests did not act as strange as these men were acting.

Seeking encouragement from Mistress Simone, wherever she might be, Phallex reached down and opened his fly. Pulling his default member free of his black tuxedo trousers, and giving it a shake, he said, "All right, who wants it first?"

"Look out!"

"The heretic has withdrawn its weapon!"

Phallex stood, penis in hand. *Weapon?* He had no weapon. Weapons were for hurting, and he had never hurt anyone. At least, not against their will. "I'm sorry," he said. "I cannot proceed any further unless I get a verbal from Simone."

"Abomination," said the young man with the knife, who stood near the window now, "your witches are dead. They've been sent back where they belong."

"I don't understand," Phallex said. *Dead?* Surely the man was making this up. A fantasy. Phallex was used to fantasies. "Listen, if you wish to employ a necrophilia package, we need to sign—"

A harsh blow on the back of his neck caused Phallex's knees to fail. He lost visual, followed by a good deal of motor power; he fell.

"Limits," he said, face down on the thick red carpeting, penis wilting and eyes utterly dark. "You need to review the limits—"

A boot hit him, hard, in the midsection, lifting his body off the floor. As he rolled to his side, another boot smashed into his mouth. He tried to stand but his hands scrabbled uselessly. His knees still did not respond.

"Codes," he managed to say, through damaged lips. "There is, there is a *code*. There is—"

Something hit his head hard. *Twice.* Something metal. Against his better judgement, Phallex went dormant.

HE BECAME AWARE OF HIS REPAIR systems, fully activated, trying to fuse ruptures of his primary motor drive. The dynamos in his knees were not functioning and his eyes remained dark. Audio was reduced but gradually improving, as neural bio-receptors were re-connected, one by one. There was no data at all coming from his left arm. His face, he knew, was irreparably disfigured.

He was being carried. Roughly. Hands gripped his legs, his shoulders.

"Let's put this down," a voice said. "I can't go any farther. Its fluids foul my hands."

"I have it by the head, so cease complaining. Earlier I spotted a place we can put it. You'll see. It'll be spectacular." A chuckle.

"Let's make it lighter still. Cut some more off."

"You saw how long it took to do *that*. This is a better idea. Just follow me. We're nearly there."

Taking initiative was difficult for Phallex and, with the damage done to him, was especially difficult now. Being carried like deadweight—presumably by the men he had come across in Simone's bedchamber—he only briefly and remotely entertained notions about defending himself, but had no idea how to begin.

"Why don't we just leave it here?"

"I told you to shut your mouth and bear up your end. You'll see what I have in mind. Be patient."

Going up stairs now. Phallex heard grunts, the sound of boots on stone, more complaints. The East Wing? The Tower? Rudimentary vision re-linked just then, and he cracked an eye open to see a dim, stone ceiling far above him, and patterns of lichen. A white dove, wings beating loud, like hands clapping, passed overhead.

Only after he felt his back rubbing against smooth stone did he fully realize where he had been taken. Too late, he attempted to pull free of the young mens' grip, to hold on, but when he stretched to grab at the ledge, he saw that his left arm was entirely missing. Clenched fingers of his right hand scrabbled on stone, then on nothing; he was falling down the laundry chute.

AGAIN, HE WAS AWOKEN BY HIS repair systems, madly working on his fractured infrastructure. He lay still, rolling only periodically, altering his position to allow his endoskeleton a chance to knit. Most of his dynamos were not working, and he had lost a great deal of fluid.

He opened his eyes to see gloom. Adjusting his irises to their largest aperture, he was eventually able to discern a ceiling, several metres above him and, within, the darker, gaping mouth of the laundry chute. He recalled the file of the plunge, reviewed it, and watched memories of his encounter with the three men. They had done this to him. Intentionally. They had hurt him without his clearance.

Some time later—he could not tell how long, because his clock was not functioning—Phallex managed to sit up. With one arm, this proved to be a challenge. Also, his repair systems, unable to mend the severity of damage done to his right knee, had amputated the leg just above the joint. Phallex looked down at himself, gently, incredulously touching what was left of his body with his remaining hand.

His tuxedo and black boots were gone. His default penis was missing. Knives had carved his skin.

Naked, broken, he struggled to pull himself up with his right hand, holding onto the edge of a wooden table, standing in the semi-darkness and balancing on one leg. He had never been in the laundry chamber before, but he knew he was below ground level. Up near the ceiling, an opening on the far wall let in a sliver of sunlight. Servants had once worked down here. He knew their faces from the storage chamber. There were none here now.

Against the mildewed wall to his left rested several poles used to beat sheets clean. Phallex hopped over to these and grabbed one, to use as a crutch.

He left the laundry chamber and slowly limped the dark and puddled corridors.

CORRUPT MEMORY FILES RAN AT RANDOM intervals as he wandered. Watching them, he bumped against stone walls, retraced his steps, found himself in black, dead ends. The images flickered through his processor. One by one, faces of his Mistresses appeared: Simone, with her crooked teeth and loud laugh; plump, gentle Lenore, lying next to him in the grand, soft bed, her breasts lolling, her sweat-beaded chest rising and falling; tiny Camille, who never wished to be fucked but often asked just to be held, throughout the long winter nights.

Was it true they were all dead?

Lost in the basement of the dark and deserted Chateaux, this bleak situation seemed likely to him now.

"There are some people out there, in the countryside," Camille once told him, as he held her, stroking her hair, "who do not approve of what we do here."

(He had stopped hobbling to relive this.)

"Why? What are we doing wrong?"

Camille laughed, but without humour. "Our Order, in fact, is despised by great numbers of people. We are not as easily contented as you, Phallex. You wake up when we call, do what you're told, and go back to sleep when we say you can. You thrive on our pleasure and the pleasure of our guests. You know nothing about guilt, or shame, or any other negative forces found inside us. We can be a very small-minded and dangerous species. That's why our Order doesn't often leave the Chateaux."

"Would they hate me, too?"

Camille nodded; he felt her head move against his chest. "They hate me, too, because I like only women. They are afraid of that, for some reason."

Leaning his head against a cool stone wall, reeling, Phallex felt these audio and visual memories erase; he was unable to retrieve them. Parts of his processor, he realized, were permanently ruined.

He would never again hear a Mistress groan with pleasure, or go dormant, smiling, knowing he had done his job well.

Spinning on the crutch, jaw clenched tight, he blindly negotiated the corridors of the cellar. The three men had never meant to participate in a scenario. They had been *destroying* Mistress Simone's bedchamber, just as they had destroyed the Mistresses themselves, and then destroyed him—

Sudden, bright daylight surprised Phallex. At the bottom of narrow stone stairs, he stood for a moment, blinking, looking up.

He ascended, step by difficult step, and paused at the top.

Wind hushed against his naked skin. The sun warmed him. Countryside stretched as far as he could see: quiet fields, the distant forest, the far-off hills. A pair of dirt tracks led away from where he stood. Beyond the trees, thin columns of grey smoke rose, almost invisible against the cloudless blue of the sky. Villages were out there, hamlets and townships; he had often heard visitors speak of them. *Where people lived*.

Phallex lost power for a moment and swayed, eyes closed. When the glitch had passed, he wondered if the three men lived nearby, and if more such as them lived over the hills, in the villages there. He shuddered.

Mangled face grim, Phallex withdrew his largest member from his abdominal pouch and screwed it resolutely into place. Leaning on his crutch, he limped forward.

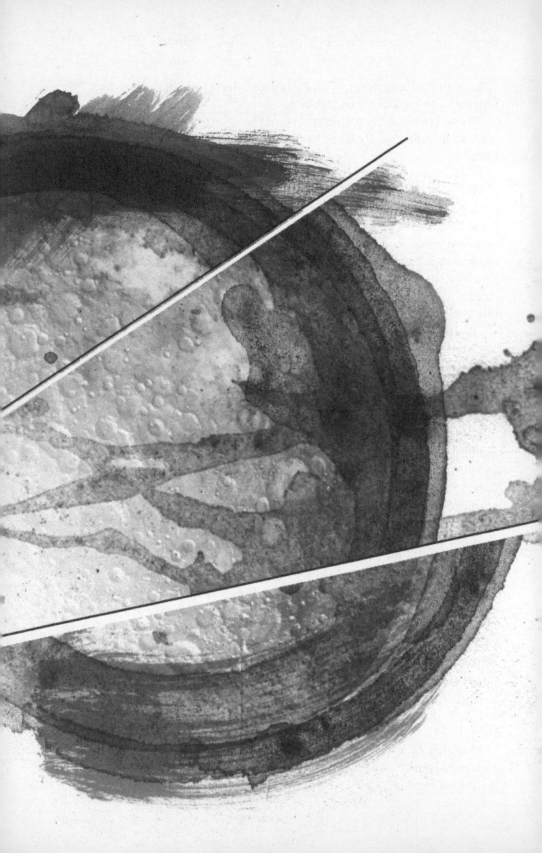

About The Author

Brent Hayward was born in London, England, grew up in Montreal, and currently lives with his family in Toronto. He is the author of three acclaimed novels, *Filaria*, *The Fecund's Melancholy Daughter*, and *Head Full of Mountains*, all available from ChiZine Publications. His short fiction has appeared in various publications. By day, he works in the aerospace field. He can be reached through his website, brenthayward.com.

Publication History

Cleaner—*OnSpec* #33, Summer 1998

Broken Sun, Broken Moon—previously unpublished

Arc of a Complex Spike—hardcover edition of *The Fecund's Melancholy Daughter*, ChiZine Publications, 2011

The Carpet Maker—*Chilling Tales* #1, Edge Publishing, 2011

The Brief Medical Career of Fine Sam Fine—*Tesseracts 14*, Edge Publishing, 2010

Glassrunner—*Horizons Science Fiction*, Summer 1993

Out On the Photon Highway—*OnSpec* #26, Fall 1996

The New Father—*OnSpec* #21, Summer 1995

The Vassal—hardcover edition of *The Fecund's Melancholy Daughter*, ChiZine Publications, 2011

Lizards—ChiZine.com, June 2011

Lake of Dreams—previously unpublished

Phallex Comes Out—ChiZine.com, July 2006

(Previously published stories lightly edited from the originals.)

PRAISE FOR
BRENT HAYWARD

"[*The Fecund's Melancholy Daughter's*] uncompromising originality leaves the reader with few familiar signposts. Reading it is like waking up in the wrong bed, in the wrong apartment, under the wrong sun. . . . By turns surreal, macabre and stunningly violent, *The Fecund's Melancholy Daughter* is dreamlike in its strangeness and complexity. Like a dream, it is difficult to define and difficult to shake. The imagery lingers like archetypes dredged up from the sleeping mind."
—Mark Dunn, *The Globe and Mail*

"[*The Fecund's Melancholy Daughter* is] beautifully written and morally ambivalent, this complex tale will appeal to readers of Gene Wolfe and China Miéville."
—*Publishers Weekly* (starred review)

"Toronto's Brent Hayward has a knack for creating incredibly lush alternative worlds and mythologies, and *Head Full of Mountains* may be his most complex and demanding work yet. . . . [The protagonist's] journey suggests an allegory of human development progressing through different stages of life, but readers will probably come up with many other interpretations as well, perhaps seeing in it a nightmare of isolated and introverted consciousness, or the endgame of technologies that have left humanity behind. The result is one of the more different and difficult SF novels of the year, but also one of the most rewarding."
—Alex Good, *The Toronto Star*

"Hayward's debut [*Filaria*] is a powerful, beautifully written dystopian tale. . . ."
—*Publishers Weekly* (starred review)

". . . *Filaria* is simply one of the best books written in the last decade and is the best science fiction/fantasy book that I have read in a long time."
—Examiner.com

"A disquieting, claustrophobic, compelling hybrid of China Miéville and J. G. Ballard. I first read *Filaria* almost two years ago: its subterranean imagery has been stuck in my midbrain ever since."
—Peter Watts, author of *Starfish* and *Blindsight*

OTHER BOOKS BY BRENT HAYWARD

Filaria
The Fecund's Melancholy Daughter
Head Full of Mountains

BROKEN SUN, BROKEN MOON

Distributed in Canada by
Fitzhenry & Whiteside Limited
195 Allstate Parkway
Markham, Ontario L3R 4T8
Phone: (905) 477-9700
e-mail: bookinfo@fitzhenry.ca

Distributed in the U.S. by
Consortium Book Sales & Distribution
34 Thirteenth Avenue, NE, Suite 101
Minneapolis, MN 55413
Phone: (612) 746-2600
e-mail: sales.orders@cbsd.com

Library and Archives Canada Cataloguing in Publication

Title: Broken sun, broken moon / Brent Hayward.
Other titles: Works. Selections
Names: Hayward, Brent, author.
Description: Short stories and a novella.
Identifiers: Canadiana (print) GBB8M0113 | Canadiana (print) 20190045035 | Canadiana (ebook)
   20190047720 | ISBN 9781771484763 (softcover) | ISBN 9781771484770 (PDF)
Classification: LCC PS8615.A883 A6 2019 | DDC C813/.6—dc23

CHIZINE PUBLICATIONS
Peterborough, Canada
www.chizinepub.com
info@chizinepub.com

Edited and proofread by Brett Savory

Canada Council   Conseil des arts
for the Arts   du Canada

We acknowledge the support of the Canada Council for the Arts which last year invested $20.1 million in writing and publishing throughout Canada.

ONTARIO ARTS COUNCIL
CONSEIL DES ARTS DE L'ONTARIO
an Ontario government agency
un organisme du gouvernement de l'Ontario

Published with the generous assistance of the Ontario Arts Council.

Printed in Canada

BROKEN SUN, BROKEN MOON

B R E N T   H A Y W A R D

For Frances and Oliver, perfects

Contents